SHADOW MOUNTAIN

By

Honor Stone

ISBN: 1-4033-8983-7 (E-book)
ISBN: 1-4033-8984-5 (Paperback)

Library of Congress Control Number: 2002095449

This book is printed on acid free paper.

Printed in the United States of America
Bloomington, IN

1st Books - rev. 10/24/02

CHAPTER ONE

As the evening sun settled behind the Rocky Mountains, a cool breeze licked at the faces of the two young boys who sat on the front porch steps, whittling. Raven Morgan, the elder, a nine-year-old, looked at his brother's notched and crooked piece of wood. "You are doing a fine job, Hawk. What is it going to be?"

Seemingly offended, but only for a moment, Hawk gave a sideways glance and answered, "Smart as you are, Raven, and you can't tell?"

Amused at his seven-year-old brother, who sometimes seemed older than his age, Raven smiled. "Well, I have an idea what it is, but if you tell me, then I'll know if I'm right."

Continuing to scrape the small blade against the wood, Hawk finally spoke. "It's going to be a peace pipe. One like Grandmother told us about."

After a long moment, Raven placed his knife in its sheath and said, "Yep, that's what I thought it was."

Hawk looked over at his brother's work. "You still making bear claws for a necklace? Thought you had enough by now."

Staring out at the red and purple majesty of the sky outlining the tallest mountain peak, Raven spoke softly, "Just a few more. It has to be perfect. It has to be just like Grandmother told me in her stories." Returning to the present, Raven ruffled his brother's curly blonde hair, then stood and took hold of the broom which was propped against the banister. As he began to sweep the steps free of wood shavings, he said, "It's getting dark, Hawk. You can finish it tomorrow."

Hawk put his knife away and laid his project aside. He felt the broom swish across his bare feet and he jumped back. "Ouch!" Looking up to see his brother's wide grin, Hawk frowned playfully and stood.

1

Raven was on the lowest step now, which put his little brother in a higher position. With hands on hips, Hawk said, "You should be wearing an apron when you do a woman's work!"

"Oooh! You'd better run for cover, little brother!" Raven exclaimed, as he pretended to chase Hawk into the house.

The two laughing boys were met at the door by Sarah Mason, a woman from town who had been sitting with their grandmother during her illness. The serious look on Sarah's face halted the boys' laughter. "Your grandmother is very ill, but she wants to see both of you. And you must be very quiet and listen to what she has to say. There is no time for questions. Just listen to her."

Raven put his arm around Hawk's shoulders and the two began walking slowly toward their grandmother's room, a frightening lump forming in their throats. Just before they opened the door, Sarah said, "Boys!"

They turned to look at Sarah. With tears welling up in her eyes, she told them, "Be sure to tell her you love her."

The door creaked as the boys quietly slipped through to see their grandmother, Laughing Brook Morgan, lying so still on the bed. Her illness had taken her body well beyond its fifty years of age. Her wrinkled skin, once so smooth and beautifully toned, like sienna, appeared to be more gray than it had even that morning. Her white hair swirled down over her shoulders, looking like the Rocky Mountain rivers she had described to them. Only her high cheek bones, her prominent beak-like nose, and the colorful geometric designs on the blanket that covered her bore witness to the fact that she was full-blooded Indian. Her dark eyes opened slowly and she raised a bony hand to reach for the boys. "Come here," she whispered.

The boys quickly approached and sat on the side of the bed. Hawk took her feeble hand in both of his and softly said, "We love you, Grandmother."

2

The woman smiled. Her eyes closed momentarily as her effort to speak tired her. "Raven ... Hawk ... I must leave you now ... to make my journey. The Great Spirit says it's time."

Hawk's heart began to pound so hard he thought it would burst. *This cannot be true! Grandmother is not old enough to die.* "But, Grandmother, I ..."

Raven touched Hawk's shoulder and whispered, "Just listen, Hawk. It's all right."

Hawk calmed himself and waited.

"Please do not be sad ... or afraid. You will not be alone. This night ... one will come for you. And you ... must go with him. He has been ... with you ... in spirit, watching ... over you. You may have seen him ... in visions, ... but now you can ... know him."

The old woman's breathing became more shallow, her eyes closed, and her hand almost slipped away, but Hawk hugged it tightly to his chest and laid his cheek against it. He fought back the tears as he whispered, *"No, God! Not yet, please!"*

The woman opened her eyes slightly and continued, her voice growing weaker. "Sarah has my letter. You must ... give it to this man. He will ... teach you ... many things. You must have ... no ... fear. Nothing ... can harm you. And you will ... understand ... many mysteries, ... things I have not ... told you."

Raven quickly knelt on the floor by the head of his grandmother's bed. Leaning in close to her ear, he asked, "Grandmother, who is this man?"

Her eyes closed, and with her last breath she whispered, "He is your father."

———————

On the mountain, as was his daily evening custom, Dark Wolf sat on the large, warm, flat rock, his legs folded, his back straight, his gaze fixed eastward in the direction of the small town nestled in the foothills far below. The gentle breeze brushed his raven-black hair over his bare shoulders. He did not move. This daily meditation took his mind to a place where he found peace.

Sitting firm as a stone, he silently prayed for his sons who were no longer with him, and for his mother who had taken them under her wing.

A hawk cried as it soared somewhere in the distance. Almost immediately, the sky darkened ominously, and a deep rumbling thunder echoed along the mountain ridge. As the first scattered drops of rain began to tap his skin, Dark Wolf raised his hands to the sky and bowed his head. He knew that his mother was now gone to the Great Spirit in whom she trusted. And he knew what he must do.

CHAPTER TWO

A single oil lamp burned on the table in the cabin, and a small fire crackled in the fireplace, dispelling the cool of the late spring night. The boys sat in silence with their small bags on the floor beside them, hats and coats on the table, ready for them to don as they departed. Sarah had helped them as much as she knew how and now was in Grandmother's bedroom preparing the woman's dead body for the journey.

Raven felt such turmoil within. Finally he would meet the man who Grandmother had said was his father. She had always told Raven that he looked like his father did when he was a young boy, and that he got his shiny, straight, black hair and the beautiful Indian skin from his father. He was excited, frightened and angry; excited at the prospect of getting to be with his father and feel like a son; frightened at not knowing where his new home would be and what it would be like without Grandmother's love and teaching; and angry because his father, obviously, had not wanted him and his brother in his life, and now was being forced to take them because of Grandmother's death. But it helped to ease his anxiety when he remembered the things Grandmother had told them. Out of respect for her and her teachings, he determined in his heart that he would trust this man and not fear, though he believed it would take some time for him to learn to love him. But one thing he vowed to himself he would not do. He would not try to dissuade Hawk's excitement.

Hawk looked at the clock and said, "What time is it?"

Raven said, "The short hand is on the twelve, and the long hand is almost on the twelve. That means it is almost twelve o'clock midnight."

Hawk looked at his brother and asked, "Raven, do you think he's really coming to get us?"

5

"Grandmother said he will come. He will come." Raven had not doubted until this very moment that their father would come, but he did not allow the doubt to linger for more time than it took to think it.

Hawk began to get sleepy. He walked over to the table, sat on his stool, leaned forward and laid his head on his coat. As he drifted into peaceful slumber, his heart was filled with joy at the prospect of finally being with his father, whom he had heard so much about from Grandmother. He tried to imagine what it would be like seeing his father's smile, hearing his voice, feeling his strong arms around him for the first time.

Sarah had finished dressing the boys' grandmother in a beautiful hand-crafted, beaded, pale, soft deerskin dress, and had braided her thick, white hair. Her beaded headband was in place over her peaceful brow, and the moccasins were on her dainty feet. The blanket was folded at the foot of the bed. It would cover her as her son took her back to the mountain from whence she came so many years ago. And her spirit would join with her husband's spirit on a higher plane.

Closing the bedroom door behind her, Sarah returned to the living room and smiled softly at the sight of Hawk sleeping at the table. She sat down in the rocking chair near Raven. "Are you all right?" she asked.

Raven straightened himself in the chair and answered, "Sure, I'm fine."

Sarah noticed Raven was clutching several of his whittled bear claws, and he seemed to be nervously massaging them around in the palm of his hand. She leaned forward and looked at him intently. "I imagine if I were in your shoes right now, Raven, I'd be pretty sad, and pretty scared. I'd be missing my Grandmother, and I'd be afraid of the unknown ... you know, what the future will bring." Noting some small hint of acknowledgement in Raven's posture, she sat back in the chair and added, "But that's just me, 'cause I'm a girl. Boys are much braver." The chair squeaked as Sarah began rocking slowly.

Raven watched her for a long moment and finally spoke. "Grandmother said we have nothing to fear. She said our father is coming for us."

Sarah continued to rock. "That is so true, Raven. You will see. Your father is someone wonderful. Someone beyond all you can imagine."

"You've seen him?"

"Once I saw him. It was when Mr. Thomas Cutler died, and your grandmother had brought you boys to the graveside service at the Cutler cemetery. It was about six months ago."

"You mean he was there in the crowd and nobody told me?" The tone of Raven's voice revealed his hurt.

"No, Raven. He was not in the crowd. He was on a horse in the edge of the woods. The way he was dressed, body and face painted, and the horse all painted up, they blended in perfectly with the colors and lights and shadows of the forest. They stood motionless. No one even knew they were there."

"Then how is it that you saw him, Sarah?"

"Well, when everyone else walked away, I was still standing at the grave side, and I looked into the forest, thinking deeply about something ... I can't remember what ... but a movement caught my eye. Then I saw him. It's like he wanted me to see him. He raised his hand slightly and held it still, sort of like a greeting. I raised my hand a little ways and held it still. I looked at his eyes and he looked at mine. Then I watched as he lowered his hand and turned his horse about. They left as quietly as they had appeared."

A touch of anger in his voice, Raven asked the question he so needed answered. "I am nine years old, Sarah. Why has my father not come for us before now? Why has he not even come to see us?"

Quickly sitting forward and reaching out to touch Raven's arm, Sarah answered, "Raven, your father *has* been here to see you. Your grandmother told me that, since I saw him that day in the forest, he has been here many times. He has knelt by your bed and watched you sleep. And he has left things for you ... gifts."

"Like what?"

Releasing his arm, Sarah quickly looked around the room and back at the boy. Suddenly, it came to her. "Well, like that knife you use to whittle out all of those bear claws. If you look carefully at the handle, I believe you will see it's made from a deer antler. And there's that leather knapsack you put your lunch in when you and Hawk go into the woods to play. Oh! And the headband with the crow feathers in it. And Hawk's headband with the hawk feathers. And ..."

Raven held up a hand and said, "Okay, I understand that he has been around sometimes, but why couldn't he give us these things himself? Why did he just leave them? Why didn't he talk to us?"

"Raven, he will tell you boys everything in time. But you must give him a chance. You will understand many mysteries. He may be afraid that you boys are angry at him. Perhaps he is afraid that you will not like him. I don't know. That's all I can say right now, but everything will be all right. I promise you."

———————

As he had so many times before, Dark Wolf slipped silently through the large open window at the back of the house and entered his mother's room. He wanted to see her alone again before he went in to meet his sons. In the dim glow of the oil lamp beside the bed, he noticed how calm and peaceful she looked, her hands folded together on her stomach. He sat on the bedside and laid a large, powerful hand over her cold, boney ones. He could see that the illness had taken its toll on her. The dress she had worn so proudly at the various celebrations during their life on the mountain now hung loosely over her withered frame. He stared at her face and determined he would not cry, for her spirit had been reunited with that of his father, and Dark Wolf knew there would be no more sadness for her. He leaned forward and stroked her cold cheek with his fingers.

Now it was time to go and meet his sons. He stood and walked to the door, his moccasins making not even the slightest sound. Just as he reached out to grasp the door handle, he heard one of the boys talking to Sarah.

Raven stood, quickly dropped his bear claws into his pocket, and looked toward the door to his grandmother's room, his eyes wide. "What's that?!"

Sarah sat forward, "What's what? I didn't hear anything."

"I didn't hear anything either, Sarah, but I know something is there. I can feel it." Pointing toward the door, he whispered, "There, in Grandmother's room. Someone is there!"

Dark Wolf lifted the latch and opened the creaky door. He smiled and stepped closer to his son. Very softly, he said, "Well, I must be slipping. The red man is known for his ability to go about undetected. But you knew I was here."

Raven quietly took a deep breath. He was overwhelmed by the size of the man standing before him, dressed in long deer skin pants with fringes down the outside seam, a beaded deerskin vest, a belt of braided rawhide strips, and light-colored moccasins. A necklace of leather and beads hung down and its beaded thunderbird laid upon his massive chest. On his right side, attached to the belt, was a leather sheath which held a large hunting knife. Staring up at the largest, most impressive man he had ever seen, Raven said proudly, "I am a red man, too, sir."

9

Dark Wolf knelt and gently put his hands on his eldest son's small shoulders. A deep sense of pride flooded his heart and he smiled. "Yes, you are. And your senses are very keen. I will never be able to sneak up on you, will I, Raven?"

At hearing his name spoken so tenderly by this quiet voice, Raven softened slightly and curled his lips into a smile. But the smile did not reach his eyes, and he did not move to embrace his father. The big hands released his shoulders as the man stood.

Dark Wolf's gaze fell upon his younger son, who was sleeping soundly at the table. Deciding not to disturb him just yet, he turned to Sarah.

Sarah put forth her hand. "I'm Sarah Mason, and I'm very pleased to finally meet you face to face, Mr. Morgan. I've heard so much about you from your mother."

"And *I* have heard much about *you* from my mother as well. I want to thank you for all you have done here."

"It has been my pleasure. I only wish I could have done something to keep your mother from dying. The boys will miss her so much. But I know they will be in good hands now." Remembering that Dark Wolf might need some refreshment, Sarah said, "Please sit down for awhile. Would you like some coffee? I can put a kettle on the fire."

Holding up one hand, Dark Wolf answered, "No, thank you. We need to leave very soon. I will take my mother's body out first. Then I will come back inside for my sons."

Raven watched as his father reentered his grandmother's room and gently covered her with the blanket. Her withered body looked so small in comparison to the man who carried it. He saw his father go to the large window and, holding his mother tightly against him, slip silently out into the darkness. He turned to Sarah and asked, "Why does my father not come and go through the front door?"

"Well, I imagine he wanted to see his mother alone when he came. And he wants to leave the same way he came in." As an afterthought, Sarah said, "And he probably doesn't want to take a chance on anyone seeing him coming here."

"Who would see him, Sarah? We live here in the woods away from everyone."

Not knowing what more to say, Sarah told him, "Raven, just trust in him. Will you do that?"

After a long moment, Raven began putting on his coat and answered, "Okay, Sarah. I will."

The clouds had thickened and now covered the moon, but Dark Wolf's eyes adjusted quickly to the darkness, and he moved swiftly to strap his mother's cold, lifeless body to the travois behind his black horse and tuck the blanket tightly around her. He then moved to the rear of the second horse, also a black with white face, and unrolled a blanket to pad a smaller travois. He had anticipated that the boys might both want to sleep on the way up the mountain, but if not, their belongings and supplies could be carried there. Now he felt sure Hawk would find comfort in the soft bed. And he would cover him with a buffalo hide he had brought along.

Returning through the window, Dark Wolf noticed that Raven had donned his coat and hat, and had his leather bag in his hand. He reached out and took the bag Raven offered him, then picked up Hawk's smaller one. Part of a feather stuck out through a small tear, and he knew that his son would bring his headband. He smiled. "I'll take these out and secure them, then I'll be back for you and Hawk."

Before he left the room, Sarah hurried forward with a small package tied with string. "Here is some food I have prepared for the journey. Please take it. And here's some fresh water, too."

11

Reaching out to take the package and canteen, Dark Wolf said, "Thank you, Sarah."

The bags, water, and food secured, Dark Wolf turned back toward the house. He stopped dead in his tracks and stood silent and still. He heard something move off to the right a few yards. He waited and listened, straining his eyes in the darkness to see if it was man or beast. After what seemed like an eternity, he heard the snort of a buck deer as it warned its family of danger. Then several deer could be heard running up the small bank into the woods, and the snort came again, only much further away. Dark Wolf breathed a sigh and continued to the house.

Hawk stirred momentarily as his father gently sat him up and leaned him against his chest so that he could put his coat and hat on him. Hawk tried to open his eyes and look around but his head fell with a thud back onto his father's chest. His little arms slowly encircled Dark Wolf's neck and he mumbled something that sounded like, "I knew he'd come ... I told you." His arms slipped downward as sleep overtook him again, and his father carried him outside. The cool air made Hawk curl up momentarily. But when his father laid him gently in the travois and covered him with the buffalo hide, he snuggled down and soon slept soundly.

Sarah sat sideways on the windowsill, her feet on the floor inside the house, watching the boys and their father prepare to leave.

Raven waited for his father to lift him onto the second horse. He wondered why it had a saddle on it, since Indians didn't normally use them, but he was thankful for the secure feeling it afforded him as he noted the distance between himself and the ground below. His feet quietly slipped into the stirrups.

Before mounting up, Dark Wolf led his horse toward the house and stopped below the window. "Sarah, I need to ask a favor of you."

Sarah, noting the seriousness in his voice, replied, "Anything, Mr. Morgan. Whatever I can do to help."

"First, you can call me by my Christian name, which is 'Jon', or by my Indian name, which is 'Dark Wolf'."As the dim lamplight reflected on his handsome face, Dark Wolf smiled up at Sarah for a moment, then he continued. "Next, I would like for you to wait at least two days before you tell anyone that my mother has died. Can you do that?"

Without hesitation, Sarah answered, "Whatever you ask, I will do." She thought for a moment, then added, "There may be questions. People might wonder about where she is and where the boys are. What should I say?"

"You may tell them that her people came to get her body for a ceremony in the Indian way, and they have taken the boys with them." Holding his finger up before him, he stressed, "You must make sure they know the boys were not kidnapped, but went willingly and happily. They must not know yet that I have come. And if they ask what direction they went, tell them you don't know. Tell them they came at night."

Sarah nodded. "I don't pretend to understand everything, but I will do as you ask. I don't want any trouble for these boys. Their safety is my greatest concern, so I will do it. You can count on me."

"I know I can, Sarah." Dark Wolf nodded and added, "And you may see me from time to time. I will need to know what people are saying, and I won't always be able to hear it for myself. Please listen, but say nothing. Even if they press you, please say nothing."

"Okay. I will stay here for the next two days and put the cabin in order. Then I will return to my home in town and do as you ask." Sarah stood and said, "Go quickly. Daylight comes early in this season of the year. You must be well on your way."

With fluid motion, Dark Wolf effortlessly swung his leg up over the horse's back and mounted, as though the travois poles were not even there. He looked at Sarah. "May God, the Great Spirit, be with you, Sarah Mason."

"And may he go with you and the boys, ... Dark Wolf."

CHAPTER THREE

Sarah closed the window, then found a warm blanket on the corner shelf. She put out the flame on the oil lamp and went into the living room. Wrapping up in the blanket, she sat in the rocking chair and stared into the crackling fire. Her thoughts were on the wonderful lady who had died, and on the son who was that lady's pride and joy. Now he would be the father the boys needed, and would find the pleasure in knowing his sons. She only wished she and her husband could have had sons or daughters. Her husband had died on a timber job several years back, and she just could not bring herself to become involved in a new courtship, though there had been suitors. Now, at nearly fifty years of age, Sarah had abandoned the idea of ever having a family.

She closed her eyes and pictured in her mind the grandmother's smiling face, even when she was feeling her worst. And as Sarah drifted off to sleep, she visualized Dark Wolf, so big and powerful-looking, much like his white father had been. In her dream, he traveled slowly, quietly through the darkness until finally the darkness enveloped him and she saw him no more.

———————

Dark Wolf and Raven rode steadily upward through the woods into the foothills above town. Neither spoke. Raven struggled to sort out his emotions and to fight off his feeling of drowsiness. Dark Wolf watched and listened, his main concern being to arrive at the other side of the pine grove and make camp. They could sleep there by the lake until dawn.

Raven's eyelids grew heavier and his head bowed. Awakened by the feel of his body slipping sideways from the saddle, he gasped and grabbed at the pommel. Instead his hands clutched the horse's mane, and the animal stopped. Suddenly he was lifted from his horse by a

15

powerful hand and placed on the other horse. He now sat in front of his father. He started to protest, but the strong arms quickly covered him with a blanket. As the horse began to walk again, Raven felt one strong arm slip gently around him to hold him close. His body warm now and comfortable against his father's stomach and chest, he laid his head to the side against the arm that held him. Giving in to his exhaustion, Raven closed his eyes and soon drifted off to sleep.

Dark Wolf thanked the Great Spirit for holding back the rain during this journey, and for allowing him to be with his sons again.

After several more hours of plodding along through the darkness, by the light of the moon, Dark Wolf saw the large stand of pines a few hundred yards ahead. He knew there would be little time for him to sleep before daybreak, but decided he would take advantage of what rest time he was afforded. He knew his sons would have many questions and would be eager to see their new home and explore the land.

The horses tethered and a fire built, Dark Wolf laid himself down between his two sons on the buffalo hide. He pulled another hide over them and closed his eyes. His right hand rested on the handle of his knife. He felt Hawk snuggling up against his side and heard him mumble. Dark Wolf wondered if Raven would ever feel the need to come close to him. He understood anger and pain, and he also realized that sometimes it never went away.

As the morning sun shone on the front of the house, Sarah had already swept and cleaned. She had eaten a bite of breakfast and now sat on the front porch steps where, just one day before, Raven and Hawk had sat talking and whittling. She missed them so much already. She would try to keep herself busy throughout the day, packing and storing away all personal belongings left behind, but each thing she touched would be a reminder. She sighed heavily as she entered the house, determined not to cry.

Tomorrow she could leave this place and return home. A nervousness came over her as she considered how she would handle it when word got out about the death of Laughing Brook Morgan and the disappearance of her body and her grandsons. The fact that Dark Wolf did not want his presence known at this time confirmed her suspicions that this good family was carrying some dark secret. She was sure that secret was somewhere in the words of Grandmother Morgan's letter. But she had not read it, so she did not know the nature of the secret.

Dark Wolf awakened and sat up quickly. His sons were not beside him. He threw back the cover and looked from side to side. As his eyes swept the perimeter of the camp, he breathed a sigh of relief at the sight of his younger son sitting on a rock on the opposite side of the camp, chin in hand, staring at him.

The boy's eyes lit up, and Hawk smiled as he said, "Good morning, Father."

Dark Wolf returned the smile and said, "Good morning, Hawk." After a few seconds, he asked, "Where is Raven?"

Hawk pointed off to the left and said, "He's up by the lake."

Seeing his elder son's silhouette, standing tall and dark against the background of sun-bathed cliffs, Dark Wolf's heart swelled with pride.

Hawk's voice broke his concentration. "Father, I have many questions. Grandmother said you would answer them. Do you want them all now, or do you want me to ask you just one or two a day for a long time?"

Dark Wolf could not contain his laughter. He walked over and picked up his son. He held him close as he began walking toward the lake. He answered, "Well, I think it would be best if all three of us could sit down together. You see, I have many things to tell you."

Satisfied for the moment, Hawk hugged his father's neck and said, "I'm so glad to be with you, Father. Thank you for coming to get us." Turning to look up the trail at his brother, he yelled, "Raven! Look! Father is awake now!"

Raven smiled softly at his brother's obvious excitement. He waited until they reached the spot where he was standing, then he spoke, "Good morning, Father. I didn't water the horses yet, but I will. We didn't want to wake you." He started to walk past them to get the horses, but Dark Wolf put Hawk down and stopped Raven.

"I should have been the first one awake. Let's go get the horses taken care of, then we'll have some of the food Sarah gave us." Reaching his arm out toward his younger son, he said, "Come, Hawk."

After the horses drank their fill and were again tied in place near the camp, Dark Wolf and his sons enjoyed biscuits with blackberry jelly and some thick bacon.

Raven suddenly remembered the letter his grandmother told him to give to his father. He pulled the folded, sealed envelope from his bag and straightened it out. Handing it to his father, he said, "Grandmother told me to give this to you. She said it is very important."

Dark Wolf took the envelope and tucked it into his pouch. "Thank you, Raven. I will have to read it later. We need to move on now. I want to get you boys settled in your new home. Then I will take my mother, your grandmother, to her resting place."

Swiftly, Dark Wolf and his sons broke camp, packed the second travois, and headed on up the mountain. The boys rode together on the white-faced horse, Hawk in front. Dark Wolf took note of how gentle and careful Raven was with his younger brother, as though he were a treasure. And, indeed, he was, so like his mother ... the blonde curls, the blue eyes, the beautiful smile. He even seemed to have her overall pleasant nature, no matter what was going on in his life.

Dark Wolf marveled at how much Raven's disposition was like his own. When tragedy and change happened in his early life, he, too, had become quiet and distanced himself from others. His mother had taught him much, but he often answered many of his own questions by listening, and by quiet observation of others and of life.

Now Dark Wolf knew it was his turn to teach and to answer. He only hoped that Raven would give him a chance to be the father he always wanted to be, and to show his love for his sons.

CHAPTER FOUR

The large cabin stood in a clearing among huge pines. Large patches of pure white snow could be seen all around. Some were still deep, giving an idea of the harshness and magnificence of the winter storms on the mountain. It was early afternoon when they arrived, and the boys explored their new home, claiming their room and putting their few possessions away or on display to designate ownership of space within the room.

Dark Wolf wrapped his mother's body again from head to toe and told the boys to follow him. As they slowly walked out of the woods and across a clearing to the edge of another wooded area, Dark Wolf carrying his mother's stiff corpse, Hawk asked, "Where are you taking Grandmother?"

"To her favorite place. A place where she used to go and enjoy being part of the earth. She would sit for hours and have her visions when she was younger. My father and I would often find her here. This is where I believe she would like for her body to rest. But her spirit is already gone. This will honor her and show our respect for her."

Four tall poles had been set and a deerskin bed stretched over a rectangular frame, which had been attached to the poles. The death stand was just taller than Dark Wolf's head, but he was able to lift his mother up and place her in the soft bed.

Hawk asked, "Father, can we lay some branches around her?" He looked around for some small twigs he could reach on the lower branches of some young pines, and as he ran toward them, he added, "Grandmother told me she loved trees and thought it would be wonderful to be one!"

Dark Wolf and Raven joined Hawk, and with the help of Dark Wolf's knife, they had all gathered enough to surround her and cover her with greenery and wood. Dark Wolf lifted Hawk up and let him place the branches around his grandmother as Raven handed them to him. Then he lifted Raven up to take a look. Raven leaned close to his grandmother's tightly wrapped form and whispered, "I remember what you told me, Grandmother. You rest now. Everything will be fine."

For a few minutes, Dark Wolf stood with his sons in silence, looking up at the stand where his mother's body lay. Then he turned away and the boys followed.

Hawk asked, "Where is my mother, ... and my grandfather?"

Dark Wolf turned to the right and began walking toward a small lake, which still had just a hint of ice at the water's edge. The boys followed him around the lake to the side opposite the cabin. They saw a small fenced plot beneath some shade trees at the far end of the clearing. A squeaky gate was opened and they stepped through to see two small grass covered mounds, a rough wooden cross marking the head of each. A rectangular piece of wood had been fastened to each cross, naming the deceased. The boys looked at the first one. Not yet skilled in reading, Hawk asked, "What does it say, Raven?"

Raven hesitated, then answered, "It says *'Jonathan Morgan, died 1835.'* That's all it says." Stepping over to the second grave, Raven said, "This is our mother's grave, Hawk. It says, *'Ravena Deep Waters Morgan, died 1845.'* And that's all it says. You were just a little baby when she died, Hawk."

Sitting down on the ground between the two mounds, Hawk breathed a deep sigh and laid his right hand on his mother's grave. Raven sat down beside Hawk and put his arm around his little brother's shoulders.

Dark Wolf's heart ached at the sight of his two sons sitting there between the graves of two people they never had a chance to know. They looked so small and lost and helpless. He walked forward and quietly sat down behind them. His reasons for not being with them since their mother's death seemed selfish and foolish now. He silently

21

vowed that he would do everything in his power to make sure his sons would never be alone in this world.

Having done all she could do at Grandmother Morgan's house, Sarah Mason decided to step outside and enjoy some sunlight and fresh air. She opened a cabinet, took out the well-worn Bible she had stored there with the other books, and went out onto the front porch. She sat on the porch swing and opened the book. When she did, an envelope slipped out, slid down her long skirt, and landed on the floor beside her feet. She picked it up and started to place it back in the book, when she noticed the name *"Thomas Cutler"* in the top left corner of the envelope. It was not fully addressed, as if delivered by mail, but the words, *"Mrs. Morgan"* had been written on the envelope, as it would have been if delivered by messenger, or in person by the writer.

Reasoning within herself that both Mr. Cutler and Mrs. Morgan had now passed on, and she wouldn't be offending anyone by looking, Sarah removed the thick contents from the envelope and read them.

More time had passed than Dark Wolf realized. The air was becoming chilly, and the western sky was now turning purple and red with the setting of the sun. He stood and reached for his sons' hands. The boys stood and took his hands, and together they walked back to the cabin.

After they reached the house, Dark Wolf assigned the boys the tasks of washing up and setting the table for supper. He lit some oil lamps, built a fire in the large fireplace, and fried some potatoes in a skillet there. The boys divided the remainder of the biscuits and smoked meat Sarah had given them, placing some at each place at the table. They were delighted to find a jar of blackberry preserves in the package.

During supper, Raven spoke. "Grandmother told us about how her family used to sit together in a circle in a teepee, and how the chief would tell stories and talk about life."

"That's correct, my son."

Raven took another bite of food and swallowed it down, then asked, "Do you have a teepee, Father? Maybe we three could sit down together and you could tell us about life."

Excitedly, Hawk added, *"Yes! Yes!* And you can tell us about Grandfather Morgan and about our mother!"

Dark Wolf smiled.

After taking his last bite, and without looking up, Raven added, "And you can tell us where you have been all these years, Father." He then looked at his father and waited for a response.

Dark Wolf realized that it would be difficult to explain how his father and his wife had died. It would be painful for all of them, but the boys did have a right to know, and he needed to put it behind him as well. He looked into Raven's eyes and softly said, "Okay, son. Tomorrow we sit down and talk. Just the three of us."

"In the teepee?" Hawk reminded.

With a chuckle, Dark Wolf answered, "Yes, in the teepee." Standing and removing his plate from the table, Dark Wolf added, "But now it is time to clean up and get to bed. We have much to do tomorrow. And there will be no time for rest until all is done."

Their first night on the mountain and at home in the cabin with their father, the boys soon slept soundly. It had been a long difficult day for all of them. Dark Wolf remembered the letter from his mother, and took it from his pouch. He smiled as he began reading.

"Dark Wolf, my son,

Hawk and Raven are a delight. I thank the Great Spirit that I was able to live to know them and teach them. Be patient, my son. All things take time."
Dark Wolf's smile faded as he continued reading.
"I have known, and my visions have been strong, but I could not tell you until I knew Raven and Hawk were safe with you. Our benefactor's son is the serpent. Do not trust him. He has robbed you of two treasures already — your father and your wife. He had you sent away for his own selfish reasons. The Spirits have not allowed him so far to take any more from you. But there is another treasure he will do anything to obtain. Your sons will help you find it. Watch for the crow. Expect trouble. Make good warriors of your sons. Let the eagle and the black wolf give you understanding. May the Great Spirit be with you, Dark Wolf.

Your mother,

Laughing Brook Morgan"

Dark Wolf read the letter again. He surmised that it must have been written not long before she died, as it appeared to have been scribed by feeble hands. Numbness and a feeling of nausea set in as the shock of his mother's words overwhelmed him. He felt as though he were being crushed, his world caving in around him. He could not move. He could not breathe. It was all he could do to find the strength to fold the letter and put it back inside the envelope.

Dark Wolf looked up at the door of the room where his sons lie sleeping peacefully. He desired that their lives would only know peace, but he realized now that he could not shelter them from reality, as he had been sheltered before his own father died.

CHAPTER FIVE

After looking in on Raven and Hawk and stoking the fire once more, Dark Wolf grabbed a blanket and his leather pack and went outside, closing the door quietly behind him. He built a small campfire in a clearing not far from the house. Wrapping the blanket around his shoulders, he sat before the fire. He pulled some eagle feathers from his pack and arranged them in a fan-type pattern on the ground between himself and the fire. With a stick, he drew the shape of a wolf in the loose dirt at the base of the feathers. He then took out some white stones and placed them in a circle around the feathers and the drawing. Dark Wolf looked at the emblems before him and spoke several phrases in his mother's native tongue, praying for the eagle and the wolf to bring a vision. He needed knowledge and understanding of his mother's words. And he needed to know what to do for his sons.

Dark Wolf knew he was well educated in both the Indian ways and in the white man's world. He had studied law and had seen the corruption of government and mankind. He had traveled abroad, experiencing many things. He had fought many foes in his travels. And he had returned to the mountain where he fought the bear and survived. But now it seemed he knew nothing, as though he were empty.

Staring deeply into the fire, Dark Wolf blocked everything from his mind. Soon his vision began. He heard the sound of rushing water as the form of his beautiful wife appeared. She was clothed in white silk. It flowed over her body and rippled in the gentle breeze. She smiled, reaching toward him, and whispered, "Come. You must see." The sight of her tore at his heart, and Dark Wolf felt the tears slowly slithering down his cheeks.

As he closed his eyes, he saw himself stepping closer to his wife. Suddenly her image changed and she became the eagle. Taking flight, she left his body there on the ground, but he could now see through her eyes. The first flight took him back to the day when his father died. He was that young boy of fifteen, standing in front of his mother, trying to protect her. Angry, drunken white men were on their horses, yelling at his father, also a white man and of large stature, taunting him about having an "Injun" wife and a "half-breed bastard" son. Their horses danced around nervously as the men fired their guns into the air and threatened to kill all three of them. His father, Jonathan Morgan, had listened to their words long enough. He quickly pulled his rifle up and shot the man closest to him, killing him instantly. Several more shots were fired, and Jonathan Morgan finally dropped to his knees. Before his body fell into the dust, he looked at Dark Wolf and his mother, his eyes revealing both love and a fire-filled spirit.

A commotion caught Dark Wolf's attention as another white man appeared on the scene and fired his revolver so swiftly, taking each drunken man down before he had a chance to think. The riderless horses ran through the lower meadow, into the forest, and out of sight. Dark Wolf recognized the man as Isaac Cutler, the son of his father's best friend, Thomas Cutler, who was a cattle rancher in the valley. Isaac dismounted and rushed over to Dark Wolf and his mother, Laughing Brook. As the man's horse stepped nervously aside, Dark Wolf noticed the brand on the horse's hip. It was a Circle C, and it matched that of the horses ridden by the white men whose dead bodies were now scattered on the ground. He said nothing. Isaac Cutler seemed so compassionate as he expressed his sorrow and helped Dark Wolf bury his father. He stated that he had come on business for his father, but now it would not matter. Also, for their safety, he would take Dark Wolf and his mother home to the Cutler ranch and see what his father would suggest for them, then he would send some of his men to come and take away the remaining bodies.

The eagle took flight again and soared over time to land at the Cutler ranch. It was now night when the eagle landed, the black wolf was there. Dark Wolf could see through its eyes as it began to slink through the darkness toward the huge house. Sitting quiet and still in the shadows outside the window, the wolf showed him another scene. It appeared as though Isaac Cutler had just told his father the news of Jonathan Morgan's death. Thomas Cutler sat quietly at his desk, staring into the fireplace, and finally spoke, his voice weary, "Jonathan Morgan ... dead. I can't believe it." With powerful-looking hands, the big man smoothed his thick, white, well-groomed hair and leaned back in his chair.

Isaac pulled some papers from his inside coat pocket and handed them to his father. "Guess you won't be needing these now, Father."

Thomas Cutler took the papers and tossed them onto his desk. "No, I don't suppose they are of any use now."

Isaac walked to a wing chair opposite his father's desk and sat down. "Father, we don't *need* another partner to help us run this ranch. We can take care of it ourselves."

A definite angry tone entered Thomas Cutler's voice as he spoke to his son. "Isaac, what do you know about anything? All you do is bring worthless, no good drifters in here to do a half-assed job at whatever needs done! You pay them to do nothing, and then they go to town and drink like fools, creating all kinds of problems for the townspeople!"

Isaac stood and tried to defend himself, "Father, I'm trying to ..."

Thomas interrupted him, "Isaac, this land ... this ranch ... this family used to be highly respected. Since I have given you some authority, we've become a *laughingstock!* You are nearly twenty-five years old. You should have a wife and children ... sons to carry on the Cutler name. You take the pure Cutler blood and mix it with that of empty-headed whores. You are a disgrace, and from this moment on, you have *no more authority! None!* Jonathan Morgan

28

was going to help me restore the good standing and prosperity of this ranch."

Rushing forward, with hands stretched outward, in a pleading fashion, Isaac countered, *"But, Father, I tried to save Jonathan's life! And I shot down and killed every man who had a part in hurting him and his family! I even brought his squaw and the half-breed boy back so we could protect them! I thought it was what you would have wanted!"*

Thomas Cutler softened for a moment. "Son, that is one thing you have done correctly. We will provide them a good home, and a safe one." A new anger mounting in his voice, Thomas added, "But if I ever hear you call Mrs. Morgan a *'squaw'* again, or Jonathan's son a *'half-breed'*, I will *knock your teeth down your throat! Now get out of my sight!"*

Slinking through the shadows again, the wolf followed as Isaac Cutler came out of the house and stalked angrily toward the bunkhouse. Isaac slammed the door against the inside wall as he entered. He stomped over to one of the beds and yanked back the covers. A rough-looking cowboy swore and sat up. Isaac grabbed the man's shirt and said, "Come with me. I need to talk to you."

The man scratched his head through tousled hair and grumbled as he staggered sleepily out into the night. Holding onto a porch post, he said, *"Dammit, Isaac!* What's so all-fired important that it couldn't wait until morning?"

Isaac whispered loudly, "Shut up, Zeke, and listen to me! My father is very upset about Morgan's death. He's coming down hard on me. Wanting to take all my authority away. If that happens, you and all your friends in there will have to go. So you are going to whip them all into shape and start doing things right around here. You got that?"

Zeke laughed. "So, your daddy found out about your plan, huh?"

"No! He doesn't know that I'm involved in Jonathan Morgan's killing." Putting his thumbs behind the lapels of

his tailored jacket, Isaac flipped his head back, smiled, and added, "In fact, he thinks I'm somewhat of a hero."

Suddenly becoming more awake, the grizzly-looking man asked, "What do you mean?"

Strutting slowly around in a small circle, Isaac bragged, "Well, I rescued the squaw and the kid and brought them back here."

Zeke's eyes widened and he stepped down off the porch to stand with Isaac. "You *what?* I thought you were going to kill them all and end the problem. You really are as stupid as your pa thinks."

Without warning, Isaac punched Zeke in the mouth, mashing his lower lip and knocking him backwards. Zeke grabbed at the post and pulled himself back to his feet.

Nursing his bloody lip with the back of his hand, he swore and said, "You can punch me all you want to, Isaac. That ain't gonna change the fact that you still got a problem. As long as that boy is alive, you ain't never gonna get Jonathan Morgan's land."

Isaac knew Zeke was right, but refused to acknowledge that fact. "Well, as long as that woman and that boy are under my control and right where I can see them, everything will be fine. And I can use them to get back in my father's good graces. Eventually, I believe that boy will be gone and the land will be up for the taking. When it is, *it's mine.!*"

Zeke scratched his head again. "So I guess the boys you sent up there to do your dirty work won't be coming back?"

"You guess right, Zeke."

Shaking his head, Zeke said, "Well, looks like we'll have to hire some more hands. Ain't hardly enough now to do half the work. Which way did they go after they killed Morgan?"

Isaac stepped closer to Zeke and leaned forward. With a sardonic grin, he said, "I killed them all." Standing straight again, he continued, "I told you. I had to be a hero. I couldn't have them coming around, drinking and shooting their mouths off about it, now could I?"

Zeke slowly shook his head again. "You really are one crazy bastard, Isaac."

With lightning speed, Isaac pulled his pistol and cocked it. Leaning in again, he held the end of the barrel against Zeke's chin and whispered, "Yes, I am. Now you think about that tomorrow when you go up on that mountain and get rid of those bodies. Take a couple of the hands with you." Releasing the hammer, Isaac turned and walked away. "I will get what I want, at all costs, Zeke." Waving his gun in the air, he repeated his last words, *"At all costs!"*

Immediately, another scene unfolded before Dark Wolf, once again inside the huge Cutler ranch house, and this time he saw himself there, at twenty-two years of age. The beautiful love of his life, Ravena Castell, had just recently become his bride, and Thomas Cutler had invited them to a small celebration dinner with the Cutler family. Dinner was over and they had all retired to the parlor. Dark Wolf's mother had enjoyed the meal with them and had been escorted home to the small cabin at the foot of the mountain. Thomas's wife, Elizabeth, and Ravena were sitting across the room talking and laughing as they sipped their wine.

Dressed equally as elegant as his host, in black velvet dinner jacket and black tie, and holding a glass of deep red wine, Dark Wolf stood facing Isaac before the fireplace. Thomas Cutler had excused himself momentarily and had left the room. Isaac, now thirty-two, his dark brown hair graying prematurely, blew a puff of cigar smoke toward Dark Wolf. He took a sip of his wine and asked, "Have you ever thought about selling your land and moving into town where your beautiful wife can enjoy the fineries of life and age gracefully?" He turned and looked at Ravena for a long moment. Turning back to face Dark Wolf, he added, "The wilderness is no place for such a rare beauty."

Dark Wolf softly answered, "My wife chose to come to this life with me. She will fare just fine." Holding up his glass, he looked across the room at Ravena and added, "And she is very happy, Isaac." He took a drink and turned back to Isaac.

Isaac raised his glass and smiled. After taking a long drink, he referred to Dark Wolf by his Christian name as he continued, "You know, Jon, there are many people ... well, *white* people ... who have a real problem with so much land being owned by an *Indian*. Why, it didn't seem so *wrong* when it belonged to your father, Jonathan Morgan, because he was a *white* man. But there are some who might try to put pressure on you to sell ... for propriety's sake. They might even try to take it from you."

Still trusting this man as his friend and savior from death, he looked deeply into Isaac's eyes and explained, "There was a time when the earth belonged to all mankind. Now it has been torn apart and divided up in ways that could never be considered by an intelligent man as equitable and fair. I did not choose to possess a document that bears my name in ownership of this great part of Mother Earth, but in the *white* man's mind, from what I learned of his law, these documents ... my father's Will, and the subsequent Deed, give *me* the right to live there and call it my home."

Isaac grunted and shifted on his feet. "Well, if you ever change your mind, I might be interested in taking it off your hands. And together we could look after it and care for it as your father would have."

Setting his wine glass on the mantle, Dark Wolf softly said, "I will look after it in my own way, Isaac, and I will use any means necessary to protect it." He turned to walk away and Isaac followed.

As the two men walked back to where the women sat, Isaac said, "Well, times are changing, Jon. Just remember what I said."

Thomas Cutler reentered the room and his wife stood. Dark Wolf reached his hand out to Ravena. Taking his hand, she stood.

"Must you leave?" Thomas's voice revealed his disappointment. "I thought you might stay the night and go in the morning."

Dark Wolf said, "I thank you, Thomas, for the kind offer, but Ravena and I noticed earlier that the moon is quite full tonight. We will have plenty of light for our journey." Grinning mischievously, he leaned closer to Thomas and added, "And you know, Thomas, there is nothing more romantic than enjoying the company of someone you love in the light of the moon."

Thomas and Elizabeth giggled and looked at each other, then back at Dark Wolf. After a hearty laugh, Thomas waved his hands toward them and said, "Well, be off with you then!"

After bidding his parents goodnight, Isaac followed Dark Wolf and his wife out onto the porch. He took another puff on his cigar and repeated his last words, "Times are changing, Jon."

Just before Dark Wolf stepped off the porch, he turned back to Isaac and said,

"The heart of the white man seems to change, more selfishly, as time goes on, my friend. The heart of the red man either rejoices in or cries for God-given treasures, such as this earth, the sky, the waters, the creatures, and mankind. That will never change."

Dark Wolf, his eyes still closed, shook his head, wishing the vision would end, but again the eagle took flight through space and time and landed where he now sat. But it was a day long past. His wife was there, walking toward the lake to bathe. Her long golden hair swayed gently in the wind, and she carried with her a new pink dress she had made. She turned around, smiled, and waved at Dark Wolf before she disappeared over the bank.

Shaking his head more fiercely, Dark Wolf felt the tears as they ran down his cheeks. *"No! No!"* he whispered. But he entered the wolf and slinked along into the edge of the woods. As the riders came, he saw his wife quietly rush through the dark water toward the shore and grab at her dress. All but one man rode toward the lake, where Ravena struggled to get up the bank. As if to spare Dark Wolf the pain of witnessing the horrible scene that followed, the wolf turned its head away. With the gruesome sounds of the men's angry pleasure and his wife's muffled agonizing screams continuing in the background, the wolf's fiery eyes stared intently at the horseman standing silent in the edge of the woods. A large tree hindered a clear view of the man's identity. Suddenly a puff of white slithered out from behind the tree, and the smell of cigar smoke filled the wolf's nostrils. The man's horse moved forward a step and Dark Wolf saw the rider. Again, Isaac Cutler had made his way into a tragic event in Dark Wolf's life. And Dark Wolf now understood that Isaac Cutler was the cause of it all.

The wolf turning its head again, Dark Wolf now saw himself running from the cabin toward the lake. Turning again, he saw the men scramble and run to mount their horses. Isaac was nowhere to be seen. Only the men he had hired were seen riding away, laughing and cursing.

Now the eagle screamed and Dark Wolf saw through its eyes as it soared to a new time and place. Landing high atop the edge of a rock cliff, the eagle cocked its head and watched as a strange rider wound his way slowly up the mountain. His head was down, as though he searched for something. Stopping his horse, he dismounted and squatted. Digging his fingers into the soil, he let the dirt sift through his hands and fall to the earth again. Swiftly and silently, an arrow sped through the air and pierced the man through his heart. He fell to the earth, a gurgling sound escaping his lips.

Another person, whom Dark Wolf could not readily identify, came on foot, dressed in layers of heavy clothing, a wide-brimmed rumpled hat, and badly worn boots. The person was strong, as the dead body was lifted with ease onto broad shoulders and carried into a nearby cave. After a long while, when the second stranger emerged from the cave, Dark Wolf gasped as he recognized that person as Hattie Gray, the woman who lived near the pinnacle on the opposite side of the mountain. He watched as she lumbered over to the dead man's horse and grabbed the reins. She led the horse a few hundred yards down the mountain, released the reins, and smacked the horse's hind end with an arrow, stinging it as she roared long and loud. The terrifed animal screamed and ran swiftly out of sight down the mountainside.

Dark Wolf saw the woman mount her horse and slowly ride away toward the top of the mountain. When she disappeared above the rock cliffs, the wolf appeared at the mouth of the cave. Immediately Dark Wolf was drawn in and caught sight of the shimmering gold layers which made up part of the cave walls. But the wolf moved further into the darkness of the cave. Seeing the vision through the wolf's nocturnal eyes, Dark Wolf's spirit balked, causing the animal to stop momentarily. A pungent smell, as of death, filled his nostrils. The wolf forced his way ahead and rounded a curve in his path. Entering a large open space, Dark Wolf saw not only the body of the one arrow-pierced man whose death he had just witnessed, but the remains of others. There were fifteen in all, placed carefully around the perimeter against the wall, clad in filthy, stringy remnants of what had once been their clothing. The bones of some had been picked clean by carnivores. Some were still in various stages of decay. But all faced the entrance of this large room with haunting stares and gaping jaws. It was a hideous sight.

The eagle returned, and another flight began at the mouth of the cave and ended at the Cutler cemetery. He remembered that day. He had camouflaged himself and his horse with earth colors and had stood in the forest watching the graveside ceremony in honor of his father's dear friend, Thomas Cutler. It appeared that he had died suddenly in his sleep one night, a mystery no one seemed anxious to investigate. Isaac had shown less than the expected remorseful attitude at the time, but had shut himself away at the ranch for a long while afterward.

The wolf appeared, and immediately Dark Wolf was in the darkness outside the Cutler home. From his father's study, Isaac's voice rang out, *"I'm* in control now, Zeke! Don't you forget it, either."

His usual boldness abounding, Zeke replied, "Oh, yes! You were in total control of your bowels when you came racin' off that mountain, too." He reared back in his chair and laughed heartily.

"Shut up, you son-of-a-bitch!" Isaac roared. *"You didn't see how close that arrow came to my head!"*

Zeke smiled and said, tauntingly, "Ooooh, Isaac, maybe that Injun has come home and has got you all figgered out. Maybe the arrow missed you because it was supposed to."

Isaac leaned back in his father's chair and stared thoughtfully at the ceiling. "No, Jon has not come home. He doesn't know I'm involved in any of these deaths ... his father, his wife, and now my own father. If he were back, he would come to see me. And he would not have missed the old man's funeral."

Leaning forward in his chair, Zeke said, "Maybe he doesn't want you to know he's back. He could be waiting for just the right moment to get his revenge, Isaac. Remember the men who you hired to kill his wife? They all came back to town all right ... tied ass upwards across their horses *with their throats slit!* And the men you sent up one at a time to look for the gold — how many were there? ...

Fourteen? Fifteen? Their horses all came back alone, lathered and shakin', terrified, like they was runnin' from a monster. It was like nothin' I've ever seen. But the men were never seen or heard of again. Doesn't that scare you a little bit, Isaac?"

Still staring upward, Isaac lit a fat cigar and answered, "No. I can understand a man taking vengeance on the men who killed his wife. But nobody knows *I* had a part in any of it." Turning to look at Zeke, Isaac smiled and added, "That is, nobody but you, Zeke."Staring at the ceiling again, Isaac continued, matter-of-factly, "Of course, my father knew. And he threatened to kill me and give everything to Jon. Can you imagine it, Zeke? A half-breed owning all of this? And me left out in the cold, wondering where my next meal would come from? *Me?* There is no way in hell I could let that happen. So now I don't have to worry about it anymore."

Zeke stood and shook his head. "Isaac, do you even care about anyone or anything besides yourself?"

Isaac laid his cigar down in the ash tray, stood and slowly walked toward Zeke, his hands clasped behind his back. "Why, of course I do, Zeke. I care very much about getting that land and getting the gold that's on it. It should have been mine anyway."

Turning toward the door, Zeke said, "I'm going to the bunkhouse. See you in the morning, Isaac." He stopped suddenly when he heard the familiar click of a pistol being cocked.

Isaac softly said, "No, Zeke, ... no, I don't think you will see me in the morning."

Zeke went for his gun as he turned around, but he was too late. A bullet hit him in the forehead and he fell backward onto the floor with a thud.

When the man's body hit the floor, Dark Wolf opened his eyes. The vision was over. His fire was still burning low. Only a few minutes had passed, but Dark Wolf's body felt exhausted, as though it had lived and suffered every experience shown in his vision. His heart ached with the agony of his new knowledge. He tried to dismiss it as he stood and kicked dirt onto the fire until it went out.

Quickly returning to the cabin, he entered the large upstairs bedroom and stood for a long moment looking at his sons, who still slept soundly. He decided he would begin at first light. They would have their meeting in the teepee, and he would explain everything to them with the new understanding afforded him by the vision. He would let his sons choose their horses from the wild herd in the hidden valley. The boys would explore the land that would someday belong to them, and together they would find the treasure of which his mother spoke.

Dark Wolf made a pallet for himself on the floor between his sons' beds. He smiled as he mentally added one more item to the next day's agenda. Raven and Hawk would meet Hattie Gray.

CHAPTER SIX

In restless sleep, an all too familiar dream came to Dark Wolf — one that forced him to relive a most painful scene from his past. He dreamt that he was standing at the edge of the lake, looking down at his wife's dead body. She had been gagged, arms stretched above her head and her wrists tied to stakes on the ground. Her legs had been spread slightly and her ankles also tied to stakes. He was fairly certain she had been raped, had most certainly been beaten, and was now dead. He untied her and sat for a long time, holding her naked body in his arms. He cried and vowed to the Spirits that he would avenge her death. Suddenly remembering that his babies were waiting for him at the cabin, Dark Wolf covered his wife with her new pink dress, which had been trampled by the men's horses, and carried her back to the house. He cleansed her wounds, brushed her hair and dressed her in her Indian wedding dress, made with white leather and decorated with beads. He placed an eagle feather in her hand and slipped her white moccasin boots on her feet. He kissed her cold, bruised lips and stroked her golden hair. Suddenly her blue eyes opened wide and looked at him with fear.

Dark Wolf awoke with a start and sat up. He looked around and realized he was there with his sons. He laid back on his mat and stared at the dark shadows created by the pale moonlight streaming through the window. He lay for a long while listening to the steady breathing and occasional movements of his sons. There was so much he had missed by not being with them, he realized. And now that they were all together as a family, he was determined to make them happy and protect them. He knew it would soon be daylight, so he quietly got up and slipped out of the room to gather the items needed for his council meeting with his sons. He would let Raven and Hawk help him put up the

39

teepee. It was his opportunity to show them first hand some of the things they had learned from their grandmother.

In the valley, Sarah Mason awoke before dawn and lay staring at the shadows in the room. She had been greatly shocked by what she had read in the letter from Thomas Cutler to Mrs. Morgan. Evidently, Thomas had found out about Isaac's involvement in everything — in the murder of Jonathan Morgan because Thomas was going to make him a partner in the running of the Cutler ranch; in sending Dark Wolf away to school in the east so he could snoop around the property and steal the gold; in the murder of Ravena Castell, Dark Wolf's lovely wife, in hopes that Dark Wolf would go away and never come back; in trying again to steal the gold, thereby causing the mysterious disappearances of several men, the number of which Thomas did not know.

As Sarah understood the letter, Isaac had even tried to buy the services of a fighter from Europe who had never been defeated, even bringing his opponents to near death. He planned to use this man to hunt down Dark Wolf and kill him because Isaac was becoming afraid of Dark Wolf's silent but powerful influence over his father. Thomas stated that he had the ultimate respect for Dark Wolf, who had remained strong and true in character even when his heart and soul must have been aching from his losses. Isaac also realized his own father cared more for Dark Wolf than for him.

The letter went on to say that Isaac had even driven Circle C cattle up the mountainside so he could take the law there and accuse Dark Wolf of stealing cattle, hoping to put him away in jail or have him hanged. But before he could get the sheriff involved, the cattle were mysteriously herded back down onto Cutler property.

Thomas Cutler had written that he and Isaac had words about all of these things, and he feared for his own life, and that of his precious wife, Elizabeth. But the one thing he wanted to do before he died was try to put things as right as possible between the Cutlers and the Morgans. So he had enclosed a Bill of Sale, showing that Jon Dark Wolf Morgan had given him a large sum of money for the ranch. Thomas had explained in the letter that he had simply withdrawn money from one account and redeposited a little less than that sum, showing it as being received from Jon. In actuality, he had purchased the ranch from himself for young Jon Morgan, but it was all legal and binding.

A Deed was also enclosed giving full description and transferring all property, possessions, assets and everything to the ownership of Jon Dark Wolf Morgan. There were two stipulations. The first stated that Thomas Cutler and Elizabeth Cutler would continue to reside in the house on the Circle C Ranch until they were deceased. After both were deceased, Jon Dark Wolf Morgan was to take possession and own or dispose of the property as he saw fit. The second stipulation stated that, after the death of both his father and mother, Isaac Cutler was to be banished from the property and should receive nothing upon his departure, with the exception of a horse to ride out on. Knowing what she did now, Sarah did not imagine Isaac would submit and go quietly when that time came.

Sarah arose and began preparing for her journey home. She hoped Dark Wolf would visit her very soon, as she needed to give these important documents to him. It made her anxious to think about having the papers in her possession. If they fell into the wrong hands ... into Isaac's hands, the results could be devastating to Dark Wolf and his sons. She decided that if Dark Wolf did not come within the next few nights, she would try to find him on the mountain and deliver the documents herself.

At daybreak, a noise outside the cabin awakened Raven. Quickly he sat up and looked around, a little confused about his surroundings. Remembering that he was in a new home, he quietly tiptoed to the window and looked down into the yard. There at the edge of the yard, beneath a huge pine, he saw his father laying out the poles and materials for the teepee. He smiled and breathed a sigh of relief. For awhile he watched the big man work, his heart aching with pride that this man was his father, with joy that his father was keeping his promises, and with anticipation of the things he would learn today. Raven hurried over to his brother's bed and, laying his hand on Hawk's shoulder, said softly, "Hawk, it's time to get up. We need to go and help Father."

Hawk sat up and rubbed his eyes as he mumbled. "Where is Father?"

Hurriedly dressing himself, Raven answered, "He is out in the yard working on the teepee, Hawk. *Come on!*"

Hawk threw back the covers and sat on the edge of the bed. Quickly pulling on his pants, he said excitedly, "Oh, Raven, isn't he *wonderful*?"

Raven found Hawk's shoes and handed them to him. "Yes, Hawk. I just hope he stays this time. Come on."

The boys ran down the stairs and out into the yard, letting the screen door slam behind them. Ignoring the crisp, cold mountain air, they ran toward their father, each breath forming a visible puff, which dissipated as quickly as it came.

Dark Wolf turned around just in time to catch Hawk, who took a running leap into his arms. Raven laughed and stopped close by. Dark Wolf tousled Raven's hair. "Good morning, my sons. Did you sleep well?"

Hawk squirmed to get down and said, *"Oh, yes, Father!"* Running over to the teepee poles, he asked, "Can we help you now?"

Dark Wolf chuckled and said, "Not so fast, Hawk. First you have to go refresh yourselves and then wash your faces and hands. We will have some food, *then* we will finish the teepee. Now, go."

Hawk began running down the path toward the large outhouse off to the left of the rear of the cabin. *"Race you, Raven!"*

Raven pretended to run his best, but did not catch his little brother until they both reached the door of the building. Out of breath, he teased, "Oh, Hawk, you have beat me again. You'll make a fine Indian someday."

A small window at one end of the building afforded them enough light to see their surroundings without lighting a lamp. They both stepped up into the outhouse, and as they had the evening before, they looked again at the rough paintings and geometric shapes on the inner walls. One wall had a brightly colored quilt spread out and hanging on nails, like a mural. There were two seats, positioned about three feet apart. And in one corner stood a broom. Beside it sat a burlap sack filled with lime.

When the boys finished their business, Hawk stepped out and Raven followed. As they walked back up the path toward the cabin, Hawk said, "Raven, you know I will *never* be an Indian, like you and Father. I'm too much like Mother, with white skin and light hair. But I want to have the same heart. Will you teach me, Raven?"

Raven felt as though his own heart would burst. He loved his little brother so much. He believed the heart of a red man was filled with much pain, but he could not tell that to his brother, who looked up to him. He put his arm around Hawk's shoulders and said, "Yes, Hawk, I will teach you."

At the Cutler ranch, Isaac sat at his father's desk, leaning back in the big chair and staring at the blood stains on the floor where Zeke's body had fallen dead the night before. The body had been buried out at the fence line in a rocky area early that morning. Isaac had sent someone to report the death to the sheriff, and to claim that a dispute had arisen wherein Zeke pulled his gun in a threatening manner, leaving Isaac no choice but to defend himself.

Pounding his fist on the desk, he muttered, "*Now* who will I have to talk to? Zeke was my only friend. *Damn him!*" Deciding to make his first trip to town in months, Isaac stood and put on his hat.

He went upstairs to his mother's room. Standing outside the door, he thought he could hear her crying. Rolling his eyes upward in a disgusted manner, he opened the door and strode calmly into the room. Offering no comfort, he began, "Really, Mother. Why do you still cry? It's not going to bring Father back, you know. And if he did come back, he'd take one look at you and vomit. You are disgustingly weak. You know how Father hated weakness in anyone."

Elizabeth Cutler had believed her heartache could not possibly increase one single jot, but at hearing her son's words, she was again cut to the quick. She was angry at herself that she had become so weak and powerless against him. For the last six months, she had felt like a prisoner in her own home. Each encounter with Isaac was so unpleasant, she had stopped venturing into any common areas of the house and had been taking her meals in her suite. Elizabeth had no proof, but she somehow knew Isaac had taken the life of her husband. And because she knew that, she feared for her *own* life. A son who could murder his own father was capable of anything, she believed.

Looking away from her son, Elizabeth stared out the window and sobbed, wishing she could see Jon Dark Wolf Morgan and talk to him. She believed if he knew what was going on, he would help her. And he would know what to do about Isaac. Isaac's voice snapped her back to the present, but she refused to look at him.

"Did you hear me, Mother? I'm going to town. The rug in the study is soiled with blood stains. It's ruined, and I want to order another one to replace it." Staring past his mother, he added, "You see, there has been a rather tragic accident."

Elizabeth quickly turned to face him. "Isaac, what have you done?"

Isaac was taken aback by her question. "What have *I* done? Shouldn't you rather be asking if I'm all right? *I*, your *only son*, could have been *killed!*" He stomped childishly to the door and grabbed the handle. Before leaving the room, Isaac turned to give his mother a piercing look and said, "You had better be very careful what you say to me, Mother. *Very* careful." Slamming the door behind him, Isaac muttered angrily as he stomped down the hallway, descended the broad stairs, and left the house.

Elizabeth watched out the window until she saw Isaac ride away out of sight. Not caring about her haggard, unkempt appearance, she quickly dressed and went outside to find the only person she believed she could trust to deliver a message for her.

Quietly entering the stables, she found Seth Logan, the groom, in one of the stalls, brushing a big, black horse. Looking around to make sure they were alone, Elizabeth made her presence known. "Oh, Seth, I'm glad I found you!"

The big, gray-haired man stopped brushing and spun around in surprise. "Mrs. Cutler, it's good to see you!" Then, noticing her hair in disarray and the distressed look on her face, he asked, "Are you okay, Mrs. Cutler?"

"Yes, Seth, I'm fine ... well, as fine as I can be right now. I want you to get a horse ready to ride. Not for me ... for you. Then come to the house and I will tell you what I need for you to do. Please, don't tell anyone, Seth. Just do as I tell you." She walked quickly to the door. Before exiting, she turned back and was pleased to see Seth already putting a bridle on the big black. *"Hurry, Seth!"*

Stopping outside of the general store, Isaac dismounted and tied his horse to the hitching post. From across the street, a feminine voice called to him, *"Isaac! Isaac Cutler! Where have you been?"*

Isaac turned to see one of the local prostitutes smiling and waving from the balcony above the saloon. He tipped his hat and turned away. Ignoring her further salutations, Isaac entered the store. He walked around slowly, looking at some of the new-fangled gadgets which were offered for sale. He couldn't remember the last time he had actually been inside the store. Most all of his clothes were made by tailors who came to the ranch to measure him and let him pick the fabrics. His father had long ago made arrangements for food and supplies to come to the ranch each week, and that system was still in place. Isaac had come to town for the services of the local barber; and, of course, he had attended meetings of the local cattlemen, but only at his father's insistence. In the past, he had frequented the saloon, drinking and enjoying the company of soft, warm women in the rooms upstairs, but since his father's death, he had kept himself at the ranch. Now recollecting his last visit to those rooms, Isaac let his fingertips slide over a bolt of pink satin fabric.

A man's high-pitched voice asked, "Can I help you with something, Mr. Cutler?"

Isaac turned to see the clerk, a small-statured, balding man with a moustache and wearing round, wire-rimmed glasses. "Yes. I am in need of a new rug for my study. Do you have a selection here I might choose from? Or perhaps a catalog I might see?"

The clerk smiled and said, "Come with me, Mr. Cutler. We have a good selection of rugs in the back room. You may see something there that interests you."

As Seth dismounted and tied his horse to a low-hanging tree branch, an eery feeling came over him. All around was a deafening silence, with the exception of a gusty breeze whistling through the trees. He slowly ascended the porch steps and listened for any sounds of life. There were none. He knocked on the door of the cabin and waited. There was no answer. Seth nervously turned the knob and slowly opened the door. Cautiously stepping inside, he listened and looked all around. Deciding there was nobody home, he relaxed a little and went from room to room, noticing the obvious signs of preparation and departure. Personal items were all stored away. Nothing left out, other than the furniture, to even suggest there had been the existence of human life in this small cabin. Swiping his hand over the surface of the mantle, he noticed that there was no dust, which indicated their departure had been very recent.

Seth went back outside and walked all around the house, looking for some indication of something, though he knew not what it would be. A few yards from the back of the house, he noticed several sets of footprints, one large, apparently made with moccasins, and two sizes of smaller prints, both made with shoes or boots. There were also the tracks of unshod horses in the dust, and four grooves, fairly wide and somewhat deep, as though something had been dragged along behind the horses. Instinct told him that he should clear away the tracks. He decided that the prints made with the moccasins were obviously those of a very big person, most likely an Indian. Laughing Brook Morgan was an Indian woman, so he reasoned that someone had come to take her and the two boys away. The fact that everything in the house had been carefully put away made Seth believe this journey was planned and necessary. He grabbed a small branch and swept it back and forth across the ground to smooth the soil.

Returning to the front porch, Seth sat down on the steps and rested. He was amazed at how intuitive Mrs. Cutler had been when giving him the instructions. She had anticipated the possibility of Seth's finding an empty house, so she had a contingency plan. Mrs. Cutler told him that Sarah Mason had been staying with old Mrs. Morgan during her recent illness. He would have to take the note to Sarah Mason, who lived on the outskirts of town. This part of the plan would be a tad more stressful, he thought, as he did not want to meet up with Isaac and have a confrontation. It could mean the mission would not be accomplished, or it could mean death ... for himself and for Mrs. Cutler.

In the back room of the store, Isaac studied the choices of rugs available to him. Finally, one captured his interest. Rubbing his hand over a large, partially-unrolled rug imported from Spain, Isaac admired the rich colors and the elegant designs. "I want this one." Turning abruptly about, he began walking toward the main part of the store. "Have it delivered today."

The clerk eagerly replied, "Yes, Mr. Cutler. A fine choice, indeed!"

As he passed through the doorway, Isaac noticed a small display of imported tobacco products. He stopped and picked up a box of cigars. Tuning out his surroundings, he opened the box, took out one of the cigars, bit the end off and spit it on the floor. Setting the box down again, he lit the cigar and began puffing deeply, savoring the taste of the expensive tobacco. Pleased with the experience, Isaac again picked up the box and walked over to the counter, where a woman stood placing her purchases before the clerk. Ignoring the customer, he reached past her and laid the box down. To the clerk, he gave instruction, "Have these delivered as well."

Smiling, the clerk replied, "They will be delivered today, Mr. Cutler."

As Isaac turned to walk away, he heard the woman chortle.

Taking offense, Isaac turned back and placed his left hand on the counter. He dropped the cigar onto the floor and crushed it with his foot. His right hand then pushed back the tail of his jacket, revealing his pistol in its hand-crafted leather holster. He rested his hand on the black ivory handle. Looking the strange woman up and down, he noted the heavy, dust-covered layers of clothing, the scuffed boots, and a worn and crumpled hat covering her stringy, graying brown hair. As she began placing her goods in a burlap sack, Isaac watched her large hands covered with leathery skin. It angered him that he was within one foot of this woman and she was ignoring him. Moving his face closer to the woman, Isaac asked, "Is there something amusing about my name?"

The woman continued to ignore him.

Becoming nervous, the clerk stepped back and to the side and busied himself at another part of the counter.

With his right hand still on the handle of his gun, Isaac grabbed the woman's arm with his left hand. "I asked you a question. Is there something funny about my name?"

Wrapping the neck of the sack around her hand, the woman turned her head and looked directly into Isaac's eyes, and, with obvious control in her husky voice, answered, "Nope. Cutler is a great name."

Gripping her arm a little tighter, and staring back at the woman's piercing eyes, Isaac agreed, "Yes, and it is a very *powerful* name. So why did you laugh at it?"

Having tolerated his arrogance as long as she could, without warning, the woman swung the heavy bag of goods directly from the counter to the side of Isaac's head, knocking his hat off, cutting his cheek, and sending him sprawling on the floor. She stepped over him and removed his gun from its holster.

Isaac's eyes rolled around in his head as he tried to focus. He struggled to raise himself up, but the woman pushed him back down, placing her foot heavily on his throat. She cocked his gun and pointed it downward toward his face. Staring down at him, she said in a serious tone, "Like I said, the Cutler name is a great name. *You* don't deserve to wear it. Your father was a good and honorable man. *You* are a pile of *horse shit!"*

With that, the woman removed her foot from Isaac's throat, tipped her hat to the clerk, and left the store. After tying down her supply sack, she mounted her horse and began riding slowly down the street. When she passed by the nearest watering trough, she dropped Isaac's gun into it. She muttered to herself, "I should have killed the weasel long ago when I had the chance."

Coughing and holding his throat, Isaac managed to get to his feet. The clerk came around the counter, picked up Isaac's hat, and began dusting it off. Isaac grabbed the hat out of the man's hands and put it back on his head. He leaned against the counter and continued to rub his throat. Finally finding his voice, in a raspy tone he asked, "Who *is* that woman?"

Returning to his spot behind the counter, the clerk replied, "She's the crazy woman from the other side of the mountain. Some folks even call her a witch."

Isaac whirled around and slammed his fist on the counter. Grabbing the clerk's shirt, he pulled him closer and yelled in a hoarse tone, *"Dammit, man! I want to know her name!"*

Terrified, the clerk stammered, "Her n-n-name is H-Hattie Gray."

CHAPTER SEVEN

The morning mist finally lifting as the sunlight crept through between the huge pines, inside the teepee Raven and Hawk sat facing their father, separated only by a small fire which burned in their midst. Both boys wore with great pride the head bands Dark Wolf had left for them during one of his secret visits to the cabin in the valley. Hawk had brought his peace pipe which still needed finishing, and Raven had brought his wooden bear claws. Dark Wolf had examined both projects with great admiration, promising to help Hawk finish his pipe.

As Raven's bear claws each had a hole carefully bored through the thickest part, Dark Wolf had given him a thin leather cord to thread through them. The necklace having been completed, Raven had lifted it over his father's head, and Dark Wolf now wore it proudly around his neck. In return, Dark Wolf had pulled from a pouch the original bear claw necklace of which his mother had told the boys in her stories. Raven had to fight back the tears as his father had placed it on him. Fidgeting with the large necklace, which hung down below his chest and onto his stomach, Raven smiled at his father.

Dark Wolf had presented Hawk with a small beaded deerskin vest which he, himself, had worn as a small boy. Hawk now sat there, grinning with pride and rubbing his fingers over the rows of colorful beads.

The boys watched as their father unwrapped and took out a long peace pipe and began crumbling dried tobacco leaves and packing the fragments into the bowl portion. Picking up a burning twig from the fire, Dark Wolf lit the pipe. Closing his eyes, he drew in several deep breaths and the tobacco began smoldering in the pipe. The sweet smell soon filled the teepee, surrounding them. He passed the pipe to Raven.

Raven held the pipe for a few seconds, staring at it and feeling uncertain of what he should do. He remembered his grandmother saying that the smoke from the pipe had a soothing effect and that it would clear his mind and open it to deeper spiritual awareness and meaning. Putting the pipe to his lips, he slowly drew in a deep breath. He held the smoke in his lungs for a few seconds, fighting hard to smother a cough as he passed the pipe to Hawk, then exhaled.

Not sure exactly what to do, Hawk attempted to imitate Raven's actions, but after taking a few short puffs and exhaling quickly, he began to cough. He passed the pipe back to his father.

Dark Wolf took another deep draw and held it inside as he laid the pipe down. Exhaling the sweet smoke, he looked at Hawk and then at Raven. "Where shall I begin?"

Raven quickly answered, "Tell us about our grandfather, Jonathan Morgan."

Smiling softly, Dark Wolf began, "My father, your grandfather, Jonathan Morgan, was a very fine man ... a good and kind man. He was very tall and big in stature." Winking and smiling, he said, "And my mother always said he was very handsome." As visions began to flash inside his head, Dark Wolf continued, "My father came upon my mother's village not long after it had been savagely attacked by some white soldiers. Only a few of her people remained alive. At first they were afraid of my father, but he began helping them in every way possible, and finally gained their trust. My father was not a red man, but he lived with my mother's tribe for a long while before he married her. He loved the Cheyenne people and their ways. He learned many good things, which he taught me as I grew to be a young man."

Hawk interrupted, "Will you teach us these things, Father?"

"Yes, Hawk, I will. But it will take time."

"Teach us something now, Father. Something that Grandfather taught you."

Dark Wolf smiled at his sons. "Here is one thing that you need to know right now, today. When you are first learning your surroundings, you look with your human eyes." With two fingers pointed toward his eyes, Dark Wolf motioned outward. Taking on a more serious tone, he continued, "But after you become familiar with your surroundings, you must become part of them, part of the earth. Then you will know what belongs and what does not. And you will know when danger is present. Not danger from the forest, the river, the other creatures who dwell on the earth, or even from the spirits ... but danger from man." Looking at Raven and then at Hawk, he asked, "Do you understand?"

Both boys nodded.

"Well, then today while we are out exploring your new surroundings, you shall practice what I have just taught you." Returning to the previous subject, Dark Wolf said, "Now, more about your grandfather."

Scenes kept flashing through his mind as he spoke to his sons, and he presented the scenes in such a way that Raven and Hawk could visualize them, too. He explained how he and his father had spent much time together, walking, talking, working, playing, wrestling, competing, laughing, and even teasing his mother. And he told of how his mother and father together taught him to have the heart of a red man and to love and respect the earth. In addition, he had learned of the Great Spirit, God, who created the earth and all living things. He also told how his father taught him to be a peace-loving person.

"I was only fifteen when my father died. It grieves me to remember these things, but you need to know them. Some white men came here to our cabin. My mother and I were outside bringing in water. Father came out of the cabin and met the men in the yard. The smell of whiskey was in

53

the air. The strangers were drunk and talking loudly. They were still on their horses, waving their guns around and threatening to kill all of us. They said it was not right for a *white man* to have a *squaw* and a *half-breed* son.

"My father saw one of the men aiming his gun at my mother and me. I stepped in front of my mother, but my father pulled his pistol with lightning speed and shot the man. He fell from his horse, dead. The other men began shooting my father over and over again. It took many bullets to make him fall to his knees. Finally, the shooting stopped and my father looked at me and at my mother before he fell forward into the dust. There was great love in his eyes, and a fire I will never forget."

Raven asked, "How did you and Grandmother survive?"

Holding up an index finger, Dark Wolf said, "Ah! Now *that* is an interesting thing. Another white man appeared from out of the forest and shot each and every man, killing him instantly. He stayed and helped us bury my father, then he took us down into the valley, where we lived in the same cabin you boys lived in."

"Who was the man, Father?" Hawk asked.

Struggling to keep the anger and pain from his voice, Dark Wolf answered, "His name is Isaac Cutler."

Hawk said excitedly, "Grandmother said Mr. Thomas Cutler was Grandfather's best friend."

"Yes, Hawk. Thomas Cutler was a good man. He and your grandfather were very much alike. And I know it sounds as though his son, Isaac, was a good man, too, because he helped us. But I have come to learn that a snake can wear beautiful skin and have a deadly bite. You will understand what I mean when you hear more.

"I lived in the small cabin in the valley with my mother, and Mr. Thomas Cutler made sure I had a tutor who could teach me what I needed to know so that I could finish school and attend a University in the east. I studied medicine and the white man's laws and learned how difficult it is sometimes to trust his words. God, the Great Spirit, looked after my mother while I was gone, and I came home each summer."

Smiling for a moment, Dark Wolf continued, "When I finished my education, I returned home again. But this time I brought a wonderful surprise. It was your mother. Her name was Ravena Castell."

Hawk interrupted, "Grandmother said she was very beautiful, and that you loved her very much."

"Yes, Hawk, your mother was very beautiful. She was a tall, strong, quiet woman, with golden hair. She had grown up in the city, but she was not like most city women who want to be pampered and spoiled. She was studying at the same University as I was, and she hoped to someday own horses and a small ranch somewhere out here in the west. So I brought her from the city to live here on the mountain. She loved the earth, and she loved life." Picturing her again in his mind's eye, Dark Wolf went on. "And she loved me. In her quiet way, the depths of her love showed in everything she did. Her kindness flowed so freely, like a river. So I gave her the name 'Deep Waters'.

"We were married and came to live here in the cabin. Your grandmother did not want to live here with us because of the painful memories of Father's death, so she stayed in the valley. But we visited her often. We even attended dinner parties at the Cutler Ranch from time to time. But Isaac Cutler began to talk about buying this land from me. He said it wasn't right for a red man to own so much property. I told him that I would keep it and take care of it as my father would have."

Adding a few more sticks to the fire, Dark Wolf went on, "We were very happy together here. And we had you, our two wonderful sons. You brought such joy and sunshine to our lives." His eyes suddenly brimming with tears, Dark Wolf stared past his sons. "Then one day during the summer after *you* were born, Hawk, your mother was up at the lake, bathing. I was here in the cabin with you boys. I was chanting an Indian song, and you were dancing, Raven. You were only two years old, but you were dancing. I was holding you, Hawk, and you were watching your brother dance. Then a strange sound came to my ear and I saw through the window that there were horses and riders at the lake. I laid you down, Hawk, and told Raven to sit still and watch after you." His words choking him, Dark Wolf softly said, "I ran to the lake and the white men rode away, laughing. I was too late. I couldn't save your mother. They had beaten her and killed her. And I swore that I would kill every one of them for what they did."

Raven choked back the tears that wanted to flow. Hawk wiped his eyes and asked, "Did you kill those bad men, Father?"

"Yes, Hawk, I did. Every last one of them. But the Spirits have shown me that there was one more man. He was hiding in the edge of the woods, watching them. And now I know that *he* sent them to do this evil thing, hoping that I would leave the mountain."

"Isaac Cutler?" Raven asked.

"Yes."

Hawk asked, "Is that when you took us away, Father?"

"Yes, Hawk. I wanted you to be safe. I knew your grandmother would take care of you. It seemed as though a shadow of death surrounded me, and anyone who was near me would die. I had lost my father and my wife, and I did not want to lose my sons. When something is lost, it leaves a void ... an empty space. That space must be filled. With darkness? With light? With something else? Every man chooses."

Raven asked, "What if it hurts so much that a man *can't* choose?"

"Then the man has already chosen. He has filled the space with pain. The pain overtakes him and he cannot hear the guidance of the Spirit. The truth has escaped him."

Raven looked intently at his father and asked, "Can a man change?"

"Yes, in time."

"That's good."

"Why do you say that is good, Raven?"

Staring deep into his father's eyes for a long moment, Raven answered, "It means that our pain will go, and you can be my father, and I can be your son."

Dark Wolf marveled at his son's perception. He nodded his head slowly in agreement.

Impatiently, Hawk cried, "Go ahead, Father! What happened next?"

"After I destroyed my enemies, those who took your mother's life, I went far away."

"Where did you go?"

Dark Wolf picked up a stick, and, in the loose dirt, drew the shape of a ship and two large circles representing two bodies of land. "I boarded a big ship, like this, and sailed across the sea. I visited many countries and searched for truth. My heartache became too great for me to bear, and I grew very angry. Angry at life, angry at myself, and angry at the Great Spirit."

Hawk scooted around closer to his father and looked up at him.

Continuing, Dark Wolf told how he had studied various cultures, religions, disciplines, as well as methods of fighting. "Some wealthy white men spent large amounts of money and made great productions out of watching me destroy anyone who was foolish enough to go up against me. I became like someone not human. No one could stand against me. I countered every surprise with a surprise of my own. If I did hit the ground, it was by choice to set my opponent up for the final blow. There was no stopping me. I no longer cared about life ... mine or anyone else's."

Raven imagined that he could feel his father's pain, and he began to see him through more understanding eyes.

Dark Wolf continued, "Then one day a white man came to me and told me that a cattle rancher here in Colorado wanted me to come for an exhibition match, but I later learned that he wanted to hire me to kill someone. That cattle rancher was Isaac Cutler. You see, the name I used when I was fighting was not my real name, so he did not know it was me he was trying to hire. And he still does not know. But he will know before all of this is over, my sons. He will know."

Raven laid some more twigs on the fire, letting his father know that he was content and wanted to know more. "And *you* were the man he was wanting to kill?"

Dark Wolf continued, "Yes, Raven. It was then that I came to my senses. Without telling anyone, I left in the night to sail back to America. No sooner had I returned home than I found out Mr. Thomas Cutler had just died."

Raven said, "Sarah Mason told me that she saw you in the forest when she was at Mr. Cutler's service at the graveyard. She said you waved at her."

"Yes, that is true."

"Did Isaac kill him, too, Father?"

Dark Wolf nodded slowly, "Yes, he did, Raven. Thomas Cutler must have learned the truth about his son, and Isaac felt he had to stop him from telling anyone."

Suddenly Raven remembered something. "Father, Mr. Thomas Cutler brought a letter to Grandmother. She did not tell us what it said, but she kept it hidden. Maybe Sarah found it when she was putting our things away. We should go and see her."

"I will do that, Raven. Thank you. I do know there is a treasure on this mountain that Isaac wants to own at any cost. I learned of the treasure in your grandmother's letter you brought and in my visions last night."

"Why didn't he just come and take the treasure while you were away at the University, or away all those years learning to fight?" Raven asked.

"I know now that he *did* try to find and take the treasure while I was gone, but someone stopped him. I suppose you could call her a sort of guardian angel."

"Who is it, Father?" Hawk asked.

"Her name is Hattie Gray, and you will meet her very soon."

CHAPTER EIGHT

Seth tapped on the window at the rear of Sarah Mason's house. As he waited, he stroked the big, black stallion's nose and whispered to him to be quiet.

After what seemed an eternity, Sarah appeared at the window and opened it. "Seth, what are you doing here? Come on in!"

Seth stepped inside and closed the door quietly behind him. Refusing the seat Sarah offered, he said, softly, "No, thank you, Sarah. I've got to get back to the ranch." Handing her the note, Seth said, "Here is a message from Mrs. Cutler to Jon Dark Wolf Morgan. It is urgent, so if you see him, please give it to him."

Noting the urgency in Seth's voice, Sarah said, "All right, Seth. I will. You tell Mrs. Cutler not to worry. Jon is supposed to come see me in a day or two. If he doesn't, then I will go and find him." Sarah tucked the note away in her apron pocket.

"Good. Now I gotta get back before Isaac sees me. He's here in town somewhere." Starting to open the door, Seth remembered something he wanted to ask. He stepped back away from the door and whispered, "Where is the old Indian woman and the two boys? Mrs. Cutler will want to know."

Sarah hesitated, then finally answered, "Laughing Brook Morgan died. Dark Wolf came and took her body and took his sons back up on the mountain." Sarah then stressed, "But you must not tell *anyone* what I have just told you. Not anyone except Mrs. Cutler. And be *very sure* Isaac is not around when you tell her. He must not know Dark Wolf is back. Not yet."

Seth nodded, tipped his hat, and stepped outside, closing the door quietly behind him.

Sarah hurried to put the message with the other documents she would give to Dark Wolf. She only hoped he would come tonight.

———————

It was only mid-morning, but after the ordeal in the general store, Isaac was ready for a strong drink. He took out his handkerchief and wiped the blood from the side of his face, then threw the bloody cloth on the ground. He crossed the street and entered the saloon. There were only a few people in the room. Isaac stepped up to the bar, demanding a shot of whiskey. The bartender, a big, husky man, set a shot glass in front of Isaac and filled it. Isaac swallowed the whiskey down in one gulp and tossed a coin onto the counter. As he walked toward the door, he caught sight of a big, black horse passing behind the buildings on the opposite side of the street. It looked like the black he had bought not long ago, but Isaac couldn't be sure without a closer look. He hurried out onto the street. Quickly mounting his horse, he rode down the alley beside the general store to the back street.

Turning in the direction he had seen the horse heading, Isaac spotted the black horse running at full gallop away from town. His hand slapped the leather holster. Looking down at his empty hand, Isaac swore. His gun was not in its holster. *Well,* he told himself, *I'll chase the horse thief down and kill him with his own gun!*

———————

Dark Wolf stood and walked to the entrance of the teepee. Pushing back the flap, he allowed the sunlight to enter for a moment as he stepped outside and looked at the horizon and the sky. As he reentered the teepee, he said, "My sons, the day is passing quickly and we have much to do. We will talk more another time."

Hawk and Raven began to toss loose dirt on the fire to put it out, but Dark Wolf stopped them. "Wait! I must tell

61

you about your names and what they mean to the Cheyenne people."

Raven and Hawk looked at each other excitedly and grinned. Hawk chuckled. Raven sat straighter as he watched his father pick up a small bowl which held a dark, blackish paint-like substance.

Dark Wolf knelt down, and, holding the bowl in his left hand, said, "Your mother loved birds, and so she named you boys after two of her favorites. The Cheyenne word for bird is '*ve'keso.*' And now I will tell you some of the characteristics of the bird you have been named after, as well as what each symbolizes." He dipped his right forefinger into the liquid and said, "Raven, come and stand before me."

Raven stood and came around the fire to his father.

With his finger, Dark Wolf began to paint feather-like designs on Raven's forehead, just above his eyebrows. He continued the feather like designs down both temples and onto the top of his cheeks. Another bowl containing a bright yellow liquid was picked up and Dark Wolf used his little finger to paint a diamond shape on the bridge of Raven's nose and covering the sides just against the cheeks, then pulled his finger forward on each side to fill in the yellow diamond, bringing the point to the end of Raven's nose, resembling a beak. He looked at his oldest son and said, "You are my firstborn son, and I am very proud of you. The raven is a bird who has strong family ties, staying with his own kind much of the time. But he is able to survive well around other creatures. He is strong and highly intelligent, and his cry fills the air when he speaks to one who will listen. He adapts well to his environment and is not afraid when confronted by a more dangerous creature, like the bear.

"You, like the raven, will not fear the bear, but you will not go out to look for the fight. You have seen that one creature must respect all others in order to live in harmony.

You will not faint, and your keen senses will keep you on the right path. And just as the raven will show us the way today, your spirit will always be there to guide your brother, Hawk, as he continues on his journey of life."

Raven nodded to his father and his fingers closed around the bear claws on the necklace which he wore. He smiled softly at Hawk and quietly sat down. The pride showed on his face as he sat straight and tall.

———————

Elizabeth Cutler paced back and forth in her room, wringing her hands, hoping that Seth would come back with some word from Dark Wolf before Isaac returned. Deciding to keep herself busy until Seth came, she began looking through the dresses in her closet for a good one to wear in case Dark Wolf would come by tonight. She would put some effort into making herself presentable. She selected a green velvet dress with black satin trim around the neck, waist and sleeves. She laid the dress on the bed and started to ring for Jessie Hill, her servant girl, to bring some hot water for her bath, when a movement outside her window caught her eye.

Elizabeth's heart sank when she saw Isaac returning from town, and her tears began to flow freely when she saw that he was leading the black horse. There was no rider, and no body strapped across the horse, so she could only surmise that Isaac had killed Seth and left him laying where he fell. Elizabeth Cutler collapsed into a nearby wing chair, buried her face in her hands, and cried. She had lost her only remaining friend on the ranch. She only hoped he had finished his task before Isaac slew him.

———————

Dark Wolf turned to look at Hawk, who still sat near him, eagerly waiting for his name to be called. "Come, Hawk, and stand before me."

Hawk quickly jumped up and stepped in front of his father.

Dark Wolf studied his son's hair, face and eyes for a moment, then dipped his finger into the black liquid and then into the white liquid. Mixing the paint into a streaked gray as he touched the boy's skin, he painted the same type of feather-like strokes on Hawk's forehead, just below his golden curls, and down his temples and upper cheeks. Picking up the bowl of white liquid again, Dark Wolf dipped a finger and carefully pulled a stroke of white down along the bridge of Hawk's nose to the tip. He dipped into the white again and drew a smooth line from the tip of his nose upward to outline the top half of each nostril, making the white markings resemble a sharp beak. Finally, he set the bowls aside and spoke. "Hawk, you are my youngest son, and you also make me very proud. You, too, are very brave. You have your mother's beautiful light-colored skin and golden hair. Your spirit shows in your eyes. I see in you great strength and power. And I have seen you run like the wind ... like the soaring of a hawk, watching for its prey.

"Many birds are called 'hawk'. Even the eagle is sometimes called by that name. The hawk is keen of eye and very strong. He is a bird of prey — a great hunter for the food he needs in order to survive. He symbolizes strength and wisdom. Courage also makes the hawk a bird to be respected and honored. You, Hawk, are keen-sighted. You don't miss anything with your bright eyes. And you will go out to hunt for food and the necessities of life without fear. Just as the eagle and hawk are guides for life and carriers of the spirit to the Better World, you will help others to find their way and go in peace. You have a good heart, Hawk. If you keep that heart, you will be honored in your house and out in the world around you."

Hawk nodded and said, "I like that! I'm glad Mama named me 'Hawk'."

Raven put his hand on Hawk's shoulder and said, "Hawk is a good name for you, my brother." Suddenly remembering something he wanted to ask his father, Raven said, "Father, can we see your scar where you fought the bear? Grandmother said you were very brave. She was proud that you did not let the bear kill you."

Dark Wolf turned his back to the boys and swiftly peeled the soft leather vest from his shoulders and lowered it to his waist. The boys could see the huge claw-induced scars which began at the top of their father's right shoulder and continued downward and diagonally to his left side.

Raven tried to imagine what it must have felt like and how it might have looked when it first happened. "Can I touch it, Father?"

"Yes, if you wish."

Both boys stepped up and rubbed their fingers over the scars, feeling the ridged tissues and the depths between. Raven was overwhelmed by the size of his father's back. It looked so strong and powerful, even with the scar, which Raven believed must carry with it some torturous memories. He asked, "Where is the bear now?"

As Dark Wolf pulled his vest up over his broad shoulders, he turned and smiled softly at his sons, then answered, "In the cabin."

Hawk's eyes grew wide with amazement, and he said, "*I* didn't see a bear in the cabin, Father. Where is it?"

Dark Wolf said, "We sit on it in front of the fire."

Raven began laughing, and as Hawk understood his father's answer, he, too, joined in the laughter.

Dark Wolf threw some more dirt on the remaining fire to smother it as he added, "His claws are on the necklace on Raven's chest. A symbol of victory." Stepping over to the entrance, he raised the flap and allowed the boys to go out before him.

"What are we going to do now, Father?" Raven asked.

Pointing to a distant rock cliff, Dark Wolf answered, "We are going to find a wild herd in the valley below those rocks, and you will choose your horses. Then we will explore and find the treasure that Isaac Cutler wants so badly."

Raven stood in the sunlight for a moment, holding the bear claw necklace up closer to his face. He looked at it again with greater awe than when his father had first given it to him. As he dropped it back down onto his chest, he thought, *This is a treasure beyond any we might find today.*

———————

Slamming the door behind him, Isaac Cutler, stood on the front porch, puffing on a cigar. From the window, he had seen the delivery wagon coming up the road toward the house, and as it came closer, he recognized the groom, Seth, seated beside the driver. Isaac leaned against a banister post as the wagon came to a halt at the edge of the yard. He laughed and shouted, *"Ha! Well, it looks like you got lucky, Seth! You didn't have to walk all the way back after all! Ha!"*

Knowing better than to speak his mind to Isaac, Seth simply stepped down from the wagon, thanked the driver for the ride, and began helping him unload the rug to carry it into the house. As they passed Isaac at the top of the steps, Isaac growled, "Where's my box of cigars?"

Before the door closed behind him, Seth answered, "On the wagon."

Isaac followed the two men into the study and watched as they began moving furniture aside in order to take up the old rug. After a few moments, he became bored and strolled out of the room, calling back over his shoulder, "When you are finished there, *get my cigars!*"

Picking up one end of the desk, Seth muttered under his breath, "Yeah, you'll get your cigars. I'd like to shove them all down your throat."

The driver, an impressionable young man with curious eyes, picked up the other end of the desk as he whispered, "Is he *really* as rich as everyone says?"

Seth stopped and sat his end of the desk down and leaned on it. "Son, you better be asking if he's as *mean* as everyone says he is. And the answer would be *'yes'*. And he's dangerous."

The young man began tugging on the desk as he said, "Well, I just figured I could work for him here on the ranch. He probably pays good money, don't he? I mean, you'd know, right? 'Cause *you* work here."

Helping the man move the desk again, Seth asked, "What's yer name, son?"

"My name is Ben Thomas. I would have introduced myself when I picked you up on my way from town, but you didn't seem to wanna talk none."

Seth looked at the other man and said in a very serious tone, "Ben Thomas, let's get this rug laid, and you go back down that road and never look back." Then, pointing to the blood stain on the old rug, Seth added, "And you can thank the Good Lord that you walked out on your own two feet instead of being carried out like the man whose blood is on this floor. Money don't mean nothin' if you can't live to enjoy it. Isaac Cutler only has what he has because his fine father died and he claimed it for his own. And he will make sure *nobody* enjoys his money but his own self."

Upstairs, Elizabeth Cutler had been awakened by a loud banging noise. In her grief over her imagined loss of her good friend, Seth, she had cried herself to sleep. Still in the wing chair, she sat forward and rubbed her forehead and eyes, trying to focus and remember why her heart was so heavy. She wondered whether the loud noise could have been a door slamming or a gun shot. Suddenly remembering the events of that morning, Elizabeth sat back in the chair again and whispered wearily, "Poor, dear Seth."

As she sat there thinking about her trusted friend and his certain demise at the hands of her own son, she heard

Isaac's voice shout from somewhere down the hall, *"Seth! Hurry up with that rug business and get my cigars!"*

Elizabeth's heart leapt for joy as the meaning of Isaac's words quickly sank in. She silently rejoiced. *Seth is alive!* Ringing for her servant to bring hot water, she began undressing and preparing for her bath. She would proceed with her original plan to prepare herself for a visit, trusting that Seth had gotten the message delivered.

Hearing the front door slam, she ran to her window and pulled the lower end of the curtain up to cover her nearly naked body. With great anticipation, she watched as Seth walked to the wagon and fetched a small box. She breathed a sigh of relief and hurriedly reached out to open the window. When she did, the drapery fell away and she stood there in her corset and undergarments. Knowing she had to hurry, she leaned out the window and softly called, *"Seth!"*

The big man slowed his pace and looked around for the source of the voice.

Again, Elizabeth called out, *"Seth! Up here!"*

Looking up, Seth saw Elizabeth at the window, her feminine frame barely clothed. He caught his breath and quickly removed his hat. He tried to turn away, but his curious male nature held his stare in the direction of the upstairs window. The white skin of Elizabeth's bare shoulders looked so soft. Attempting to shake off these strange thoughts and feelings, Seth finally found his voice and whispered, "Mrs. Cutler, what are you doing?"

Noticing the strange way Seth was staring at her, Elizabeth blushed, grabbed the drapery and again pulled it in front of her. "Did you get the message delivered?"

"Yes, ma'am. I'll talk to you later." He stood for another moment looking at her, then smiled softly as he put his hat back on and continued forward out of sight and into the house.

Elizabeth heard a tap on the door.

Jessie, the servant girl, a lovely young woman with long, strawberry blonde hair, entered the room with two large buckets of hot water and began preparing the bath. She noticed the green dress lying out on the bed. "Oh, Mrs. Cutler, that is such a *beautiful dress!* Does this mean you will be coming down to supper tonight?"

Smiling, Elizabeth answered, "Perhaps I will. I am feeling much better now. But supper is a long way off, Jessie. I think I may first go for a walk and see if the flower garden is coming to life." She laughed and added, "I *may* even go for a *ride!"*

Jessie clapped her hands excitedly. "Oh, Mrs. Cutler, I'm *so* glad you are smiling again! I'll get more water. You'll want to relax in a nice deep bath. Then we can wash and style your hair like we used to do. It's still such a beautiful auburn color."

Elizabeth sighed and looked at herself in the mirror. "I'm afraid there's more gray than auburn now, Jessie."

"Well, when we get done fixin' it up, you'll see." Jessie picked up the buckets and left the room, humming as she went down the hallway.

Continuing to undress, Elizabeth thrilled at the prospect of seeing Jon Dark Wolf Morgan and soliciting his help. She decided she would save the dress for later in the evening and put on some proper riding clothes after her bath. While at the stable getting her horse, she could talk to Seth about his morning errand.

Jessie made several trips with buckets of hot water, and finally returned and finished preparing the bath, adding a fragrant skin-softening oil, and placing soap and towels nearby.

After promising to ring for her when she was through, Elizabeth dismissed Jessie. She could not stop thinking about the way Seth had looked at her only a few moments ago. She had always taken great pride in her appearance and had confidence that, for her age, her body was still quite shapely. Out of her deep respect and love for her late husband, Thomas Cutler, Elizabeth had never allowed herself to look at or even *think* about another man. But, in the midst of all the turmoil in her life, Seth's gaze had caused something to come alive inside of her, bringing with it the hope of new-found happiness and desire.

As her body slid down into the inviting bubbly, steamy liquid, Elizabeth savored the feeling of warmth, enfolding her like a blanket. Her nostrils taking in the delicate fragrance of the water, she closed her eyes and visualized Seth's smile again. Remembering he had removed his hat upon first seeing her at the window, Elizabeth felt herself blush again, and she smiled.

———

Isaac slammed his door behind him as he stepped out into the hall. At the top of the stairs, he prepared to bellow out another order for Seth to bring the cigars, when he spotted the cigar box on the small table just inside the door. He descended the stairs and picked up the box. Entering the study, he took out one of the cigars and rolled it back and forth in his fingers. After biting the end off and spitting it in the floor, Isaac lit the cigar and set the box down on the desk.

Seth ignored Isaac and continued the rug-laying project. Ben Thomas, easily distracted by Isaac's powerful and patronizing air, stopped working and watched his every move.

Standing at the window, smoking his cigar slowly and deliberately, Isaac's peripheral vision allowed him to notice the young man staring at him. Slowly he turned his head and looked directly at Ben Thomas.

Ben looked down and fumbled around with the rug in an attempt to cover his embarrassment at being discovered staring.

Seth shook his head and muttered something under his breath, which caught Isaac's attention.

Amused at the young man and at Seth's foul mood, Isaac said, "Good enough, Seth. Put everything back now and get that old rug out of here. Then you may go finish your chores in the stable." He began slowly moving toward the doorway. As an afterthought, he added, "Brush the black again. And I don't expect to see you riding him anymore ... *ever!* This is your *only* warning." Pointing to Ben Thomas, Isaac demanded, "And *you* ... when you are all finished here, come and see me before you leave. I'll be outside waiting for you."

"Yes, sir!" Ben answered, with a smile.

Seth shook his head and grunted. He knew nothing good could come out of Ben Thomas's association with Isaac Cutler. But he also knew that Ben, stricken with a greedy infatuation for Isaac, was not willing to take his good advice. Seth, believing that Isaac was going to somehow use Ben's obvious adoration to his own advantage, determined that he would look out for Ben as much as he could so he would not end up dead, like Zeke ... the man who had been Isaac's only friend.

CHAPTER NINE

Somewhat nervous about his choice of horses, Hawk allowed his father to lift him onto the back of a young, light-colored mustang. Raven sat tall and proud upon a black and white pinto mare, which had nickered at him when she noticed him standing on a small mound at the edge of the valley floor. The boys were amazed at how quickly their father had brought the horses into submission, not by the rough treatment they had seen and heard about in the past, but by gentle, patient methods Dark Wolf's father had taught him.

Hawk grabbed a handful of mane and sat as tightly as he possibly could with no saddle under him. His father had promised to lead the horse for the first few miles until Hawk felt comfortable enough to take the reins.

Their quest to find the treasure began at the valley home of the wild horses where the grass was lush and green. The peaks above were still snow-covered and pure white. The sun shone brightly now, and its warm reflection on the snowy ground had a blinding effect. Gathering strength from the slowly melting snow, every mountain waterfall and stream seemed to laugh and sing as it tumbled down from the mountain heights toward the rivers far below.

The boys were thrilled to see with their own eyes so many kinds of vegetation and animals which, until now, had only been flat, lifeless drawings on the pages of Raven's school books. Dark Wolf had answered many questions and had given the boys time to stop and observe the various creatures and their activities.

After several hours of walking the horses along the mountain trails, they agreed to stop and rest on a small flat where a stream flowed nearby in bubbly, laughing ripples. Letting their horses rest and graze by the stream, Dark Wolf sat with his sons on a large rock which had been warmed by the sun. They shared some flat bread and deer jerky, as well as more conversation and laughter.

Raven asked, "What will happen if we don't find this treasure, Father?"

Dark Wolf answered, "We will find it, Raven."

Hawk said, "What are we going to do with it when we find it?"

"That remains to be seen, my sons. But we must not forget, it was the desire for this treasure that caused your grandfather and your mother to be killed."

"Are we going to die, too, Father?" Hawk asked.

Dark Wolf took his sons by the hand and answered with great intensity in his voice and in his eyes, "No. You will not die because of this treasure. Tomorrow I will teach you to be great warriors and to defend yourselves."

After a long silence, Raven spoke. "Grandmother told us that a true warrior does not go in search of warfare, but that he is ready to defend what is his when warfare comes to him. She said he will not run. He will go out to meet the enemy and stand tall against it."

Smiling softly, Dark Wolf released the boys' hands and said, "Your Grandmother is right. We will not go in search of trouble, but if it comes to us, we will be ready for it."

Hawk stood and hugged his father. "Thank you for bringing us to the mountain with you, Father." Quickly pushing away, Hawk announced, "I'm going down to the water and see if I can see any fish!" He ran the short distance to the stream and lay down on his belly on a large flat rock at the water's edge. His chin resting on the edge of the rock, Hawk swished his hands back and forth in the cold, clear, rippling water. He could see all sizes of rocks on the creek bed, and he noticed how some of them sparkled, even beyond the glinting of the sunlight on the water. Stretching as far as he could without falling in, Hawk plunged his small hand into the water and scooped up some rocks and sand.

Raising his hand above the surface of the water, he sat up on the rock and examined the dripping creek mud and small stones. The sand sparkled in the sunlight and twinkled with a golden color. Still looking down at his hand, Hawk called out, "Father, have you ever seen anything on earth shine as bright as the sun?"

Dark Wolf approached the rock and stooped down to look at his son's find. His gut wrenched. "Hawk, I believe you have just found the answer to the mystery in your grandmother's words."

Now looking over Dark Wolf's shoulder, Raven asked, "What is it, Father?"

"Gold."

Hawk looked at it again and asked, "Can I keep this handful, Father?"

Hesitant at first, Dark Wolf decided that the boys should have this small token to remind them about greed and how it leads to death. "Yes. Put it in your pouch, Hawk. Keep it to yourself. And always remember what it means. The treasure itself is not evil. The Great Spirit made it. It is a part of Mother Earth. But the evil comes when man's desire to have the treasure becomes so great he will do anything to obtain it."

Following his father's instructions, Hawk put into his small leather pouch as much of the moist sand and small stones as possible, then rinsed his hand in the stream.

"Now what, Father?" Raven asked.

Dark Wolf quietly walked back up to the large rock where they had sat earlier. He again sat down and finally answered, "Your grandmother said we must watch the crow. It will show us something more. We will meditate and wait."

The three sat in silence, eyes closed, concentrating on their trust that the revelation would come. They listened to the sounds of nature, the occasional stomping of the horses' feet and the munching sounds as they grazed, the breeze whispering through the branches of the aspens, the rippling water, the falling of a giant tree somewhere off in the distance.

Growing weary of waiting and being so quiet, Hawk peeked with one eye at Dark Wolf. Adjusting his posture to imitate his father, he closed his eyes again.

Just then they all heard the familiar cawing as a crow flew nearby. Opening their eyes, they watched as the large black bird swooped down toward them several times, cocking its head sideways and giving them an inquisitive glance. Finally it flew further up the mountain and landed in the top of a huge tree, which stood in front of a wall of rock, weathered and cracked with age. The crow continued to caw, as if calling to them.

Without speaking, Dark Wolf led his sons to their horses and helped them mount. They rode slowly up the mountain side, watching the leafless tree and the black bird perched on the highest branch. Occasionally, the bird would bob its head and caw loudly. Finally, after carefully winding their way upward over uneven trails among loose rocks, they came to a clearing below the tree. The crow ruffled its feathers and called to them again.

Dark Wolf noted that the huge tree was gray and twisted, its roots jutting out of the ground, a symbol of agony and death looming above them. A few yards behind the tree was what appeared to be the entrance to a cave.

Dark Wolf dismounted and walked slowly to the dark, gaping mouth of the rock face. His hand touched the cold wall at the edge of the entrance and he stopped. The pungent odor of death crept into Dark Wolf's nostrils. Keeping his hand flat against the rock, he closed his eyes. Scenes from his vision of the night before flashed in his mind, and he remembered the veins of golden rock and the dead bodies, the same odor filling his nostrils even now.

In his excitement, Hawk broke the silence. "Can we go inside the cave, Father?"

"No!" Dark Wolf turned around and walked back to his horse. More calmly this time, he answered, "No, Hawk. We must not go inside." He mounted his horse and turned it away. "We have seen enough."

———————

Ben Thomas stared unbelievingly at the twenty dollar gold piece in the palm of his hand.

Isaac laughed. "Haven't you ever seen one of those before, boy?"

"No, sir, Mr. Cutler. Not up close." Smiling, he looked at Isaac and added, "And I *damn* sure never got to hold one in my hand."

Blowing a puff of cigar smoke, Isaac teased, "Well, you go spend that on yourself tonight, Ben. You deserve it. And there will be plenty more for you to earn."

Smiling broadly, Ben shoved the gold coin into his shirt pocket and said, "I'm gonna hang onto this one for awhile and just enjoy havin' it ... at least until I earn me another one."

Isaac laughed again and put his arm around Ben's shoulders, directing him toward the wagon as they walked. He removed the cigar from his mouth. "Okay, Ben, just remember to keep your ears open in town for the next few days, and come let me know immediately if you hear anything at all about the matters we have discussed."

Climbing into the wagon and taking the reins, Ben answered, "I know what to do, Mr. Cutler. Don't you worry none. I won't let you down."

Puffing on his cigar again, Isaac said, "Good. Good. You know, Ben, you do right by me, and there could just be a place here at the ranch for you. Would you like that, Ben?"

Stifling his excitement at the prospect, Ben simply shrugged and nodded. "Sure. I'm just driftin'. Ain't got no better place to stay."

"Well, be off then." Isaac stepped back and watched as Ben turned the horses and started off down the road. "And when you come back, bring me some more of these cigars!"

Ben acknowledged the order with a wave of his hand, then smacked the horses into a run so he could hurry back to town and begin his task for Mr. Cutler.

Elizabeth Cutler, still enjoying her relaxation in the tub, continued to smile and think of Seth.

"Well, well. Look who's smiling." Isaac's voice carried a hint of sarcasm.

Elizabeth's eyes opened and she gasped. Sitting forward, she quickly grabbed a towel and covered herself as much as possible there in the water. *"Isaac! What are you doing in my room when I'm bathing?!"*

Sitting in the wing chair looking at her with a smug expression, he answered, "Oh, I just thought I'd look in on you and see how you are doing, Mother. Really, now, your modesty amuses me. I have seen naked women before, you know."

Pulling the cord, which hung near her head between the tub and the wall, Elizabeth signaled for Jessie to return. She said sternly, "Perhaps you have, Isaac, but you know this is most improper. You may leave my room now. I will be down for supper this evening and we will talk."

"I'll leave the room if you will tell me what you were smiling about. I sense that something is going on behind my back. Jessie was singing earlier in the hallway." Grabbing the green dress from the bed and holding it in his fist, he continued, "Now you are bathing and putting on fancy dresses ... for supper downstairs with me, perhaps?" Throwing the dress into the water, Isaac asked, "What's going on, Mother?"

Elizabeth had decided upon first seeing Isaac in her room, sitting there with that patronizing look, that she would absolutely *not* let him ruin her good mood, no matter what he did. She was sorely disappointed that he had chosen to toss her dress into the water, but she had other dresses to wear. She took a deep breath and quickly came up with an answer which she hoped would satisfy her son for the moment. Calmly she said,

"Isaac, it was something you said this morning before you went to town. You told me that, if your father were here and saw me in the condition I was in, he would ... well, ... vomit. Remember? Well, it's true. So I decided to just push away all the mournful, tragic thoughts and make some positive changes. I'm still alive and I need to act like it. Your father built this wonderful house ... this ranch ... *all* of it, for me to enjoy, and I am going to start doing that again."

Seemingly satisfied, Isaac stood and strolled slowly toward the door. "Good. I'm glad I could help."

Just before Isaac reached the door, Jessie arrived and tapped on it. Knowing it would frighten the girl, Isaac quickly opened the door and gave her a wide smile as he leaned forward, his face close to hers. Amused to see her cowering and the alarmed look on her face, he laughed as he walked past her into the hallway.

Stepping into the room and closing the door, Jessie saw Elizabeth struggling to lift the dress from the water and wring it out. Rushing over to help, Jessie cried, *"Oh, Mrs. Cutler, your beautiful dress! It's ruined!"*

"Now, now, Jessie. We don't want to let Isaac's childish tantrums spoil our fun. Let's get my hair washed, then I can dress in my riding clothes and take that ride. Later I'll find another dress to wear to supper."

Together they finished wringing the dress and Elizabeth said, "Just move the pitcher and put the dress in the basin. We can decide what to do with it later."

Jessie laid the wet, crumpled pile of green velvet in the basin and turned around, only to be met with a sprinkling on her face as Elizabeth playfully flipped water from her fingers. Jessie laughed as some of the nervousness began to leave her.

Elizabeth laughed and said, "There now, that's better."

———————

Hattie Gray had been back from her trip to town less than an hour when she heard a familiar voice call out. *"Hello the house!"*

She eagerly stepped out onto the porch and smiled at Dark Wolf. Then, as quickly as she had come out, the smile left her face and she went back inside. Stepping back out again, she pulled a shotgun up to her shoulder and aimed it toward the three visitors. Squinting and resting her finger on the trigger, she said, "You I know, Dark Wolf. But who are these varmints?"

Raven's heart began to beat rapidly with fear, but he did not move.

Hawk stared at the end of the gun barrel and whispered, "Father, don't let her shoot us. Tell her we aren't varmints."

Dark Wolf dismounted and said, "Easy, Hattie, you don't want to shoot these varmints. They aren't big enough to eat yet."

Hattie lowered the gun and looked the boys up and down. "Yeah, yer right. It'd be a waste of good am'nition." Suddenly, Hattie reared back and laughed loudly.

Smiling, Dark Wolf turned and winked at his sons. He motioned for them to come closer.

Raven jumped down from his horse and went around to help Hawk down from his.

Hattie leaned the shotgun against the house and stood firm with her hands on her hips.

Both boys stood very close to their father while introductions were made. "Boys, this is Hattie Gray. Hattie, these are my sons, Raven and Hawk."

Hattie reached out to shake hands with the boys as she said, "Hope I didn't scare ya too bad. I was just funnin' with ya. I'm really glad to finally meet ya. Yer pa has told me about ya. And I know he's glad to have you boys with him now." Directing Dark Wolf and the boys inside, Hattie added, "I sure was sorry to hear about yer grandmother's passin' on, though."

Raven spoke, "Yes, we will miss her." And quickly, as an afterthought, he said, "It's good to finally meet you, too, ma'am."

Hawk looked at Hattie, her long, wild, graying hair, piled kind of lopsided on her head, with strands hanging down around her sweaty face, her dusty, crumpled clothes, her worn boots. He decided he liked her, even if she did scare him. Sitting down in a hard, wooden chair near the fireplace, he said, "Hattie Gray, you really did scare me pretty good. But it's okay. I like you, anyway."

Hattie laughed and said, "And I like you, too, Hawk. You and Raven are welcome here anytime." Coming closer, she tousled Hawk's blonde curls and said, "And I promise I won't hold a shotgun on ya no more." Turning to Dark Wolf, she said, "I'm fixin' to build a fire in my cook stove and fix some vittles. I'd be right pleased if you would stay and eat with me."

Seeing the hopeful look in Raven's eyes and the broad smile on Hawk's little face, Dark Wolf could hardly decline the offer. "Thank you, Hattie, that would be nice."

Hawk jumped up from his seat and said, *"I can help!* Grandmother used to let me help her in the kitchen. Just tell me what to do."

Hattie said, "Well, all right then. I'll peel some taters while you mix up the biscuit dough." Rummaging around in a cupboard in the corner of the room, Hattie said, "I know there's a big bowl in here somewhere. We'll want to make a whole bunch of biscuits." Finding the bowl, she set it on the table and said, "Let's get this fire goin' first so the stove can be heatin' while we're mixin'."

When Hawk began handing Hattie the chunks of wood for the stove, Dark Wolf motioned for Raven to go with him, and they quietly slipped outside. Closing the door behind him, Dark Wolf said, "Let's tend to the horses before supper."

Raven had a gut feeling that his father wanted to say something to him while they were alone. But he did not ask. He would wait.

After loosing his and Hawk's horses in the corral, Dark Wolf led Raven's horse into a small stable. He showed Raven how to calm the horse, which had been accustomed to freedom in wide open spaces, and how to brush its coat gently. Holding the halter tightly in one hand, Dark Wolf advised, "Don't try to brush her belly or her hips or her legs today. Just brush her neck, her shoulders and her chest, very gently, like this." Putting the brush in Raven's hand and covering it with his own, he gently stroked the brush down along the mare's neck. The mare flinched at the first touch. Her nostrils flared, loud bursts of air escaping with each breath, and fear showed in her eyes as she stomped and tried to pull away from Dark Wolf's grip. *"Watch her feet!* She might stomp you." Releasing Raven's hand, but still holding the halter firmly, he leaned in to put his cheek against the mare's cheek and began to speak softly, "Easy. Easy, girl. Raven will take good care of you. Easy now."

Hearing his father's words, Raven gained confidence and continued brushing, following each stroke with his other hand, enjoying the silky smooth feel of her coat, and allowing the mare to get used to his touch. He could feel her muscles quivering for a few minutes, but then she seemed to calm down, and Raven carefully moved around to her other shoulder.

Dark Wolf softly said, "Keep brushing for a few more minutes. Perhaps tomorrow morning you can tie her close in and sit up on the rail and brush her back, too."

Raven became nervous as he asked, "Are we going to be here tomorrow, Father?"

"Yes, Raven. I must go to town tonight, and you and Hawk will stay here with Hattie."

Raven stopped brushing and came to stand beside his father. Looking up at him he said, "I want to go with you."

Without answering, Dark Wolf led the horse outside and turned her loose in the corral with the others. Raven followed close behind him. They walked back to the house and sat down on the edge of the porch.

"I must go alone, Raven. I can go quickly and see Sarah Mason. You said she might have a letter from Mr. Cutler. Remember? It could be very important."

Raven, panic seeming to overtake every nerve in his body, tried to speak. He could only stare and wish his father could hear his thoughts and know his fears. Somewhere off in the distance it seemed, he again heard his father's voice, though it appeared to be stifled by the loud, thunderous drumming of his own heart.

"You must stay here and look after Hawk. You can show him how to brush his horse. And you can help Hattie until I return. She will have plenty of chores for you to do. The time will pass quickly."

Raven found his voice and said, "I am afraid."

Dark Wolf put his arm around his son's shoulders. "Raven, I know that you are afraid. You fear that I will not come back to you because I left you for so long before. This I did because *I* was afraid. But I tell you the truth when I say that I love you and Hawk more than life itself, and I will never leave you alone again, not like before."

Raven leaned against his father and put his head on his chest. "Promise me that you will return tomorrow, Father. For I know if you promise it, you will do it."

"I promise, Raven." Dark Wolf wrapped his arms around his son and held him tightly. "I promise I will return ... very soon."

CHAPTER TEN

Seth watched as Elizabeth Cutler walked her white Arabian horse out of the barn and mounted. She sat so tall and lovely in the saddle. She was so stylish in her riding pants and jacket and her tall black boots. As she urged the animal into a gentle canter, Seth turned back to his work. He was thankful he had been able to tell her about his findings at the cabin and about his brief visit with Sarah Mason. He knew Elizabeth was looking forward to a visit from the Indian son of Jonathan Morgan. She had not said much, only that Dark Wolf was a true friend and would help her.

Seth blushed and smiled when he remembered her apology at standing in the window earlier that day clothed only in her undergarments. Though he had protested, she had given her explanation, declaring that she did not want to be thought of as a loose woman, like those she had seen hanging out of the upstairs windows in times past when she had gone to town with Mr. Cutler.

Though he kept himself busy, Seth could not help worrying about Mrs. Cutler riding out alone. He pulled a watch from his pocket and noted the time. If Elizabeth was not back within the hour, he would go and find her. In the meantime, he would stay near the door of the barn so that he could watch the house. As long as Isaac was still inside, Seth believed Elizabeth would have an enjoyable ride and return safely.

When Elizabeth believed herself to be out of sight of the ranch house, she smacked her horse with the riding crop and gave it free rein. It ran like the wind, so smoothly, and when she leaned forward and low and felt the sting of the horse's mane whipping her face, she was reminded of her younger days, and of her free spirit. They followed the road

83

along the fence at the very foot of the mountain until she saw the familiar cabin home of Dark Wolf's mother. She gently pulled back on the reins and began slowing the horse. When she reached the clearing, she dismounted, walked the horse into the yard, and tied the reins to a porch post.

She knew the house would be empty, as Seth had told her of Laughing Brook's death and the departure of the boys. Sure enough, Sarah Mason had provided the answers and the assurance that Dark Wolf would come. Elizabeth slowly walked into the house and looked around. A gentle breeze followed her inside and caused the rocking chair near the fireplace to begin rocking. She strolled over and sat down in the chair. Laying her head back and closing her eyes, she began to rock slowly.

A sadness welled up inside her when she thought of how her own misery over losing her beloved Thomas had kept her from visiting Laughing Brook Morgan in her time of loneliness, illness, and death. She was so ashamed that Jonathan Morgan's life had been taken and that Laughing Brook had been alone all these years, except for Dark Wolf's sons. And believing in her heart that Isaac was most likely responsible for the losses sustained by Laughing Brook and the boys, Elizabeth felt an indescribable shame. But ashamed as she might feel now, it would not change anything. She quickly prayed that all of the misery would stop and everyone could go on with the business of living life to its fullest.

Elizabeth stood and walked into the bedroom. After briefly gazing around the room and feeling the emptiness that had now pervaded the entire house, leaving it cold and stark, she decided to leave. She closed the door behind her and turned around. One hand flew to her chest and she gasped when she saw Isaac. He was only a few yards from her horse, sitting on the black stallion, staring at her with piercing eyes. *"Oh, goodness, Isaac! You scared me!"*

"What's going on, Mother?!" he shouted angrily.

Attempting to cover her feeling of alarm, Elizabeth moved down the steps and untied her horse. She calmly said, "Nothing is *going on*, Isaac. I just came to see the Morgans since I hadn't been here in a long while, but, as you can see, they are not here."

"What do you *mean*, they are not here?"

Turning her horse away from the house, Elizabeth answered, "I mean, they are not here, Isaac."

Dismounting, Isaac jerked his horse around and threw the reins toward his mother. *"Here! Hold onto him, and don't leave!"* Stomping up the steps and into the house, Isaac began to mutter and swear. He stood, disbelief and anger filling him as his eyes scanned the front room from the table at the extreme right to the cold, empty fireplace at the extreme left. He walked into the bedroom and was met with the same deserted condition.

"Damn!" The windows rattled when he slammed the door behind him as he left the house. *"Damn!"*

Elizabeth tossed the reins back at Isaac and turned her horse away. Over her shoulder she said, "I really don't know why you are so upset, Isaac. We didn't *own* them, you know. They probably got tired of living here and decided to go somewhere else. And I will miss them."

Kicking his horse in the ribs, Isaac trotted past his mother and said, *"Oh, shut up, Mother! What do you know?"* After a long moment, he said, *"Damn!"* Kicking his horse again, Isaac rode on ahead, leaving his mother to travel home alone.

Elizabeth breathed a sigh of relief that she had maintained a calm exterior, though she had been very frightened by Isaac's obvious anger. Three difficult episodes with Isaac in one day was almost more than she could bear.

Seth had been pacing in his room in the corner of the barn for several minutes, wondering what to do. He had seen Isaac ride off in the same direction Elizabeth had gone earlier. Finally, he had endured all the suspense he could handle, and had saddled a big bay mare. He was just preparing to lead her out when he saw an unfamiliar buckboard carriage, drawn by a single horse, coming up the road. He tied the bay to a rail and walked out of the barn and to the front of the house.

As the carriage arrived at the house, Seth recognized Jessie's younger brother, Curtis. "Hi, Curt! What are you doing here?"

The young boy nervously blurted out, "Can you get my sister for me? I need her to come home with me."

"Sure thing. Just stay put. I'll get her." Seth hurried into the house and called for Jessie.

Jessie came running from the kitchen. "I'm right here. What's the matter, Seth?"

Pointing toward the door, Seth answered, "I don't know. Curt is here. He says he needs you to go home with him."

As Jessie hurried past him, untying her apron, she said, *"Oh, no!* I guess Mama has gotten worse. She was not well the last time I was home for a visit."

At the sight of Jessie, Curtis jumped down from the buckboard and ran to meet her. Throwing his arms around her, he cried, "Jessie, Ma is dying. You need to come *now.* She wants you."

Jessie hugged her brother and told him not to worry. She turned to look at Seth. "Will you help me carry some things down?"

Curtis wiped his eyes and climbed back up into the wagon to wait, relieved that he had found his sister.

Seth and Jessie went into the house and up the stairs to Jessie's room to pack.

When Isaac reached the end of the road leading up to the house, he saw the rig and whipped his horse to run faster. Reaching the edge of the yard, he stopped his horse short and jumped down. Taking long strides, Isaac approached the worried youngster and grabbed the reins out of his hands. *"Who are you, and what are you doing here?"* he demanded.

The boy stammered, "I-I'm Curtis Hill. J-Jessie's brother."

"Well? What are you doing here, boy?"

Beginning to tremble, the boy tried to answer, "M-my mother ..."

Just then Jessie and Seth came out of the house, carrying a carpet bag and some other parcels. Isaac released the reins, throwing them at the boy, and approached Jessie. *"Where do you think you are going?"*

Pushing aside her fear, Jessie walked past Isaac and put her things in the space behind the wagon seat. "I'm going home, Mr. Cutler. My mother is sick and needs me now." As she began to climb into the carriage, Isaac grabbed her and pulled her back.

Seth stepped up in a threatening manner and said, "Isaac, you let go of her right now or I will *knock you out!"*

Isaac, seeing the huge fists and the fire in Seth's eyes, released Jessie. He returned the look with an evil one of his own and growled, "I'll deal with you later, Seth Logan. You can believe that."

From a distance, Elizabeth had seen her son's meanness and had heard Seth's loud warning. She urged her horse on and quickly arrived on the scene. Dismounting quickly, Elizabeth smacked Isaac across the chest with her riding crop and yelled, *"Isaac, go into the house!* We will discuss this later."

Furious, although surprised at his mother's behavior, Isaac gave a piercing look to each of the others, then turned and went angrily into the house, slamming the door behind him.

Jessie ran over to Elizabeth and began to cry as they hugged each other. *"Oh, Mrs. Cutler, my mother is dying!* She needs me ... I don't know how long I will be gone."

Comforting her, Elizabeth said, "Of course, dear. You go and stay with her. We will be fine here. I'm just so sorry."

Jessie gently pushed away and looked up at Elizabeth with tear-filled eyes, "If Mama dies, I will be needed at home to care for the younger ones. I may not be able to come back at all."

Elizabeth looked at Seth and said, "Please stay here with Curt while I talk to Jessie for a minute. I need to give her something from upstairs."

Seth gave an understanding nod and stepped over closer to the boy. "How about you come help me put these two horses in the barn for Mrs. Cutler."

With her arm around Jessie's shoulders, Elizabeth guided the girl into the house. She glanced into the study and saw Isaac slouched in his father's chair at the large desk, looking like a pouting child. The two women went quietly up the stairs and directly to Elizabeth's room, where she locked the door behind them. She indicated the wing chair and Jessie sat down. Handing her a handkerchief, Elizabeth whispered softly, "Jessie, I want to help you any way I can. I have hidden away some money, and I want to give it to you. You and your family will need it."

As Elizabeth brought a strong box from the closet and turned the key in the lock, Jessie wailed, *"Oh, Mrs. Cutler!"*

Elizabeth quickly whispered, *"Shhhhh, Jessie, please!* We must not stir Isaac's curiousity."

The girl dabbed at her eyes with the handkerchief, nodded, and quickly calmed herself.

Elizabeth continued, whispering, "Now I know you will need this money, and I know you will be prudent with it, so I want you to have it." She handed Jessie a thick envelope filled with currency. "Stuff it into your hand bag right now, Jessie. And if you need more later on, I trust you will let me know somehow. You have been like a daughter to me, Jessie, and I have enjoyed your company so much. But now it is time for you to go and take care of things at home. Besides, I'm feeling much stronger now." Smiling and waving her riding crop in the air, she added, "And much braver."

Jessie laughed through her tears. "Oh, Mrs. Cutler, I will miss you. And I thank you so much for the money. I do promise I will use it wisely."

Cupping her hands on Jessie's cheeks, Elizabeth used her thumbs to gently wipe the tears from the girl's sad eyes as she said, "I know you will, Jessie. Now you must go. Your mother is waiting."

Jessie wanted to tell Mrs. Cutler something very important, but time would not allow it to be told just now. She knew she must hurry home to her mama.

Elizabeth walked Jessie out and stood beside the carriage. Jessie hugged Elizabeth again and said, "Thank you. I will write a letter very soon. Watch for it. And please take care."

Stepping away and standing beside Seth, Elizabeth waved as Curtis turned the wagon about and started down the road.

Seth looked down at Elizabeth and in a serious tone asked, "Are you worried that Isaac might try to hurt you, Mrs. Cutler?"

Turning to go to the house, Elizabeth said, "I have worried too much about what Isaac might do, Seth. I can't live my life in fear anymore. I've had a good day in spite of him. I'll be fine." Leaving Seth standing there, Elizabeth walked to the top of the porch steps. She turned back and smiled at seeing the big man still standing there watching her. "Seth, I'm going to finish cooking the supper Jessie began preparing. When it is finished, I'd be pleased to have you join us at the table."

Blushing, Seth nodded and grinned. "I'll get cleaned up and come around directly. Thank you, ma'am."

CHAPTER ELEVEN

The sun had settled behind the mountains, and the darkening shadows had covered the valley town. The roar of thunder crowded out the silence. The rain began to pour as Dark Wolf arrived at the back street leading to Sarah Mason's home.

Sarah sat by her fireplace, reading by lamplight, a multi-colored, patchwork quilt wrapped around her. She had left her back door unlatched, hoping and trusting that Dark Wolf would come, but when the rain began, her heart sank. Just then, she heard the door open, and the fresh smell of the storm pushed its way into her house. Unwrapping the blanket, Sarah stood and picked up her oil lamp. She walked to the back room of the house and offered the blanket to the handsome man who stood before her, his wet cedar-toned skin shining like silver in the lamp light. "Here! Wrap up in this. I've already got it warmed up for you."

Dark Wolf wrapped himself with the warm quilt. "Thank you."

Sarah motioned for him to follow her into the kitchen. As she sat the lamp down on the table, she said, "Please, sit down. I've got some papers for you. I'll get them and you can look at them while I make some hot herb tea." She stepped up onto a chair and reached high up on a shelf for a large stone jar. She carefully set the jar down on the stove and stepped down. Reaching her arm deep into the jar, she pulled out the envelope she had found in Laughing Brook's Bible, along with the note from Mrs. Elizabeth Cutler. Handing the documents to Dark Wolf, she told him, "I came across the envelope when I was packing up the last of your mother's belongings. And the note was delivered to me this morning, but it's for you."

After examining the names on the envelope, Dark Wolf calmly opened it and took out its contents. He unfolded the papers and began to read the letter from Thomas Cutler to his mother. When he was finished with the letter, he read the first few lines of the first legal document. He stopped reading and looked at Sarah, who had a small fire going in the cook stove and was now busily tossing herbs and spices into a cooker full of water. He asked her, "Did you read these papers?"

Embarrassed, Sarah turned to him and confessed, "Yes, I did, Dark Wolf. If I hadn't, I would not have known how important they were to you."

Dark Wolf surprised Sarah, "Good. Now tell me what they say. I don't have time to read them all now."

Sarah made sure the brew was simmering nicely, then she sat down across from him at the table and began explaining the legal documents as she understood them. When she finished, she reminded him about the note, which she also admitted reading. She stood and hurried over to fill two heavy mugs with the aromatic tea. Adding a large spoonful of honey to each mug, she chuckled and said, "Well, if I am to be the messenger, I should get to know what is going on."

Dark Wolf smiled and began reading the note from Elizabeth Cutler. His smile disappeared when he learned of Isaac's recent behavior and the feeling of fear and despair in the woman who wrote the message. He laid the note on the table and looked at Sarah. "Thank you for these things you have shown me." He cupped both hands around the mug and slurped a small sip from it. "And thank you for the tea." He smiled at Sarah as she returned to sit across from him.

"Oh!" Sarah exclaimed. "I almost forgot to ask. How are the boys? *Where* are the boys?"

"The boys are fine. They are safe on the mountain with a friend."

Sarah continued to question, "Are you going to see Mrs. Cutler right away?"

Dark Wolf was torn. He knew that Mrs. Cutler needed him to help her, and that the problem with Isaac needed some attention, but he had promised his sons he would return very soon. After a few moments of contemplation, he answered, "I will see her in two days. Can you go there tomorrow and let her know?"

"Yes, I can do that. I will bake some pies and take to her. I've been wanting to see her anyway."

"Good. Thank you." Standing, Dark Wolf dropped the blanket onto the chair and turned to leave.

"Can't you stay here tonight and leave early in the morning?"

Walking toward the back door, Dark Wolf answered, "No. Thank you, Sarah, but I must go and listen to the talk in town. Maybe I will make my presence known."

Sarah smiled and said, "Aren't you worried about Isaac finding out? I'm sure someone will tell him."

Just before Dark Wolf pulled the door closed behind him, he said, "After all that I have learned within the past two days, I *want* him to know that I'm around."

Hattie had just finished emptying the boys' bath water from the large washtub, and was preparing their beds on the floor. "You boys have had a long day and done some hard work. I figger ya'll are plum tuckered out."

Hawk sat down beside Raven on a mat in front of the fireplace. "I'm going to go to sleep pretty soon, because you said I could help you chop the wood in the morning!"

Raven said, *"I'll* chop the wood, Hawk, and you can help Hattie stack it."

"Okay, and you promised to help me brush my horse some more, too." Hawk reminded Raven.

Engaging in more conversation about their busy day, the boys had not noticed Hattie leaving the room. Now she came to sit with them. They noticed she had washed up and put on a flannel nightgown. They watched as her large hands worked swiftly to make one long braid in her wet, stringy, gray hair. She pulled it around to the front on the right side and finished it, then tied a strip of cloth near the end to hold it.

"Hattie, where did you come from?" Hawk asked. "Have you always lived here?"

Hattie thought for a moment, then answered, "I'm not sure. I never thought about it much. I've lived up here for so long ... I just don't rightly know."

"How old are you, Hattie?" Hawk asked.

Hattie thought for a moment, then answered, "Well, Hawk, I don't rightly know *that* neither. It don't matter much, I s'pose."

Staring into the fire, Raven finally spoke. "Before Father left today he told us that you had killed the bad men who came to steal the treasure in the cave. He said you shot them with arrows."

"That's true," Hattie said.

The thunder roared and then cracked like a shooting gun as a lightning bolt lit up the sky and flashed its light through the cabin windows. Hawk slid closer to Hattie, and she put her arm around him. "Are you cold?" she asked.

"No ... just tired," Hawk answered with a sigh.

Raven asked, "How did you learn to shoot a bow and arrow so well?"

Hattie smiled. "Well, your father taught me. And I practiced ... *alot.*" Chuckling, she added, "It took me a long time to get any good at it."

Hawk asked, "But why did you shoot all those men with arrows? Why didn't you use a gun?"

Looking down at Hawk, Hattie said, "Oh, I guess I thought a silent death that just sneaks up on a man would do better. And I guess I didn't want the noise of gun fire to attract any attention from the folks in town or on the plains. Noise carries pretty far in the wide open sky out here." Grabbing an iron poker, Hattie poked at the fire and stirred it to a higher blaze. She added, "I s'pose I wanted it to be a mystery to folks. These men were greedy and up to no good. Out to take what didn't belong to them. They came onto the mountain, died real quiet like, and were never seen again. Finally they stopped comin'."

Standing up, Hattie said, "C'mon now, it's time we bed down for the night. Yer pa will want you to be rested and ready to go with him when he gets back."

The boys found their places on the floor and Hattie covered them with their blankets. As she tucked the covers around Hawk, he said, "Hattie, do you think any other bad men will come?"

Hattie let out a big sigh and leaned forward a little. "Maybe. But this time there will be three warriors on the mountain. Yer pa, yer brother, and you."

Raven was already drifting off to sleep, but he murmured, "There will be four, Hattie. We will have you, too."

Still kneeling on the floor beside Hawk's mat, Hattie chuckled and said, "Nonsense! What would ya need with an old woman like *me*?"

Hawk pushed back the cover, sat up, and threw his arms around Hattie. Squeezing her as tightly as he could in his little arms, he said, "We *do* need you, Hattie."

———————

After finding a shelter for his horse at the side of the livery, Dark Wolf untied the roll from behind his saddle. He unrolled his blanket to reveal a pair of black boots, some denim jeans, and a tan corduroy jacket. He pulled a neatly folded, white shirt from his saddle bag, and his father's stetson from a gunny sack hanging on the other side. There in the darkness, he quickly removed his wet garments and slipped into the dry clothing. After putting them on, he looked up and down the street, which appeared to be deserted, no doubt due to the rain. Dim lamplight shone from a few houses, and he could hear the music of the piano and the laughter and loud conversation coming from the Red Dog Saloon down at the corner on the opposite side of the street. Placing the hat upon his head, he stepped out into the rain.

Quickly crossing the street, he made his way to the saloon. He stood outside the doors for a few minutes, listening, wondering if Isaac Cutler might be inside. After a few moments, he heard one man say to another, "Yeah, that's right! I'm already workin' for Mr. Cutler."

Someone asked, "For Isaac Cutler? I thought you was workin' at the general store."

The first man spoke again, "Well, Mr. Cutler hired me today. Even paid me in *advance!*"

The distinct sound and sight of a large gold coin hitting the table drew the attention of those around the man, and Dark Wolf stepped closer to the window, taking the opportunity to look through and identify the braggart. He saw the man snatch up the coin quickly, as he had dropped it, and put it back into his shirt pocket.

When asked what he had to do to earn that kind of money, the man said, "I can't say, but he did promise there is more where this came from. And he will soon be putting me in charge at his ranch."

Still observing from the shadows outside the window, Dark Wolf saw one of the older men at the table rear back and laugh loudly, and heard him say, "Ain't *nobody* but Isaac gonna be in charge of anything at the Circle C Ranch. Rumor has it he shot Zeke, his foreman, for havin' them same ideas."

The first man argued again, "Well, things will be different when *I* get there."

———————

The noise inside the saloon began to die down, and the piano music ceased in mid-measure. Ben Thomas looked around to see what had caused this deafening silence. Only the squeak of the saloon doors could be heard, and Ben whirled back around in the direction everyone was staring. He saw a tall, dark-skinned man standing in the doorway.

Turning to one of the other men, he asked, "Who is that man?"

Just then he heard the sound of a chair scooting away from a table across the room, and a distinguished-looking older gentleman in a suit stood and said in a loud, deep voice, *"Well, I'll be damned! Young Jon Morgan! Where the hell have you been?"*

Dark Wolf smiled and met the man halfway across the floor. The man hugged him and shook his hand. "Jon, come sit at my table, please!" Turning toward the bar, the man shouted to the bartender, *"The prodigal has returned! Drinks for everyone ... on me!"*

The crowd cheered, not caring to know the reason behind this wonderful display of generosity, but happy to be on the receiving end. The piano player began a lively tune, and the roar of conversation again filled the room.

Laying his hand on the gentleman's shoulder, Dark Wolf said, "I'll be right there. I need to say something to the bartender." He sauntered over to the bar and set his elbow on the counter with his hand up, challenging the big man behind the bar to an arm wrestling match.

The bartender came over, laid his wiping rag aside, and accepted the challenge without a word. As he silently slipped his hand snugly into Dark Wolf's, their eyes met.

Some of the nearby onlookers began to cheer, some placed bets, and Ben Thomas took it all in with great excitement, knowing that Mr. Cutler would want to hear all about this man's reappearance.

Finally the match began, and the two big men kept staring into each other's eyes. The bartender broke into a heavy sweat as he fought desperately to hold his own against the dark-skinned man. Cheers went up throughout the room, some for the bartender, some for "Morgan", or "Dark Wolf", as some called him.

Ben noticed the one they called "Dark Wolf" seemed calm and unaffected by the contest. Then suddenly he saw the red man purse his lips and give a determined look. In an instant it was over.

The bartender wiped the sweat from his face and neck and massaged his aching arm and shoulder. *"Dammit, ya half-breed, ya almost broke my arm!"* Then he laughed and said, "I should make *you* serve all these drinks now."

Dark Wolf said, "It has been a long time, Will. Are you married yet?"

The bartender smiled broadly as he answered, "Almost. She's a keeper, Jon."

"Glad to hear it." Dark Wolf took the opportunity to look around again and see the young man at the front table. Turning back to the bartender, he said, "You are a good man, Will. You need some children before you are too old to enjoy them."

"You're right, Jon. Yes, you are ... about the *children*, I mean."

Both men laughed.

Jokingly, Dark Wolf asked the bartender, "And do you serve half-breeds in here now?"

The bartender smiled and replied, "Just the *white* half. What'll it be?"

Dark Wolf smiled and said, "I'll have a short one. Please send it over to the table. Surprise me."

"Okay, Jon. And don't stay away so long next time."

Remembering the conversation he had heard upon arriving at the saloon, Dark Wolf said, "One more thing, Will. Can you tell me the name of that squirrely boy over at the table near the door?"

The bartender looked at the men around the table, then looked back at Dark Wolf. Filling some glasses for the two men on either side of Dark Wolf, he answered, "He ain't nobody. Not from around here. Just a drifter. Name's Thomas ... Ben Thomas. Been braggin' that he's Isaac Cutler's right hand man."

"Yes, I heard. Thanks, Will." Dark Wolf turned to go. Looking back, he added, "You'll be seeing me around."

Ben Thomas watched as Dark Wolf removed his hat and seated himself at the table with the group of men, whom Ben had been told were the local cattle barons. He was certain Mr. Cutler would also want to know that Morgan was rubbing shoulders with these men. After quickly gulping down his free shot of whiskey, Ben slipped out into the dark, rainy night.

When the introductions began, Dark Wolf quickly glanced past his host's shoulder just in time to see Ben Thomas step outside and the swinging door return to its former stillness. He smiled and returned his attention to his host and the other men at the table. Fresh drinks had been served and they had lifted their glasses in a toast to his homecoming.

After listening to his host, Adam Miller, tell some things about his dealings with Jonathan Morgan, as well as his future hopes for a business relationship with Mr. Morgan's son, Dark Wolf spoke, "Adam, your boastings about my father are greatly appreciated. He was a wonderful father, and I understand that he was a very fair and level-headed business man. But you are forgetting that he brought me to only *one* meeting before he died. I was fifteen at the time. And the cattle business is not something I learned in my travels."

Adam argued, "No, I have not forgotten your attendance at that one meeting, Jon. How could I? Your suggestion was taken into consideration and has been put into practice ever since."

Another man spoke up, "Some of us weren't here at that time, Adam. What was the boy's suggestion?"

Looking around the table as he spoke, Adam answered, "Well, let me put it like this. The meeting was about to begin, and in walks Jonathan Morgan with his young son. After some considerable laughter at the boy's expense, the meeting was called to order. And there was order for about ten minutes or so, while the business of the previous meeting was recounted. When new business began, it became a bragging match, an accusing match, a threatening match, every one of us looking out for our own interest. Forget the other guy."

Now indicating Dark Wolf with his hand and looking at him, Adam continued. "This young man, only fifteen, stood and waited for us to get quiet. And I want to interject here that his father was not involved in the ruckus. He was observing the goings-on with a definite look of disappointment ... and embarrassment for his father. Anyway, everyone stopped to listen, and the boy said, 'You *all* look like very intelligent men. So I am sure you would want to make the best rules and regulations to benefit all of you. When one is hurt, all are hurt. A family of such men would look out for each other and protect the overall business.' Then he just sat down. We all looked at each other like a bunch of scolded children. But I can tell you that the meeting took on a very different flavor, and all of them since have been better. Look how we have grown! And how well we get along! Several of you came into the fold after that time, and you must admit this little association works for the good of all." Turning to Dark Wolf, he added, "Jon Morgan, we would sure like to have you raising cattle and working with us."

Dark Wolf looked around the table and then at Adam. "Why isn't the Cutler ranch represented here? Isaac Cutler should be taking care of his father's interests."

Several men mumbled to each other as they squirmed in their chairs, and Adam said, "First of all, this is not an official meeting. Some of us just decided to get together and have a steak dinner tonight." Nudging the man next to him, Adam joked, "You know, sample some of the merchandise.

Ha!" Then in a more serious tone, he added, "Unfortunately, Isaac Cutler is no kind of business man. We fear Thomas's ranch will go under if something doesn't change. We can't get near Isaac or the place, though. We've tried. He just doesn't seem interested. But enough about Cutler. Jon, we'd like to have you in our midst."

Dark Wolf stood and stepped away from his chair. As he placed it back under the table, he picked up his glass and said, "Gentlemen, I would be honored to be in such a distinguished group. I have heard that the railroad is coming westward. It could provide a good and speedy way to market our beef. Support of this venture is worth consideration, I believe."

Adam Miller bellowed out, *"Hear! Hear!"* and several of the others nodded in agreement.

Lifting his glass for a toast, Dark Wolf said, "Now in honor of Thomas Cutler, I propose that we put Isaac aside for now and concentrate on helping Thomas's widow, Elizabeth, make a profitable business of the Circle C. I will be calling on her very soon and will let her know of our supportive intentions."

All of the men lifted their glasses in agreement and drank.

Dark Wolf put on his hat and added, "Now I have some other business I must attend to at this time, but I will get back to you. Gentlemen." After tipping his hat and thanking his host again, Dark Wolf left the saloon.

Isaac had just drifted off to sleep when he heard the loud knocking at the front door of the house. He fumbled in the darkness to find a lamp and lit it. He put on a thick burgundy robe and picked up the lamp. The pounding began again and he heard Ben Thomas's voice.

"Mr. Cutler! Mr. Cutler!"

Elizabeth also heard the noise and crept to her bedroom door. She opened it in time to see Isaac start down the stairway with the lamp. She quietly tiptoed down the hallway to the top of the stairs to listen.

Seth came running from the barn and arrived on the porch before Isaac reached the front door. In the moonlight, he recognized Ben Thomas, and he whispered angrily, *"Ben, what are you doing here at this time of the night?!"*

Ben backed away from Seth, and before he could answer, the door opened.

At seeing Ben's face in the lamplight, Isaac stepped back and said, "Well, come on in, boy! Have you heard something?"

Seth started to follow Ben into the house, but Isaac's hand flattened against the big man's chest. "We don't need you here, Seth. Go back to the stables where you belong." Isaac gave Seth a gentle shove backwards and slammed the door in his face.

Ben Thomas could hardly contain his excitement at getting to tell Mr. Cutler this important news. The two men went into the study, and Isaac put the lamp on the desk.

He poured a drink for the rain-soaked young man and handed it to him. Indicating another chair, Isaac said, "Sit. Calm down, boy. Tell me what you know."

Holding the rail at the top of the stairs, Elizabeth leaned down as far as she could and strained to hear.

Ben calmed himself, took a big gulp of the drink, and caught his breath. "I know that your half-breed, Jon Morgan, or Dark Wolf, or whatever you want to call him, is in town tonight."

Isaac picked up a cigar and bit the end off of it. After calmly lighting it, he asked, "And how do you *know* this? Did someone tell you?"

"No, sir. I saw 'im with my own two eyes. He came into the Red Dog."

Isaac sat in the big chair behind the desk and continued his questioning. "And how did you know it was him?"

"Well, Mr. Cutler, some man, a cattle man, stood up and called out his name and invited him to sit at his table."

Growing impatient, Isaac leaned forward and frowned at Ben. "And that's it? That's all you know?"

Becoming nervous at the look on Isaac's face, Ben squirmed in his chair and replied, "Well, he challenged the bartender to an arm wrestling contest. I saw that, too."

Isaac leaned back and puffed on the cigar. "Oh, really? And who won this contest?"

"Morgan won. And I will say he didn't have to struggle none to do it."

Staring at the oil lamp, Isaac quietly asked, "What happened after that?"

"He just went over and sat down with the cattle men."

Still staring at the lamp, Isaac asked, "And did you move closer in the crowd so you could hear what was being said?"

Suddenly feeling he had let Mr. Cutler down, Ben answered, "No, sir. I just came straight here to tell you he was in town."

Isaac slammed his fist on the desk and said, *"Dammit, man! What do you think I paid you for? You should have listened! And you should have asked questions!"*

Ben stood. "I'm sorry Mr. Cutler. I wasn't thinking."

Though Isaac felt like shooting the incompetent young fool, he grit his teeth and managed to stay relatively calm. He opened one of the desk drawers and pulled out another gold coin. Tossing the coin on the corner of the desk, he said, "Next time pay attention, boy. Find out what his plans are and ask the townspeople what they know. But be smart about it, son. If you see him again, listen to hear if he says anything about me. Follow him if you have to. But remember, he has Indian blood and he may turn on you."

Ben picked up the coin, put it in his pocket and assured Isaac he would do better next time.

Just before Isaac closed the door behind Ben, an idea came to him. "Wait, boy." Isaac stepped out onto the porch. "Better still, after you find out what Morgan's up to, make *sure* he notices you. If it happens that he corners you somewhere, just tell him Isaac Cutler wants to see him. Then, if you can, get back here and tell me. I have a plan, and you can help me with it." Placing his hand on the boy's shoulder, he added, "There will be big money in it for you, son."

Elizabeth noticed that the lamplight was moving, creating new lights and shadows in the entryway. She quickly tiptoed back to her room and closed the door. Her heart leapt for joy at hearing that Jon Dark Wolf Morgan was back. She believed he had gotten her message by now and would soon come to see her. Snuggling down in her bed again, Elizabeth thanked God for answering her prayer for help.

CHAPTER TWELVE

Jessie sat with Curtis and her other younger brother, Eli, and little sister, Rachel, while Dr. Smith attended to their mother. It seemed an eternity to Jessie since the doctor had gone into her mother's room. The children were quiet, often looking at one another with fear, and looking to Jessie for hope. The thunder cracked and lightning split the sky. The youngest child, Rachel, reached for Jessie. She was lifted to the warmth and safety of Jessie's arms, and she hugged her tightly.

Finally, the old doctor came into the room, his drooping shoulders and bowed head showing weariness and defeat. He raised his eyes to look at Jessie and slowly shook his head.

Jessie knew she had to be strong for the little ones, but she could not stop the tears from filling her eyes and spilling onto her cheeks. Her heart ached so badly. Her father had died last fall, and now she was the only one left to care for these young people who still depended on their mother for everything. She took a deep breath and pushed aside the urge to break down. "Doc Smith, can we go in for a moment? I need to explain this to the children."

The doctor laid his hand on Jessie's shoulder. "Yes, you take your time. I will go talk to the undertaker and let him know of her death. He will come around tomorrow and help you." He put his coat and hat on and picked up his bag. Before he opened the door to go out, he turned back and said, "If you or the children need anything, just let me and Abigail know. We will help any way we can."

Jessie stared at him for a long moment, the tears still brimming in her eyes. She knew she needed to talk to him soon for a physical condition of her own, but deciding she should wait, she took a deep breath and simply said, "Thank you so much, Doc. I will send Curtis around if we need anything."

As Jessie began to explain their mother's passing and try to give comfort to the three sobbing children before her, she felt the first flutter of new life within her own abdomen. She caught her breath, and one hand went to her stomach. She had been able to hide her condition from Mrs. Cutler by the clever ways she wore her housekeeping aprons, and by the way she moved about quickly when in Mrs. Cutler's company.

Jessie could not contain her tears as panic stuck her. *What shall I do? How can I take care of these three, let alone another?* She suddenly remembered the money Mrs. Cutler had given her, and began to find comfort in the fact that the family would not starve. But imagining the humiliation she would suffer as the townspeople found out about her, Jessie broke down again. She bowed her head and held all three children as she cried. *This should not have happened to me!*

When Sarah Mason reached the front door of the small house facing the alley, she heard the loud crying. Putting aside the formality of knocking, she opened the door and entered. Following the sounds, Sarah found Jessie and her siblings at the bedside of their dead mother. Rushing over to them, she picked up the youngest one and held her tightly as she said, "There, there, Rachel. It will be all right. Mommy will be in heaven with Jesus. And you'll see her again someday. Shhhh, now, it's all right."

Jessie looked at Sarah and seemed to find strength in her presence and in her words. She calmed herself and slowly directed the two boys into the other room, away from the source of all the sadness.

Sarah followed, carrying Rachel, and closed the bedroom door behind her. She answered the question in Jessie's eyes. "Doc Smith stopped by and told me what happened. I'm so sorry. Your Mama was such a sweet lady. Everyone will miss her." Sitting down in a rocker in front of the fire, Sarah began rocking and humming softly. Soon, little Rachel was asleep, only an occasional sob escaping her lips.

The boys agreed to lay on a mat before the fire. Jessie covered them with a thick blanket, and soon they were asleep.

Sarah continued to rock, and Jessie took a seat in a high-backed chair near her, laid her head to the side, and began staring into the fire.

Noticing Jessie's apparent physical exhaustion, and the look of despair in her eyes, Sarah spoke softly, "Jessie, you must be worn out. Why don't you go to bed? I will look after these three until you awaken. We'll be fine." Kissing Rachel's forehead, she added, "I've always wanted to rock a little one like this, you know."

Jessie slowly leaned forward and wearily hung her head. Beginning to nervously wring her hands, she said, "Sarah, something has happened to me, and I don't know what to do about it."

Continuing to rock, Sarah softly coaxed the girl, "Jessie, what is it? Can I help?"

Looking at the older woman, Jessie choked back a new river of tears and said, "Sarah, I'm going to have a baby."

Sarah stopped rocking. She stood and walked to the small bed in the corner of the room and laid Rachel down. After removing the child's tiny shoes and socks and covering her with a blanket, Sarah returned to sit beside Jessie. Putting her arm around the embarrassed young girl, she said, "Jessie, dear, it's not the end of the world. But I know you are scared. Do you want to talk about it?"

The girl's tears streamed down her cheeks as she began, "It never should have happened. I have always been a good girl like Mama taught me to be."

"Of course, you have, dear," Sarah comforted.

Continuing, Jessie's anger began to mount, "He was drunk and he was *mean*. He would come to my room and ...

107

hurt me ... while he covered my mouth with his sweaty hand. Then he would *laugh* at me and *threaten* me. I was *so afraid*. I just could not tell anyone."

Sarah asked, "Are you sure you are with child, Jessie?"

Jessie stood and turned around slowly, holding her arms out from her sides. *"Just look at me, Sarah!* I've seen Mama's body change like this enough times. And just tonight, after Mama passed on, I felt the first little flutter of movement, just like Mama told me would happen." Sitting down again, Jessie added sadly, "Only Mama told me it would be a wonderful thing because the baby would be conceived with *love* between me and my husband. Now *no* man will *ever* want anything to do with me."

Sarah took Jessie's hands in hers and said, "Jessie, the child inside you will need your love, even if love is not what caused it to be. You *know* that. And someday, some good man with a good heart will see what a fine, loving mother you are and ask you to be his wife."

Jessie smiled through her tears and gave Sarah a hopeful look. "Do you really think so, Sarah?"

Giving the girl a hug, Sarah assured her, "Yes, dear, I really do think so." After a few moments, Sarah decided to ask the obvious question, "Jessie, will you tell me who did this to you?"

After staring at the floor for a long while and thinking about her options, and realizing that, right then, Sarah was the only friend she had, Jessie finally spoke, "I'll tell you, Sarah. The man who did this to me is Isaac Cutler."

The rain was letting up as Dark Wolf mounted his horse and rode out of town toward the mountains. He believed it had been a productive day. He had been advised of Thomas Cutler's desires with regard to his ranch, his wife, and his worthless son. He had learned that Elizabeth Cutler desired to see him, and he had arranged for Sarah Mason to ease her mind and tell her when he would come. He had made his appearance in town and felt sure that Isaac Cutler would be informed. And he had been urged to join forces with the cattle ranchers, his father's loyal friends.

As Dark Wolf entered the forest at the edge of the foothills, he thought about the time he had spent that morning with his sons, Hawk and Raven. He had helped them to understand some things about their past, including the reasons for his own absence in their lives thus far. He had provided them with beautiful horses and taught them how to respect, care for, and enjoy them. He had introduced them to Hattie Gray. And he had made promises to them — promises which he fully intended to keep.

At that moment he was on his way to fulfill the most important one, and that was to be back at Hattie's when his sons awoke the next morning. It would mean he could not stop and rest for the night, but he did not want them to feel deserted again.

Hattie awoke with a start. Grabbing her rifle from beside the bed, she threw back her quilt and set her feet on the floor. She had left an oil lamp burning in the corner so that, if awakened during the night, the boys could see their surroundings. Quickly glancing around the room, she noticed that Raven was not on his mat. She also noted that the door was slightly ajar. Afraid the boy might have decided to leave, Hattie rushed to the door, opened it, and stepped outside into the darkness. She quietly pulled the door closed behind her.

The storm had ended, but the fresh smell of the rain-soaked earth lingered heavily in the air. Hattie held her rifle at her side and walked slowly across the porch. She could not see anything, but she could feel the presence of someone or something very near her. Stepping back to the door, she slowly pushed it open so that the dim light could creep across the porch floor toward the steps. Her eyes followed the trail of light. Relief flooded her soul when

Hattie saw young Raven sitting on the top step, his back resting against a post.

Hattie leaned the rifle against the wall and sat down beside the boy. Taking a deep breath through her nostrils, Hattie spoke, "The air sure does smell good right after a storm."

After a long silence, Raven finally spoke, "Hattie, is my father coming back?"

Hattie chuckled. "Now, Raven, you just haven't had time to get to know your father yet. I can tell you this; he promised he would be back soon, and that means he will do just that. Don't you worry about it none."

Raven sighed, then said, "Well, he promised he would never leave us again, and he has left us with you."

Hattie reached out and patted the boy's hand. "This is different, Raven. Someday you'll understand." Thinking of a way to coax the boy back inside the cabin, Hattie said, "When I was a girl, I remember someone saying, '*a watched pot never boils.*' Well, that's silly. Of course it'll boil, if it's got a fire under it." She chuckled for a few moments, then added, "Oh, it *seems* like it will never boil when yer watchin' it, but it does. That's sort of like what yer doin' now. Yer watchin' for yer pa, and it seems like he'll *never* get here. But if ya go inside and go back to sleep, before ya know it, he'll be here a-wakin' you up, or, more likely, he'll be here in time for a big breakfast!"

Raven stood and reached out his hand for Hattie's, "Well, I *do* want him to come back soon, so I'm going to give it a try, Hattie."

Taking his hand and standing, Hattie said, "Now, that's the spirit, boy!"

Elizabeth Cutler sat in the darkness in her room, straining her ears for the familiar sounds of Isaac ascending the stairs and going to his room. After a long while with nothing but silence filling the air, she put on her dressing gown and went to find him.

Finding him in his father's chair in the study, Elizabeth questioned him, "Isaac, who was that at the door? I heard shouting. Is everything all right?"

Turning to look at his mother, Isaac frowned. "Mother, everything is fine. It's nothing that concerns you." Turning away again, and dismissing her with a wave of his hand, he said, "Go back to bed, Mother."

"I asked you who was at the door, Isaac. And I want to know what all the shouting was about. It is distressing to be awakened in that manner."

Swinging around to face his mother, Isaac slammed his fist on the desk and shouted, *"Dammit! It's none of your business, Mother! Now go back to bed!"*

Something inside of Elizabeth snapped. She was tired of being spoken to in this manner by her own son. She stepped closer to him and grabbed his collar. Though her fiery eyes showed her anger, she spoke calmly to him as she said, "Isaac Cutler, you will not continue to treat me like this. I am your mother, and this is *my house*. And what happens in *my house* is *my business!*"

Seemingly amused by her words, Isaac smiled and his hand came up to push hers away, as he leaned forward to stand.

Elizabeth pushed him roughly back into the chair and said, "I don't know *how* it's going to end, Isaac, but it is. Mark my words, Isaac, it's going to end."

Angry now, Isaac grabbed his mother's wrists as he stood. Continuing to hold her wrists up near her face, he forced her backwards toward the doorway. At the doorway, Isaac growled into her face, *"Nobody* is going to tell me what I *can* and *cannot* do. Not even you, Mother." Having said that, Isaac pushed her so hard her back and head slammed against the wall on the opposite side of the entryway. His fists balled up at his sides, he shouted, *"Stay out of my sight!"* Grabbing the door handle, he stepped back into the study and slammed the door behind him.

As the door slammed, Elizabeth slid down the wall and sat on the floor, trying to focus. The pain in her body from hitting the wall was great, and she could hardly catch her breath. After a few long moments, she struggled to her feet and carefully made her way to the top of the stairs and to her room. As she fell onto the bed, she prayed that the nightmare would soon end.

CHAPTER THIRTEEN

The tantalizing smell of smoked bacon cooking on the stove filled Dark Wolf's nostrils as he quietly stepped up to the door of the cabin and knocked. He smiled as he heard the sound of small feet running to open the door. The door swung open wide, and Hawk came rushing out to greet him. Dark Wolf stooped down and swept Hawk into his arms. "How is Hawk today?"

Hawk hugged his father's neck tightly and answered, *"Oh, Father! I'm fine! I'm so glad you are back!"*

Dark Wolf laughed and set Hawk down again. He noticed Raven standing in the doorway, smiling, a look of relief on his face. "And how are you today, Raven?"

Raven stepped forward and took his father's hand. Tugging at him, he said, "Come on. You are just in time for breakfast, Father."

Hattie was just setting the last hot dish on the table when the three fellows came inside and closed the door. "We've got bacon, eggs, fried taters, hot apples, and a whole *heap* of biscuits! And here's some poor man's gravy for the biscuits, Dark Wolf. Hope you like it."

They all took their places at the table. Dark Wolf said, "I'm sure I will, Hattie. This all looks and smells so good." Noting how the boys were quickly scooping large portions from the various dishes, he grinned and asked, "Has Hattie worked you like horses while I was gone?"

Hawk, his mouth too full of food to speak, simply nodded.

Raven smiled and pushed another fork full of potatoes into his mouth.

Hattie said, "My lands, yes! I worked the orn'riness right out of 'em. They'll prob'ly amount to somethin' after all!"

Dark Wolf laughed. Dipping the food onto his plate, he said, "Well, let's hope so. I'd hate to think your efforts have been wasted, Hattie."

It had been after midnight when Sarah Mason returned home from comforting Jessie and helping her with the children. Still she had arisen early, remembering that she was to bake pies and take to Elizabeth Cutler, along with a message from Dark Wolf. She put the pies carefully into the compartment under the carriage seat, and took her place to begin her journey. Jessie's situation had been heavy on her heart and mind since she awoke, but she resigned herself to the fact that it would all work out somehow, and she would do whatever she could to help the poor girl. The air smelled fresh and clean after the much-needed rain of the evening before, and Sarah began to hum a pleasant tune as the horse trotted along the road leading away from town.

The soreness in Elizabeth's body caused her to move slowly during her morning ritual of preparing herself to face the world, as well as the challenge of dealing with Isaac. She had just finished washing her breakfast dishes, and stood looking out of the open kitchen window, when she saw Isaac ride away. Noticing Seth coming toward the house, she quickly dried her hands and headed for the front of the house. She opened the door just as Seth stepped up onto the porch.

"Good morning, Seth!"

Removing his hat and blushing slightly, Seth answered, "Good morning, Elizabeth."

Smiling sweetly, Elizabeth asked, "Is there something I can do for you, Seth?"

"Oh, no, ma'am. I was wondering if there might be anything I could do for *you*." Fidgeting with his hat, he continued, "I mean, with Jessie gone and all ... well, I thought maybe there might be some chores I could help with in the house."

Not wanting to thwart his kind offer, Elizabeth had to think fast, and finally came up with an idea. "Well, now that you mention it, Seth, there are a few things I need done that will take the strength of a man. But I will not expect you to do them all in one day." Noting Seth's smile, she added, "Goodness knows you certainly have enough to do with caring for the horses and keeping things maintained on the outside!"

"It's no trouble, Elizabeth. Really. I'm all caught up out there for now." Stepping closer, Seth said, "You just tell me what you want me to do."

Holding the door open, Elizabeth smiled and warned, "All right, Seth, come on in. But you may regret your offering after you see some of these tasks."

Laughing together, they entered the house and she directed him in and out of each room, listing the projects she would need help with.

Isaac tied his horse outside the Postal Office and walked up the street to the alley in which Jessie lived. He stepped up to the door of the house and pounded on it. When Jessie opened the door, Isaac pushed his way in. He saw her younger brothers and sister sitting at the table with papers, small brushes and paints. "Well, well. Are we having an art class this morning, children? How nice!"

Jessie rushed over to stand between Isaac and the children. "What do you want here, Isaac?"

Slowly, Curtis pulled his little sister over to him and held her tightly against him.

Isaac smirked and said, "Jessie, you don't seem the least bit glad to see me. I thought sure you would miss me just a little." Stepping close to her, he ran his fingers down the right side of her face. "I know *I* miss *you*, Jessie."

Jessie cringed at his touch and closed her eyes as a wave of nausea came over her. She quickly recovered and stepped away from Isaac. "We have just lost our mother, Mr. Cutler. We are in mourning and can't entertain guests right now. Could you please go?"

"Ha, ha, ha! 'Can't entertain guests right now'," he mocked. "Well, sure, I can go. But I promise you, Jessie, I will be back." He stepped closer again and grabbed Jessie's hand. Pulling her to him, he said, "Yes, Jessie, I will be back."

Jessie struggled to free herself from his grip, but he grabbed her hair and held her head firm. She could feel his hot breath on her face. Not wanting to frighten the children any further, her fiery eyes met his and she whispered angrily, "You don't touch me in front of these children! Let go of me right now!"

Isaac released her and pushed her backward. Opening the door, he gave her a look of warning. Glancing at the children, he saw the look of fear on their faces. Amused, he stepped out of the house and pulled the door almost closed. Sticking his head back inside, he gave a sardonic grin and taunted, "Have a nice day, children."

Jessie rushed to the window to watch and make certain Isaac was actually leaving. She could hear him laughing and mumbling. *He truly is a madman,* she told herself. And she could not help wondering what she would do when he *did* come back.

Ben Thomas came out of the hotel where he had spent the night in a soft bed for the first time in months. With the money he had received from Isaac Cutler, he had also treated himself to a hot bath and a shave. He believed he could get used to this life style, and was thrilled at the prospect of doing whatever it took to stay in Isaac's good graces so that he could afford it.

After lighting a cigar, Isaac stepped out of the alleyway just as Ben passed by. "Hey, there, Ben!"

Ben turned around to see Isaac. Somewhat embarrassed, he lamely answered, "Oh, hello, Mr. Cutler. I was just coming to see you."

Walking all around Ben, looking him up and down, Isaac teased, "My, aren't we all gussied up? And smelling so *sweet*, too."

Laughing nervously, Ben said, "Well, yes, it's been a long time since I got cleaned up real good. Thought it was about time."

"Certainly, certainly," Isaac agreed. "Can't blame a man for wanting to do a little something for himself, now can you?" Putting his arm around Ben's shoulders, he began walking down the street. "Come, on, now, Ben. Let's have a drink and talk some business, shall we?"

Dark Wolf and his sons had left Hattie's mountain home soon after breakfast and returned to their side of the mountain around mid-morning. As they reached the clearing in the forest on the upper side of the cabin, Hawk stopped his horse and pointed. Excitedly he exclaimed, *"Look, Father! Indians!"*

The other two horses stopped and Raven asked, "Who are they, Father?"

Carefully studying the sight before him, Dark Wolf remained silent. He saw several teepees set up not far from the one he and his sons had erected the day before. A fire circle had been prepared. Strange horses were turned into the corral. There was no movement in the camp; however, as he looked to the left in the upper side of the meadow, he counted at least fifteen Cheyenne sitting in a circle around his mother's death stand. They were too far away for Dark Wolf to distinguish the gender of each, but he believed he heard a female voice singing a spirit song. Deciding it to be safe to continue on toward the cabin, he finally answered,

"They must be Mother's people. We will go down to the cabin and tie the horses out on the other side. Then I will go and greet them." Urging his horse forward, Dark Wolf said, "Come, my sons. This will be a good day."

Trusting their father's judgment, the boys followed quietly. As they passed behind the strange teepees, the laughter of children could be heard. Hawk gasped and whispered, "Father, may I play with the other children?"

"Hawk, you must wait until they come out. You do not go in. Do you understand?"

"Yes, Father," Hawk answered. "May I sit on the front porch and wait for them to come out?"

"Yes, Hawk, you may."

Turning to his brother, Hawk asked, "Will you sit with me, Raven?"

Raven shrugged and answered, "Yes, Hawk, I will sit with you. But you have to be quiet and wait like Father said."

After taking their few supplies inside the cabin and tying the horses out, the boys took their places on the porch steps, Hawk staring intently at the teepee from which came the young voices and laughter, anxiously awaiting the first appearance of an Indian child.

Dark Wolf walked up through the meadow toward the other Cheyenne people. As he approached, the oldest of the group, a man not much older than himself, stood to greet him. Dark Wolf felt a rush of excitement flood through his body as the elder spoke.

"I am Two Falls, brother of Laughing Brook. We have come to honor her in her passing to the spirit world. My father has welcomed her now."

A strange, unexplainable feeling came over Dark Wolf as he heard the elder's name, but he stifled the urge to comment aloud, only offering to introduce himself instead. "I am Dark Wolf. I am Laughing Brook's son."

Two Falls nodded and indicated a place on the ground next to where he had been sitting. "You may join us here in the circle."

Dark Wolf quietly sat down beside Two Falls and looked around at the faces of the others on the circle. Each one silently nodded a greeting, and the Indian maiden continued to sing in the Cheyenne language a beautiful song of life and death.

Growing impatient with having to wait for the children to emerge from the teepee, Hawk stood and began pacing back and forth, making more noise than necessary, in an attempt to attract the attention of those inside. Raven warned, "Hawk, you had better be still."

Just as Hawk was about to defend himself, a motion caught his eye and he turned to see a little Cheyenne girl step out of the nearest teepee. She stood for a moment staring at Hawk and Raven, then she pulled back the flap and leaned down to speak in her native language to the other children.

Raven stood and waited, his arm around his little brother. "Stay here, Hawk."

"I'm not going anywhere, Raven." Looking up at his brother, Hawk asked, "Do you know what she said?"

"No, but here come the other children."

Unable to bear it any longer, Hawk pulled away from his brother and ran down the steps, stopping in front of the girl. She was a little taller than he, so he looked up and said, "Hi! My name is 'Hawk'. What is *your* name?"

The girl smiled and said, "I am 'Calm Rivers'." Looking past Hawk at Raven, she asked, "And his name?"

Hawk answered, "That is my brother, 'Raven'. He doesn't say much."

The children all gathered around Hawk, and some reached out to touch his curly blonde hair. He laughed, and they all laughed, some speaking in their native tongue and laughing again.

"Come up and sit on the porch with us," Hawk invited. "We can talk for awhile."

Calm Rivers spoke to the other children, and they all began climbing the steps and seating themselves at the edge of the porch, dangling their legs over the side.

"How is it that you are brothers, and you look so different?" asked Calm Rivers.

Raven spoke. "Hawk looks like our mother. I look like our father."

Hawk asked, "Calm Rivers, are you the only one who can speak like us? Will you teach us to speak in your language? What are the names of these other children?"

Raven smiled, amused at his brother's excitement and continuous questioning.

Calm Rivers laughed. "Hawk, you ask many questions. First, let me tell you the names of the others." As she began to introduce the other children, she walked behind them and touched each on the head as she said the name.

Hawk jumped down from the porch to walk in front of the children. As each one was named, he bowed graciously and then moved to the next one. They all laughed at his antics.

Ben Thomas had received his new assignment from Isaac Cutler and had begun packing his saddlebags for the journey. After filling an extra canteen and strapping a second bed roll behind his saddle, he went into the general store to purchase some jerky and other food items to take along. As he was picking up his purchases and turning to leave, he noticed a jar of peppermint sticks on the counter. He emptied one hand and pulled a coin from his pocket. Tossing it on the counter, he asked, "How many sticks of candy will that buy?"

The clerk picked up the coin, smiled and answered, "This will buy five sticks, Ben. Shall I wrap them in paper for you?"

"Yeah. And hurry it up. I've got a long ways to go."

Having heard the local gossip that Ben had been hired by Isaac Cutler, the clerk could not contain his curiosity. As he handed the parcel to Ben, he asked, "Did things not work out for you with Mr. Cutler, Ben? Because I could still use your help here. You don't have to leave town."

Ben grabbed the package and stuffed it into his jacket pocket. "Just don't you worry about it, old man. Mr. Cutler and I are doing just fine. In fact, he is sending me out to do something for him right now." He again picked up the supplies and started for the door.

Quickly the clerk spoke again, "Where are you headed, Ben? What does he want you to do?"

Stopping at the door, Ben turned around and said, "It's really none of your business, but I can tell you this; there's a certain half-breed that had better watch out!"

Isaac stood on the saloon porch, watching as Ben mounted his horse and rode toward him up the street. As Ben passed by him, Isaac grinned and gave a slight nod. Feeling proud of himself over his brilliant idea and his assignment for Ben, Isaac went back inside the saloon, purchased a bottle of whiskey, and made his way upstairs to the room of his favorite whore. As it was mid-morning, the saloon had no noisy crowd. Only a few businessmen had come for a liesurely breakfast and some story-swapping. Isaac's voice boomed throughout the establishment, *"Sadie, my love! Move on over! Your man's comin' in!"* A woman's high-pitched squeal and laughter erupted just before the door slammed.

Sarah Mason knocked on the door of the Cutler Ranch and waited patiently, adjusting the cover on her basket of pies. She was startled when the door was opened, not by Elizabeth, as she had expected, but by Seth, the stable hand. "Oh! Goodness! I was expecting to see Elizabeth ..."

Stepping into the open doorway, Elizabeth smiled broadly and said, *"Sarah! Oh, Sarah! It's so good to see you!"* She hugged Sarah tightly and added, "Please, come in." Directing Sarah into the house, she continued, "I'll make tea and we'll talk. You *will* stay for awhile, won't you?"

"Why, yes, Elizabeth. I brought some pies, too."

Elizabeth turned to Seth, who was still standing near the door. "Seth, did you hear that? Sarah brought some of her delicious pies! You should stay and have some with us."

Smiling to see that Elizabeth was genuinely happy with Sarah's visit, Seth bowed slightly and said, "I'm sure you girls will have things to talk about. I'll go check on things in the barn, *and* to make a list of the chores you've given me to do. Then I'll come back later and start on them." Waving his hand to Sarah, he added, "Nice to see you again, Mrs. Mason."

After closing the door behind Seth, Elizabeth turned again to Sarah. "Here, let me take your wrap. We'll put the pies in the kitchen and get the tea started. Come!" She took the basket and hurried away.

Sarah followed Elizabeth into the kitchen. "Elizabeth, I have been so worried about you, but you look *wonderful!"*

After lighting a fire in the stove and filling the teapot with water, Elizabeth sat at the table and took Sarah's hand in hers. "Oh, Sarah, I cannot begin to tell you how miserable I have been since Thomas's death. It's only been in the last two days that I have begun to come alive again."

Giving Elizabeth a sideways glance, and grinning, Sarah asked, "And does our handsome Seth have anything to do with your 'coming alive', Elizabeth?"

Blushing and releasing Sarah's hand, Elizabeth stood and went to the cupboard for the tea tray, cups and accessories. She chuckled and said, "Now, Sarah, what ever could you mean? Oh, certainly, Seth is a handsome man, and he has been very kind to me, but I actually began coming back to myself just before Seth stepped into the picture." Having readied the tea tray, Elizabeth started to pick it up. A stab of pain shot from her neck down her back and made her gasp. She grabbed at the back of her neck and began rubbing the muscle.

Sarah rushed over to her and put her arm around her shoulders. "Elizabeth, what happened?"

"I'll be fine. Would you mind carrying the tray to the parlor for me?"

Taking the tray and following Elizabeth again, Sarah asked, "Elizabeth, what is going on? I can sense that things are not as good as you are letting on."

When they took their seats, Elizabeth began serving the tea as she answered, "Sarah, these months since Thomas's death have been very difficult. But my worst problem has been my own son."

Sarah sipped her tea in silence, allowing Elizabeth time to think about things and talk them out.

"Isaac has just been horrible. There is so much I could tell you, but what good would it do? I will say that last night I finally tried to stand up to him and put him in his place." Taking a sip of tea, Elizabeth became silent and stared at the floor, reliving the incident in her mind.

Sarah waited, then softly asked, "What happened, dear friend?"

Returning to the present, Elizabeth took another sip of tea and smiled. "Well, somewhere out there in the foyer, there should be some of my skin, ... and a dent where my head met the wall." Then laughing softly, she said, "You know how hard-headed I can be, Sarah."

Setting her teacup down, Sarah stood and said, *"Do you mean to tell me Isaac has taken to knocking you around?"* Angrily, Sarah began walking back and forth and saying some of the things she wanted to tell Elizabeth. "Oh, how *angry* that makes me! I know he is your son, Elizabeth, but he is just plain evil. Just last night I sat with Jessie and helped her get the children to bed." Stopping briefly, she looked at Elizabeth and said, "Their dear mother passed on last night, so they needed comforting. Poor things."

"Oh, no, Sarah. Jessie was so distraught when she left here, afraid that her mother would die. She didn't think she would be able to come back."

Pacing again, Sarah continued, "Well, I'm sorry to say that is not the least of her worries. Elizabeth, Jessie is with child."

"But how ...?"

"Now I'm telling you this because I am sure you would want to know." Sarah sat down beside Elizabeth and put her arm around her shoulders. "*You* are going to be a *grandmother*, Elizabeth."

Looking a bit confused, Elizabeth said, "But, Sarah, that would mean ..."

"Yes, Elizabeth. Isaac is the father."

Elizabeth stood and looked down at Sarah in horror. "Are you telling me that Jessie and Isaac have been sneaking around here in my house? Why would they feel they had to sneak around? I mean, I would have been happy for Isaac to marry Jessie."

Standing to face Elizabeth, Sarah calmly said, "Elizabeth, Jessie did not want any part of Isaac. Do you understand what I am saying to you?"

For a moment Elizabeth stared at Sarah in disbelief, then she slowly sat down again on the sofa. "Sarah, did Isaac force himself on Jessie?"

"Yes, Elizabeth. More than once." Sarah sat and took her friend's hand. "You see, she was worried you might notice the changes in her body and question her, but she enlarged her aprons and carried things in front of her so you couldn't see."

Elizabeth pulled her hand away and stood again and began walking about. "Oh, Sarah. I must go and see her. I must let her know that I don't blame her. I must see what I can do to help." Her mind racing, she stopped and tapped her chin with her fingers. "Do you suppose she would bring her brothers and sister and come here to stay? We certainly have enough rooms for them all! We could ..."

"Wait, Elizabeth. Calm down. You seem to be forgetting one very important thing."

"What's that?"

Sarah looked solemnly at Elizabeth and said, "Isaac lives here. Neither she nor her brothers and sister could have any peace as long as Isaac is around."

Sitting down again, Elizabeth sighed. "Oh, yes. That's true." Sadly, she admitted, "Sarah, Isaac is my son ... mine and Thomas's. How did he become so evil?"

She looked at Sarah and said, "Do you know, Sarah, that Isaac was responsible for the deaths of Jonathan Morgan and Ravena Morgan? And I know in my heart that he killed his own father, my wonderful Thomas."

Sarah took a deep breath and said, "Elizabeth, it's time to do something about Isaac. When Dark Wolf comes, you must tell him what's going on. And let him do what needs done ... for all our sakes."

A look of hope in her eyes, Elizabeth asked, "So he is coming to see me, then?"

"Yes. He will be here tomorrow."

CHAPTER FOURTEEN

On the mountain, preparations were being made for an evening feast. There would be dancing and singing around the fire circle.

Dark Wolf smiled as he stood alone, slowly scanning the scene before him. He had planned this day to show his sons the art of war and how to defend themselves against their enemies, but the Great Spirit had seen fit to bless him with much more. He was amazed as he watched the Indian maidens scurrying about at the commands of the older women, carrying sticks and water bags, working with the corn meal and flour to make cakes, laying their brightest costumes out to freshen in the sunlight and breezes.

The oldest men of the group were instructing the youngest braves, including Hawk and Raven, in the art of making weapons and tools for hunting. Games to test strength, skill, and cunning were being set up by the young warriors. Paints were being prepared to decorate the horses for the races that would soon begin.

As Dark Wolf approached his sons, Hawk patted the side of his leg and stuck out one foot. He said, "Look, Father! We have Indian clothes and moccasins now!" Then Hawk held up a bow and arrow he had made. "And look, Father! Two Falls helped me make this for hunting rabbits and turkeys and deer. But we are going to practice on some targets first."

Touseling Hawk's golden hair, around which he now wore his headband, Dark Wolf praised him. "Hawk, that is good. We will eat well, and your family will never go hungry when you know how to hunt." Turning to Raven, he said, "And what have you made, my son?"

Holding up a long straight stick with a sharp stone attached to the end, Raven calmly answered, "A spear for fishing and hunting, Father. Hawk and I will teach each other, so we can become good at using both."

Dark Wolf smiled at his oldest son. "Perhaps you both can teach me as well."

Hawk said, "Oh, Father, we are going to swim across the lake, too! Will you watch us?"

Squatting down in front of his son, Dark Wolf said, "Yes, I will watch. But you know the water is still very cold right now."

"Oh, yes, I know, Father. But if we swim really fast, we won't freeze."

Raven added, "The women will meet us on the other side with warm blankets. We will be fine."

Two Falls nodded and motioned for the boys to go with the others and line up for the target practice. When they were alone, Two Falls spoke. "Dark Wolf, let us walk."

Dark Wolf walked slowly alongside Two Falls and waited for the older Indian to speak.

"You are afraid for your sons. I feel it. I see it in your eyes."

"Yes, Two Falls, I am."

After several long moments, he finally spoke again. "You already know that you have an enemy who pretends to be your friend."

"Yes."

"A messenger will visit your camp tonight. He will come as a snake."

Dark Wolf stopped dead in his tracks. "What does he want?"

Two Falls stopped and turned to face Dark Wolf. "He wants to take your son, Hawk, the one who trusts everyone too much."

His heart pounding loudly in his ears, Dark Wolf could barely find his voice or hear himself speak, but he formed the words, *"No! I cannot let that happen!"* He turned his head to look for Hawk in the distance, and breathed a sigh when he saw his golden-haired son among the other young

127

boys. A cold hand touched his arm, and a chill went through him. He spun back around to face Two Falls.

"You must stop him *after* he takes your son." Pointing to the very spot where Isaac had hidden years ago and watched as Dark Wolf's father was murdered, Two Falls continued, "In the edge of the woods ... there ... you will stop him, but you must not kill him."

"Not kill him? What good can it do to let him go? He will return to my enemy and give a bad report."

Two Falls started to touch Dark Wolf again, but drew his hand away. "Dark Wolf, when that time arrives, you will know what to do. Do not be afraid. The snake will slither away, as he came." Indicating a nearby log, Two Falls said, "Sit here with me."

Dark Wolf sat facing the cabin and once again searched the distant scene until he found his youngest son.

"The Great Spirit has seen your grief. He knows of the great losses you have suffered on this mountain ... this mountain of shadows. But light comes, and peace will be yours."

Continuing to watch his sons, Dark Wolf asked, "What of the enemy ... the one who sends the snake?"

"For the sake of many you will go to him."

Frowning with anger at the thought of seeing Isaac face to face, Dark Wolf asked, "What then?"

Two Falls laid eighteen twigs on the ground in a circle pattern near Dark Wolf's feet. Finally he laid a finger in the center of the circle and answered, "Here, in the midst, you alone will confront him."

Staring at the twigs, Dark Wolf waited for Two Falls to tell him more. When nothing more was offered, he asked, "Will it be over then?"

Standing and beginning to walk back toward the camp, Two Falls answered, "That is all I can say, Dark Wolf."

It was high noon when Isaac made his way back down the stairs to the saloon.

He stopped and tossed a coin on the bar. "Willie, boy! Give me one more for the road."

Will poured a shot of whiskey and slowly slid it toward Isaac. As he picked up the coin, and turned away, he heard Isaac chuckle. He turned around and asked, "Is something funny, Mr. Cutler?"

Isaac took out a cigar, tore the end off and dropped it on the floor. "Son, have you ever been upstairs with Sadie?"

Will grabbed a rag and began wiping the counter. "No, sir. I don't mess with none of them whores."

Isaac laughed out loud. He lit his cigar, then, with a sneaky grin, he asked, "What's the matter, Willie? Ain't you man enough to handle them whores?"

A surge of anger went through Will at being insulted by the swine who sat before him, but he maintained his composure and answered, "I'm sure you could not begin to understand what I'm about to say, Mr. Cutler, but I happen to have a decent gal, and I do not intend to lose her love by keeping company with the immoral women upstairs."

Isaac's grin quickly vanished. He stood and glared at Will for a long moment. After taking a long drag from the cigar, he blew the smoke toward Will and said, "Well, maybe the right whore hasn't come along yet. Hell, maybe your *decent gal* is a whore, too! Ya just never know, Willie." Satisfied that he had upset the bartender to the point of making him see red, Isaac turned to walk away. "Ya just never know."

Will's knuckles were white where he had balled up his fists at his sides at hearing Isaac's words. He reassured himself that his sweet lady's reputation was not at stake simply because Isaac Cutler presented such an idea. However, he hoped for an opportunity to catch Isaac in a dark alley sometime so he could put him out of everyone's misery.

Upon returning home from her visit with Elizabeth, Sarah Mason found a note which had been slipped under her door. She hung her shawl on its hook and put her bag in her bureau drawer. After putting on her spectacles, she sat in the rocker and read the note, obviously written with a shaky hand.

Sarah,

I need to talk to you. Something is wrong. I don't know what to do. Please come as soon as you can.

Jessie

Sarah quickly put the note in her skirt pocket, grabbed her shawl, and again went out of the house. When she came to Jessie's house, Eli and Rachel were crying, and Curtis was trying to calm them down. Jessie was unconscious, but Sarah was relieved to find that she was still breathing. Sarah demanded, "Go and get Doc Smith." Turning to Curtis, who stood looking on, obviously terrified, Sarah yelled, *"Now, Curtis! Go!"*

Curtis ran out of the house and let the door slam shut behind him. A new wave of shrieks came from little Rachel, and Eli was shaking and whimpering. Sarah scooped Rachel up in her arms and began to quiet her, telling her everything would be all right soon. She sat down in a wing chair on the opposite end of the room and pulled Eli up onto her lap to hug him, too.

Sarah looked at Jessie again and thought, *She looks so pale, as though the life is going out of her. I wish I knew what was wrong. Lord, let her be all right!* She began humming a hymn to help herself calm down. The children

130

were finally quiet, and after awhile, she noticed they were both asleep.

Suddenly the door opened, and in came Curtis and the doctor.

Sarah motioned for Curtis to come and take Eli and lay him down on his mat in the other room. Following him, she gently laid Rachel down and covered them both. They had cried so hard, she believed they would sleep soundly for awhile. Now she could find out from Curtis what had happened.

Dr. Smith pulled the cover back and began examining Jessie. Noticing the bloody stains on the lower part of her dress, he realized that Jessie was far too young for this hemmorrhaging to be a part of her normal menstrual period. He asked, "Curtis, when did this bleeding start?"

Curtis came to the doorway of the room and answered. "Mr. Cutler was here and he was being mean to her, and it started after that.."

Sarah could not believe her ears. *"What? Isaac Cutler came here?"*

"Yes, ma'am, twice."

Somewhat perturbed at Sarah, the doctor said, "Let's not worry about Mr. Cutler right now." Turning again to Curtis, he asked, "Did he hit her?"

Curtis nodded his head slowly, "Yes, she told him something and he got angry. He pulled her hair and then hit her. She fell down, then he kicked her."

Shaking his head in unbelief, the doctor asked, "Where did he kick her, Curtis?"

"In the stomach, sir."

A wave of nausea went through Sarah. She decided she had better tell the doctor about Jessie's pregnant condition. She spoke up, "Curtis, can you go into the other room for a minute? I need to talk to Doc Smith privately."

Frowning, the doctor waited for the boy to leave, then he began, "Sarah, I don't think ..."

Sarah interrupted him, "Doc, you listen to me, and then you will know what to do for Jessie."

The doctor folded his arms in front of him and said, "Hurry up, Sarah! She is hemorrhaging."

Placing her fists on her sides in aggravation, Sarah leaned forward and said softly, "Well, she is also pregnant with Isaac Cutler's baby, so you had better be careful!" Noting the look of surprise and disgust on the doctor's face, Sarah shook her finger at him and added, "Don't you be thinkin' what you're thinkin', Doc. You know she's a good girl. He raped her when she was working out at the Cutler ranch. Now I'll shut up. You just take care of her!"

Doc returned to his examination, cutting and peeling the soiled skirt and undergarments away from Jessie's lower body. Sarah held out a sack that she had found in the corner, and the garments were dropped into it.

"I will be right back, Doc. I'm going to get Curtis to help me with some rags and hot water." Sarah hurried from the room.

To Sarah's surprise, the boy had already put a kettle of water to heat in the fireplace. "Thank you, Curtis. You are a fine brother. Now we need some clean bed sheets to make some rags."

They worked together to tear the sheets into wide strips. Then Sarah prepared a pan of hot water for the doctor's use.

When she reentered the bedroom, Dr. Smith held out his bloody hands and said, "Just give me a wet rag for my hands, then throw it in the sack, too."

Sarah set the pan of water down and pulled a rag from the bundle. "Is she going to make it, Doc?"

Doc rested his elbows on the edge of the bed and sat on the floor as he wiped his hands. "I don't know. She is very weak. I examined her and, from what I see, I believe that she is near five months along."

Sarah sat in a nearby chair. "Yes, it was just last night when her mother passed away that she felt the first movement. She told me about it last night. Poor girl. She is so humiliated, and so scared."

Doc said, "Sarah, the baby seems to have a very strong heart beat right now, as far as I can tell. But I've got to get the bleeding stopped, or we will lose them both."

"Just tell me what I can do to help you, Doc, and I'll do it."

After staring at Jessie for awhile, the doctor finally turned back to Sarah and said, "Okay. Help me get her cleaned up and bind some rags on her. I want to take her to my house where Abigail can help me look after her. Can you take the other children home with you for a few days?"

"Yes! I would be delighted to take care of them until she is able to come home again." She stood, "Well, Doc, let's get to work!"

Elizabeth decided to write a letter to Jessie. As she sat with pen in hand, staring out of the window by the small desk Thomas had provided for her in his study, so many thoughts rushed through her mind, she barely knew how to begin. Finally, she dipped the quill pen into the ink, laid it gently to the paper, and began.

> *My dearest Jessie,*
>
> *I miss you terribly, although I am learning quickly how to do many things for myself. Seth has been a great help, and has even completed some of the larger tasks you and I had talked about doing.*
> *Please don't be angry at Sarah, but she was kind enough to let me know that I will soon be a grandmother. A grandmother! I'm smiling, because I know it will be a sweet child with you as the mother. I extend my deepest sympathies for my son's behavior.*

> *Understand that I have no ill feelings toward you.*
>
> *Jessie, God is very real, and he is sending an angel of vengeance to bring judgment upon Isaac. It will happen very soon.*
>
> *I know it. And after it does, I would like for you to consider bringing your brothers, and that dear little Rachel, to live with me here at the ranch. You know there is plenty of room here, and they will all have room to run and play. And when my grandchild is born, I can enjoy watching him (or her) grow.*
>
> *Please think about all that I have said. I will write again soon, or come and see you. We can talk about it then.*
>
> *With much love,*
>
> *Elizabeth*

Just as Elizabeth finished slipping the folded letter into an envelope and placing her seal upon it, she saw Isaac coming up the road. She hurriedly tucked the letter into her skirt pocket and put her writing materials away. Calmly, she stepped out of the house and began strolling toward the barn.

"And just where do you think you are going, Mother?" Isaac dismounted and walked toward her. With an evil grin, he said, "Well, if you are going to play with the stable boy, you could at least take my horse with you. It won't look so obvious that way."

Elizabeth stopped and reached out her hand to accept the reins of the lathered animal which seemed to be gasping for breath. "I'd be glad to rescue the abused beast from having to spend another moment in your company, my son."

Isaac threw the reins at his mother, put his finger in her face, and threatened, *"I've warned you, Mother. You had better watch what you say to me!"*

Choosing not to say what more was on her mind, Elizabeth began leading the horse to the stables. To herself, she thought, *What are you going to do, Isaac? Kill me, too?* She opened the barn door and called out, "Seth! Are you here?"

Hearing the sweet voice calling his name, Seth quickly hung the curry comb up on its nail and stepped out of a stall, closing the gate behind him. "I'm here, Elizabeth!"

Watching as the big man walked toward her, Elizabeth soon forgot about her confrontation with Isaac. "Here is Isaac's horse. Could you help me rub him down and cool him off? It appears as though Isaac has ridden him very hard today."

"Certainly, ma'am." Looking at the horse's rear left flank, Seth spotted some bloody stripes. "Aw, now, look at that. He's been whipping the thing hard, too."

"I'm sure I don't understand how one person can be filled with such cruelty, Seth."

"And this horse is a good one. It'll do whatever you say. It don't need a whippin'. Let's get this saddle off and take him to the watering trough. We can soak some rags and clean up those torn places." Looking at Elizabeth, Seth quickly added, "That is, if you want to mess with it, ma'am. You might get that pretty dress dirty before we are through."

Elizabeth smiled and began walking toward the other end of the barn. "Seth, just tell me what you need for me to do. I *want* to help." Slipping her hand into her skirt pocket, she remembered her reason for coming to the barn. "When we are finished with the horse, I need for *you* to do a favor for *me*."

Seth caught up with her and answered. "Anything, Elizabeth. Anything you say."

Two Falls announced that all of the men, including Dark Wolf, would gather in his teepee just before sunset for a pow-wow. Then there would be feasting, music and dancing, and the three new Cheyenne family members, Dark Wolf, Hawk, and Raven, would be honored.

There were several hours of daylight remaining, so the competitions would take on a different setting. Dark Wolf was reluctant to let Hawk and Raven go into the forest with the others to play the war games, but Two Falls had assured him the snake would not arrive until after nightfall and would not succeed in its mission to kidnap Hawk, so he let them go. But he decided he would go, too, and keep Hawk within sight.

The women of the camp prepared cakes and began cooking a young doe which had been killed by the hunting party earlier in the day. A stew pot simmered over a small fire and the savory smells filled the air. There would be plenty of food for all.

The young men and boys were divided into two teams, Two Falls doing the selecting of each. The rules were simple. They all would go deep into the woods using their skills of stealth, sense of direction, and keen senses to help them find their way back without being captured by the other team. If they were captured, they were to try to escape, even if it meant by outrunning the captor in a straight pathway home. They all understood that it was a serious exercise, because in a true battle, all of these skills and bravery would be required to survive. And, unlike this game, in a real battle, there would be death.

Raven and Hawk were on opposite sides, which momentarily caused Hawk to become nervous. He had never sided against his brother in anything. However, having been coached in how to determine direction by the sun and shadows, and also having been fitted with a pair of moccasins for a quiet step, Hawk made sure his headband was securely in place and his feather was standing somewhat straight and tall, then squared his shoulders and began walking with the others into the forest.

When Dark Wolf started to follow a few yards behind, Two Falls grabbed his arm. "No, Dark Wolf. You must let him go. His brother will watch over him."

"But they are on opposite sides, Two Falls. How can he watch over him?"

Two Falls pointed into the forest where the boys could still be seen making their way into the shadowy woods. "See? Even now Raven is helping Hawk find his way."

Dark Wolf saw that what Two Falls told him was true. He could see Raven holding Hawk's hand as he climbed over a large log that lay in his path.

"Come, rest for awhile. You must have your wits about you at the feast tonight when the snake comes."

CHAPTER FIFTEEN

At Dr. Smith's house, Curtis sat in a chair beside Jessie's bed watching her sleep. The oil lamp on the bedside stand made a pale glow on her face. He decided he had never seen his sister look so pretty before. Even though she was pale and weak, the high lacy collar on the flannel gown she wore, and her long hair swirling down over her shoulders made her look so feminine. Curtis had not been able to see her very much in the past few years. She had worked for the Cutler's for a long time, but he remembered her sweet nature and how she seemed to care so much about Ma and Pa. She always sent home all of the money she worked so hard for. *She deserves to be happy,* he thought. *She's been cryin' too much lately.* Looking up toward the ceiling, Curtis began to pray out loud. *"God, if you can hear me, please let my sister be happy for the rest of her life. Don't let her cry no more."* As an afterthought, Curtis added, *"Oh, and God, don't let Mr. Cutler come around her no more, neither."*

Abigail Smith, the doctor's wife, came quietly into the room and stood beside the bed. "Curt, you need to go and get some rest. It's nearly dark out now. Sarah's got supper ready, I'm sure. She may need your help with Rachel and Eli."

Standing and looking at Jessie once more, Curtis said, "Okay, ma'am." He gently took Jessie's cool hand and kissed it. Tears welled up in his eyes as he laid it back down.

"You can come back tomorrow, Curt. Perhaps she will be better and can talk to you."

Brushing away the tears and shaking off the desire to release the flood gates, Curtis took a deep breath and said, "Thank you, ma'am."

Sarah chuckled at hearing a knock on the door. As she opened it, she began, "Curtis, you don't ..." To her surprise, it was not Curtis, as she had expected. Standing before her was Seth, Mrs. Cutler's groom. She stepped back and motioned for him to enter. "Come in, Seth! I thought you were Curtis. He should be back any minute now. Is something wrong with Elizabeth?"

Removing his hat, Seth said, "No, ma'am. I came to town to deliver a letter to Miss Jessie from Mrs. Cutler. But I didn't find her at home. Do you know where she is?"

"Yes, I do. She is at Doc Smith's house. She's very ill. They are looking after her until she is well again, *if* she gets well. We are all praying for her."

Rachel came into the room rubbing her sleepy eyes. She walked slowly over to Sarah and reached her arms upward.

Sarah picked her up and hugged her. "Hello, Rachel. Do you feel like eating supper now?"

The little girl nodded.

Eli came shuffling into the room and sat down in the nearest chair. He squinted his eyes a few times, yawned, and mumbled, "I'm hungry."

"Good! Supper is ready. When Curtis comes back, we'll eat." Turning to Seth again, Sarah asked, "Would you like some supper?"

"No, thank you, ma'am. I need to get back. What shall I tell Mrs. Cutler about Jessie?"

"Well, just tell her that Jessie is not feeling well. I don't want to worry Elizabeth. Tell her when Jessie is better we will come around for a visit."

Seth pulled the letter from his pocket. "Would you see that Jessie gets this letter? It's very important to Mrs. Cutler that she get it."

"Certainly, Seth. I'll see to it."

Just then the door opened quietly and Curtis came in.

Seth noticed that the boy looked as though he carried the weight of the world on his shoulders. He reached out his hand.

Curtis looked up at him and shook his hand. "Jessie's sick, Mr. Seth."

Laying his big hand on the boy's shoulder, Seth said, "I know, Curt. Sarah told me. But don't you give up on Jessie, now. She's a good, strong woman."

Seeming to find some degree of hope and comfort in Seth's words, Curtis smiled and said, "Yes. Yes, she is. Can you stay awhile, sir?"

Putting on his hat again, Seth said, "I'm sorry, Curt. I need to go and let Mrs. Cutler know about Jessie. But I'll see you soon, I'm sure. You keep that chin up, now!"

Seth left and Sarah closed the door behind him. Turning around, she set Rachel down and said, "Let's eat! Jessie wouldn't want us to get sick, too, now would she?"

As they sat down at the table, Sarah asked, "Curtis, would you say grace?"

They all bowed their heads and Curtis began, "God, it's me again. First I want to thank you for this food. And I want to thank you for Miss Sarah takin' us in. Then I want to ask you to bless my sister and let her get well real fast. And last, God, I would like for you to get that Isaac Cutler for what he done to my sister. Get him good. Amen."

"Amen!" echoed Eli, then Rachel.

When Curtis looked up, he saw Sarah staring at him with a sad look on her face. "Curtis, be careful what you say in front of the little ones. I know you are hurting, but don't let your anger make you mean, like Isaac Cutler. And don't you worry; God will deal with him. You can believe that."

The sun had just set and the shadows faded into night when all of the young men and boys emerged from the forest. Dark Wolf had been unable to rest, concerned that the two sons who had finally been restored to him would now be lost to him forever. He was filled with immeasurable relief at the sight of Raven and Hawk coming toward him smiling. Raven held the end of a rope in his hand. At the other end was Hawk, tied round about, and unable to move his arms. Dark Wolf laughed and hugged his two sons.

Raven said, "I captured him as soon as we started back. He's been my prisoner all the way." Then, playfully rubbing his brother's golden hair, he added, "And I had an awful time getting him to be quiet. He did try *very* hard to escape."

Falling to the ground and rolling from side to side, Hawk said, "I'm sure glad to be home. My legs are tired, and I'm hungry." Looking up at his father he said, "Could you please take this rope off of me?"

Laughing again, Dark Wolf grabbed the rope knot and lifted Hawk off the ground. Throwing the boy over his shoulder and walking toward the camp, where a large fire gave light to the entire area, he said, "I don't know. What do you think, Raven? Should we set your brother free?"

Raven smiled up at Dark Wolf and answered, "He is hungry, and I don't want to have to hand feed him, so I say we let him go!"

Hawk began kicking his legs and squealing, "*You better let me go!* I'll capture you next time, Raven, and I'll tie you to a *tree!*"

Dark Wolf sat Hawk on the ground and removed the rope from him.

Hawk rubbed his arms and said, "It felt like a snake was wrapped around me, squeezing me. I didn't like that."

Instantly, Dark Wolf was again reminded of Two Falls words about the snake which would come into the camp tonight. He knew it would be soon, as darkness had fully descended.

He only wished he knew exactly what to expect, but that was not the way it was to be. The Spirit would show him as he needed to know.

In the study, Isaac paced the floor. He had been drinking, and he was angry. Just the thought of having a child to aggravate and complicate his life was repulsive. As he paced, he began to mumble, "Well, I don't have to worry about *that* anymore. I took care of the little tramp. It's all over now. No child for this old boy!" He opened another bottle of wine and began guzzling it down. The burgundy liquid ran down his chin and onto his white shirt as he took the bottle from his lips. Falling into his father's plush chair, he cursed aloud and threw the bottle across the room. *"Where's that boy? Why isn't Ben back with that boy?!"* Isaac mumbled out a few more curses, then laughed and passed out.

Elizabeth, hearing the glass shatter and Isaac's loud voice, put on her dressing gown and tiptoed to the top of the stairs. After waiting several moments and hearing nothing but Isaac's loud snoring, she returned to her room and quietly closed the door. She was so worried about Jessie. Seth had not known much about what was wrong, but she hoped that Jessie and the baby would be all right. She smiled at the thought of someday holding the infant in her arms. But she knew that could never happen until there was peace in the house. Trying to dismiss all the cares of the day, Elizabeth took a book from her table, deciding she would read until she was able to sleep.

Jessie stirred slightly and tried to swallow. She grimaced at the attempt, her mouth seeming so dry and her throat feeling raw. She rolled her head slowly from side to side and tried to open her eyes. But her lids were so heavy.

Lying still for a few moments, she mustered the strength to push out a breathy sound. "Curtis."

Abigail Smith rushed to the side of the bed and took Jessie's hand in hers.

Still unable to open her eyes, Jessie smiled and repeated, "Curtis."

"No, Jessie. It's me, Abigail Smith, the doctor's wife. I sent Curtis home to rest for the night."

Suddenly recalling what had happened and her pregnant condition, tears began to stream from the corners of Jessie's eyes and run down into her ears. She squeezed Abigail's hand and whispered, "My baby."

"Honey, so far your baby is doing all right. But you are very weak, so you must lie still." Releasing Jessie's hand, she laid it gently on the bed and said, "I'll get my husband and he can tell you what you want to know. I'll be right back."

Jessie managed to raise her hands to her face and wipe the tears from her eyes. The tears continued to run down her temples, but she finally managed to open her eyes enough to see the dim lamplight and the shadowy corners of the strange room. She wished she were home with her brothers and her sister, and that none of this had happened. More than ever, she wished she could feel her mother's arms around her and hear her say everything would be fine. A new wave of tears came just as the doctor entered the room.

He took Jessie's hand and sat beside her on the bed. "Are you in great pain, Jessie?"

Jessie squinted and tried to blink away the tears. Hoarsely, she answered, "My heart aches, ... but I don't feel much of ... anything else." Trying to lick her lips, she added, "My mouth is so dry."

Turning to his wife, he said, "Get her some water, Abigail. Just a little." He turned back to Jessie and said, very seriously, "Jessie, the baby's heartbeat seems to be still very strong, but you lost a lot of blood. Do you remember what happened to you?"

Nodding slowly, Jessie fought back new tears. Finally she said, "Yes, I remember."

Abigail returned with a small cup. The doctor raised Jessie's head slightly and helped her take a few small sips.

The cool water touching her lips and tongue felt heavenly, and Jessie savored the moment. She put her lips outward indicating she wanted more. After a few more sips, the doctor set the cup aside on the night stand.

Jessie grabbed at the edge of the covers and tried to push them down. "I need to get home to the children."

Pulling the covers back up around her, the doctor said, "Now, Jessie. You just lie still. The children are staying with Sarah Mason until you are feeling better. Don't you worry about a thing. You must take care of yourself and your baby right now."

Beginning to cry again, Jessie smiled and said, "Thank you so much." Her voice quivered as she continued, "I know this looks very bad ... for me to be carrying a child ... when I am not married to anyone. I am so ashamed. But it wasn't my fault." Closing her eyes, she whispered, "...not my fault."

Dr. Smith stood and patted Jessie's hand. "You need to rest now, Jessie. I will go and tell Curtis that you were awake for awhile and that he can come and see you tomorrow."

Hoping the doctor could see her response, Jessie made a feeble attempt to nod her head just before she drifted off to sleep again.

On the mountain, a sumptuous feast had been enjoyed by everyone. While the women cleared the remainder away and cleaned their utensils, the men had gathered in Two Falls' teepee, smoking the pipe and listening to stories and prophecies told by Two Falls and several others in the group.

Dark Wolf attempted to listen carefully to the elders, but often found himself straining to hear the familiar laughter of his two sons outside. He was relieved when Two Falls made an end to the talking and dismissed the men.

Now Dark Wolf sat on one of the logs, which had been placed around the perimeter of the fire circle, his sons on either side of him. Smiling down at Hawk, he laid a hand on his shoulder and pulled him closer. There was a low hum of chatter flowing around the circle.

Hawk pointed across the circle and said, "Father, do you see Hattie over there? She came while you were in there with the other men."

Dark Wolf searched the faces until he spotted Hattie, sitting on a log with some other women, proudly wearing her crumpled hat, now with a feather stuck in one of the holes.

She waved and smiled, then pointed to the feather.

Dark Wolf laughed and nodded as he returned the greeting.

Raven sat beside his father watching the fire light flicker on the faces and in the eyes of all who sat in the huge circle around it.

Hawk looked all around, wondering why everyone had become so silent. Suddenly, Two Falls emerged from his teepee in full headdress and beaded leather clothing. He stepped into the circle and came toward Dark Wolf and his two sons. Stopping before them, he motioned for them to stand.

Dark Wolf nudged Raven and Hawk and the three of them stood facing Two Falls.

Two Falls spoke, "In celebration of finding our three new Cheyenne brothers, the son and grandsons of my sister, Laughing Brook, we will play and sing and dance. And to honor our two new braves, Raven and Hawk, we will do a special dance of the bird. The spirits come to help us when we do this dance." Looking at Hawk and then at Raven, Two Falls said, "Listen and you will hear the voice of many birds. After you see how the dance is done, you may join in, if you wish."

Raven and Hawk looked at each other and smiled, excitedly.

Two Falls walked away and took his seat. He nodded to the left and the deep noise of a single string being plucked replaced the silence.

Several high-pitched bird calls rang out. A single drum sounded in a steady rhythm, and two separate clicking sounds came forth as if sticks or gourds were being hit together. Simultaneously with all of that, several young men came dancing into the circle. On their heads and down their arms, they were decorated with eagle and several other types of feathers, reminding the onlookers of many giant birds, their wings spread. Around the tops of their knee-high moccasins, there were small silver jingly bells. The dancers bent at the waist slightly and looked toward the ground, keeping their arms outward, like birds gliding on the wind. Only their feet moved with the beat of the drums and kept the bells ringing with each step as they moved around the fire. After several measures, the fire now totally encircled by these birdmen, a small group of women stood and chanted out the words of the bird song in their native tongue. So many new bird voices filled the air.

Hawk looked around for the source of the sounds, but they seemed to be all around, coming from every direction. He gave up looking and asked his father, "Can I dance now, Father?"

"Yes, Hawk, Two Falls said you could."

Hawk stood and began jumping on first one leg, then the other. He began following one of the smaller young men and tried to imitate his motions and movements as they danced around the fire. When he got to the other side of the circle, a group of children jumped into the dance with Hawk. They laughed and jumped and completely surrounded Hawk.

Raven watched the dancer closest to him, and truly felt honored to be a part of this celebration and see how the bird family played such a big part in the lives of the Cheyenne. He pointed and said, "Father, it looks like they are gliding on air."

Dark Wolf looked in the direction Raven was pointing and nodded.

Suddenly the music stopped and the bird voices quieted to two or three high-pitched. Then came the single strumming of the low-pitched string again. And as it sung out, the dancers lowered the wings to their sides and looked from left to right, with the rhythm of the strumming. Finally, the drums began again and the dancers spread their wings to glide. The women chanted out the tune again and the dance continued.

"Do you want to dance, Raven?" Dark Wolf asked.

"No, Father. I just want to watch this time." After a moment, he added, "Father, I'm pleased to be here with you."

Dark Wolf looked down at his oldest son and his heart swelled. This was the first time Raven had expressed joy at being in his father's company.

Hawk came dancing by, surrounded by the other children, and he had to jump high to even wave at his father.

Dark Wolf was relieved to again see Hawk's golden hair bouncing in the firelight.

Hattie stood and made her way around the outside of the circle to where Dark Wolf sat. She sat beside him in Hawk's place. "Some shindig, ain't it? I ain't seen nothin' like this since yer pa brought yer ma up here to live. These might be the children of some of the same fellers I saw dancin' then. They came to celebrate when you were born, too, Dark Wolf. Yes, sirree, it was somethin'."

147

Dark Wolf became caught up in Hattie's chatter, and Raven moved to sit on the ground so he could face them both and listen to them.

———————

From the edge of the woods, Ben Thomas finally spied the young, blonde-haired, boy Isaac had told him about. He dismounted and tied his horse to a tree a short distance back from the edge of the meadow. He knew he would have to lay low in order to keep from being seen. Dropping to his knees, he began crawling toward the fire. Fortunately for him, the noise of the drums and the singing kept him from being heard as he laid down on his belly and crawled even closer. He wanted to stay at the lower end of the circle so he could make a straight run back to his horse, but he wondered, *What if the boy doesn't come outside the circle toward me? Maybe I should wait until they all bed down and try to take him then.*

Just as Ben was about to turn and crawl back across the meadow, he noticed the young boy leaving the circle on the upper side, and he was alone. Quickly evaluating the situation, he decided to keep low and circle around the right side of the cabin and to the rear, which was the direction the boy had gone. He ran the course he had mapped out in his mind, bending low as he did so. When he reached the back of the cabin, he saw the boy entering the outhouse. Ben looked from the corner of the cabin to see the crowd, still involved in the celebration around the circle. He quietly made his way to the door of the outhouse, where he heard the boy humming.

Hawk finished his business and pulled up his pants, still humming the same tune the Indian women were singing by the fire. As he opened the door and stepped out, he felt a gritty, gloved hand cover his mouth, and a strong arm surround him and pick him up. His heart raced with fear as he felt himself being squeezed so tightly. He could barely breathe, and he could not get his arms free to pull the hand away. He began swinging his legs and kicking at the man, but it did not seem to phase him. His muffled cries could not be heard over the festive sounds on the other side of the cabin.

Despite the young boy's squirming and kicking, Ben held on tight. He decided to take a direct path from the right corner of the cabin, cross the meadow at a wide angle away from the fire, then work his way through the woods until he got back to his horse. He tightened his grip on the boy and began running.

Hawk was terrified. He now felt a great aching in his chest due to the lack of air in his lungs. Comforting himself by visualizing the faces of his father and brother, Hawk slipped into dark unconsciousness.

As suddenly as it had begun, the music stopped and everyone mingled about, slowly returning to their seats. Raven shook hands with one of the braves who had danced for them and thanked him.

The brave smiled down at him. "It was a great honor for me to dance for you, Raven."

"Can you all stay here and teach us more?" Raven asked. "They could stay on for awhile, couldn't they, Father?"

Looking into the young brave's eyes, Dark Wolf knew the answer, but to spare his son any confusion, he simply answered, "They may stay as long as they like, Raven."

The young man bowed his head slightly to dismiss himself, turned and walked away.

All was calm, only soft laughter and the murmur of voices talking low around the fire.

Dark Wolf quickly stood and looked around. Hawk had not returned to his seat, and there seemed to be no sign of him in the circle. His heart ached as the realization set in that his son was gone, just as Two Falls had predicted. *But how could it happen with so many people around?!?* he wondered. Desperately his eyes made another sweep around the circle in search of Hawk.

Feeling his father's despair, Raven stood and pulled at Dark Wolf's hand. "What's the matter? Where's Hawk?" He started to step out into the circle and look for his brother, but he felt his father's large hand on his shoulder.

"Stay here with Hattie, Raven. Do not leave her sight."

Hattie reached out an arm and Raven took refuge against Hattie's side, pulling her arm around him.

Dark Wolf's eye caught a sudden movement near the opposite side of the circle. He turned his head quickly and saw Two Falls standing, looking at him. Their eyes met.

Two Falls raised an arm and pointed toward the woods across the meadow, to the spot he had told him of earlier that day — the place where Isaac Cutler had hidden and watched Dark Wolf's father and wife being murdered.

Dark Wolf started to turn away and run, but Two Falls motioned for him to go quietly and stay low. Looking once more at Raven and Hattie, Dark Wolf stepped outside of the circle and dropped to his belly. He crawled as quickly as he could, the sharp grass blades and the prickly, dry, brown grass at the root end tearing at his skin. He felt no pain as he thought about rescuing his son from this evil messenger. He only hoped he was not too late. As he reached the edge of the forest, he heard a horse nicker softly. Breathing a sigh of relief, he stood and flattened himself against a large tree near the horse to wait for the kidnapper's return.

Looking off to his right from time to time in order to judge his bearings from the position of the fire, Ben carefully made his way toward the place where he had left his horse. He noted that the boy had apparently fallen asleep, as he was no longer fighting him and trying to cry out. His body had gone limp. But he still did not dare to remove his hand from the boy's mouth. His entire plan, and all of the money he would receive, could be foiled by the slightest noise right now. Having gone deeper into the forest than he had realized, Ben looked again to the right and saw the silhouette of his horse in a direct line with the fire beyond. He turned and made his way toward the animal. Breathing a deep sigh, he sat down on the ground to rest, still holding tightly to the boy.

In the shadows, Dark Wolf listened. He heard the man's heavy breathing and an occasional grunt or sigh as he began to relax. But he did not hear his son moving or speaking. He could not wait any longer.

Before Ben even knew Dark Wolf was present, the boy was snatched from his arms and he felt a kick to one side of his head just before the other side of it hit the ground.

After making sure the man was out for a few moments, Dark Wolf sat down and held the limp body of his youngest son. He began to rock, fearing his son was dead. *Please, God, don't let him die, too! Take me, if you want another soul. Take me!*

He stopped rocking and laid his son on the ground. Laying his ear against Hawk's chest, he listened. He believed he could hear a faint heartbeat. Raising up on his knees, he placed his fingers under Hawk's nostrils and felt a shallow breath escaping. Relief flooded him again as he picked up his son and held him gently, rubbing upward on his back.

At last Hawk began to return to consciousness. He coughed a few times and took in several deep breaths of fresh air. Suddenly remembering that someone had grabbed him, he began to fight and started to yell, *"Let me go! Let me ..."*

"Hawk, it's me, your father. You are safe now."

Hawk's fears dissipated as he heard his father's voice. He hugged Dark Wolf's neck tightly. After coughing several times, Hawk said, "I knew you would rescue me, Father. I *knew* you would."

Just then, they both heard the man on the ground groaning.

Dark Wolf swiftly carried his son to the edge of the woods and stood him in the meadow. "Are you able to stand, Hawk?"

"Yes, Father. I'm fine now, but ..."

"Run to the fire, Hawk. Raven and Hattie are waiting for you there."

"But I want to stay with you, Father. I want to know who that man is."

"No, Hawk. I will take care of this man. Raven is worried about you. Go on, now, son."

The man groaned again, and Hawk began running as fast as his legs would carry him toward the fire circle.

Ben rolled onto his side and tried to push himself up to a sitting position. He shook his head and wondered what had happened. Just as he was about to sit up, a hand jerked his gun from its holster, grabbed his shirt collar, and pulled him to his feet.

"I would like to kill you right now, mister. And I hope you realize how easy it would be to do so, but the Spirits tell me I must let you live because you are only doing the bidding of the evil one who sent you."

Ben struggled to free himself, but Dark Wolf held him and asked him, "Why does Isaac want my son? *Why?*"

"Turn me loose and I'll talk to you."

Dark Wolf released him and grabbed the reins of his horse. Standing there in the shadows, he asked again, "Why does Isaac Cutler want my son?"

"He is afraid of you. Oh, he didn't say so, but I can tell. I suppose he wants your son for protection. Because if you tried to hurt Isaac, he would kill your son."

Dark Wolf's anger shifted from this man to Isaac Cutler. "I know your name is Ben Thomas. And I know that Isaac pays you well for doing his dirty work."

"Yes, he does, mister. But you might as well kill me now, because if I go back without the boy, Isaac will kill me, anyway."

Deciding to offer the young man another option, Dark Wolf said, "Don't go back."

Ben laughed, then mocked, "Don't go back? Mr. Cutler would come lookin' for me and kill me."

"Isaac would not bother to look for you. He would just figure you failed and were killed, like all of the others who have done his bidding." Handing Ben the reins, Dark Wolf said, "Only you don't have to die like all of the others, Ben. Get on this horse and ride as far away from Isaac Cutler as you can."

Ben put his hat back on his head and mounted his horse. "What about Mr. Cutler? What are you going to do about him?"

Without answering, Dark Wolf slapped the horse's rear and it bolted away into the deep night shadows of the forest, Ben Thomas hanging on for dear life.

CHAPTER SIXTEEN

Sarah finally managed to get Curtis, Eli and Rachel bedded down for the night so she could lay down and rest. She turned out the lamp beside the bed and closed her eyes.

No sooner had her head buried itself in the softness of her pillow, than she was sound asleep.

Curtis lay awake in the darkness, listening for Sarah's heavy, relaxed breathing to begin. Finally it began, and when he was sure she was asleep, he slid out from under the covers and crossed the floor to the back door. Carrying his boots and coat with him, he quietly lifted the latch and opened the door. Stepping out into the night, he closed the door and leaned against the back of the house while he put on his boots. He began walking toward the livery stable, putting on his coat as he went.

When he got there, he slipped from stall to stall until he found the mare he had used when he went to bring Jessie home. He spoke to her and stroked her cheek and neck. Then he slipped a bridle on her and led her out through the back.

As he mounted the horse, Curtis felt under his jacket to make sure his father's hunting knife was still in the sheath at his side. He swallowed hard at the thought of what he had determined in his mind to do. He let the horse walk quietly through the back streets to the edge of town before he kicked her sides to make her run.

To keep from losing his courage, Curtis visualized his sister, lying in that puddle of blood, nearly dying. He rode hard, the anger and hatred swelling up inside him. He told himself, *Isaac Cutler will never hurt my sister again!*

When Dark Wolf returned to the fire circle, the festivities were ending and everyone was preparing to lie down for the night. The fire had burned down to a low flickering flame. Hattie sat in silence with the two boys. Raven's arm encircled Hawk tightly, and all three watched as Dark Wolf came toward them.

Hawk spoke first, "Father, are you angry at me?"

Kneeling down in front of his youngest son, Dark Wolf embraced him and said, "Yes, I am angry, Hawk ... but not at you."

"What did you do to the man, Father?"

Releasing his son, Dark Wolf sat back on his heels and stroked Hawk's golden hair. "I sent him away. He will not be back, my son."

"Who was he, Father?" Hawk asked.

Standing, Dark Wolf simply said, "It does not matter now, Hawk. He is gone." Before Hawk could question him further, Dark Wolf held out his hand and said, "Come, now. It is late and we must rest while it is night. Into the cabin, Hawk. Go inside with your brother. Raven, you may light the lamp on the table. I will be right in."

"Yes, Father." Raven put his arm around Hawk's shoulders and began directing him toward the house.

Dark Wolf watched until the boys were well out of earshot, then turned to Hattie. "I ask that you stay the night here with us and be with my sons tomorrow. I must go and take care of some business in town."

Hattie grinned, "Would this *'business'* have anything to do with that weasel, Isaac Cutler?"

Dark Wolf thought for a moment, then answered, "Perhaps it is time for me to pay my old *'friend'* a visit." Picking up a thick, short stick, Dark Wolf stared toward the dying embers of the fire and added, "First I will see his mother, Elizabeth. And then, I will see Isaac." From the mere pressure of his finger muscles, the stick snapped in two as he squeezed it. Giving Hattie a sideways glance, he asked, "Will you stay?"

Hattie laid her big hand on his shoulder and nodded. "You know I will."

In the moonlight, Curtis dismounted and looked upward. Against the night sky, he could plainly see, in dark letters, the name *'Cutler'* forged in the top of the iron archway stretching from post to post across the roadway leading to the ranch house. He tied the mare loosely to one of the posts and began walking toward the Cutler ranch. His fearful heart pounded so fast and hard, he could hear the blood squishing through his veins with every beat. The closer he came to the house, the harder and louder the pounding became. His mouth was dry and he soon began to feel dizzy, as if he might faint. Nausea welled up in his stomach at the vision of Isaac lying in his own blood. Curtis leaned against a fence post beside the road and vomited. A cold sweat came over him, and he shivered as the tears brimmed in his eyes. With his coat sleeve, he wiped the bitter saliva from around his mouth. With trembling fingers, he wiped the tears from his eyes and focused his mind on what he believed he had to do.

Seth had been unable to sleep. Noticing a light still burning in Mr. Cutler's study at that late hour, he had an uneasy feeling. Something just didn't seem right. He stepped outside and looked around. The moon shone brightly and a cool breeze stroked his face. He listened for any unusual noises as he slowly walked out into the night. He heard nothing. Looking up at the moon, he decided he would sit out under the large tree near the road fence and enjoy the cool night air.

He recalled when he and his wife had first come to the Cutler ranch to work and live. Resting the back of his head against the tree, he closed his eyes and thought, *My beautiful Mary ... I miss her.* They had loved each other so deeply. When she died, Seth had been devastated. He had cherished her memory and had never loved another. As she lay on her deathbed, she had placed her soft hand in his and spoke to him gently. He remembered the pleading look in her eyes as she said, "Seth, when I am gone, do not be alone. Please marry again. You have so much love to give."

Seth looked toward the ranch house again, and he let his gaze wander upward to Elizabeth Cutler's window. There was no light coming from it, so he believed she must be sleeping soundly. She was a fine woman, faithful to her husband as long as he lived. She had recently regained the strength of her character in spite of her constant distress over Isaac's behavior. Seth had the utmost respect for Elizabeth. He believed he loved her with much the same love as he shared with Mary. *Could she feel the same way about me? But I am only a groom. What do I have to offer this wonderful woman? She deserves so much better.* He turned his face back toward the entrance road and looked at the sky. *Maybe someday, Lord. Maybe it will work out somehow.*

Just then Seth heard a noise on the road near the wood rail fence a few yards away and he thought he saw something move. He sat quiet and still, straining his eyes, hoping to identify the intruder, be it man or beast, before it noticed him.

Curtis was so near to the ranch now, and, in spite of his extreme nervousness and fear, he had managed to regain his composure enough to begin forming a plan for sneaking up on Isaac. He stopped at the last section of fence and stood for a long moment staring at the light in the lower window at the front of the house. He laid his forehead against the post and hugged it. His breath came in heavy short gasps as the panic began to overtake him again. In the silence of the night, his own breathing sounded as though someone was standing beside him. Not sure whether he was praying to God or trying to convince himself, he whispered aloud, "I just gotta do this. For Jessie's sake, I *gotta* do it."

Suddenly Curtis felt a large hand cover his mouth and another hand pry his left hand loose from the post. He tried to whirl around, but the attacker's arm quickly enfolded his midsection and he was being dragged backward toward the barn. Before he could succeed in locating his father's knife at his side, he was thrown to the ground inside the barn where he landed in a soft pile of hay. He heard a horse nicker softly. When he tried to stand up, he was pushed down again. A large shadow loomed over him. He closed his eyes and braced himself for what he believed would be the final blow. Instead, his nerves were jolted, and his eyes opened wide when he heard the gruff whisper and recognized it to be Seth Logan's voice.

"What on earth are you doing here, Curt?"

Curtis, flooded with relief, sat up and looked toward the voice. "Well, ... I ..."

"Come on, boy! You must have had some good reason for sneaking onto this property in the middle of the night. Let's hear it."

With a surge of courage and determination, Curtis stood up and squared his shoulders. He said matter-of-factly, "Isaac Cutler deserves to die, and I came to kill him."

Seth put his arm around Curtis's shoulders and guided him back outside to the tree. He sat down in the same spot he had been earlier, and Curtis sat next to him.

Speaking in whispered tones, Seth asked him, "Curtis, what is going on? Why do you want to kill Mr. Cutler?"

Curtis sighed heavily, then spoke. "Ya know when ya came by Sarah's house this evenin' and we told ya Jessie was sick?"

"Yeah, I remember."

"Well, Mr. Seth, Jessie might be dying. Mr. Cutler came by our house today and hurt Jessie real bad. She's bleedin' from the inside and she just might die."

Seth laid his big hand on the boy's shoulder. He could find no words of comfort.

Curtis continued, "Anyway, even if she don't die, I'm here to make sure Isaac can't never hurt her again." After a few moments of silence, Curtis looked up at the big man, whose face he could now see in the moonlight. "Will ya help me, Mr. Seth?"

"How did you get here? Did you walk?"

"No, I borrowed a horse from the livery, and I left it at the end of the road there." Curtis pointed in that direction. "So will ya help me?"

In silence, Seth stood and reached out his hand for Curtis. "Yep, I'll help ya, boy."

Curtis grabbed Seth's hand and pulled himself to his feet. "Well, what are we gonna do?"

After leading the boy into the barn and to the first stall, Seth spoke aloud, "We are gonna get on this big black horse, go to where you left *your* horse, and then I'm gonna take you back to Sarah's house."

Curtis took a few steps backward. "But I thought ..."

"No, Curtis. I'm gonna help you by taking you back so you can be there when your sister wakes up."

Pleading, Curtis repeated, loudly, "I *gotta* kill him so he can't hurt my sister ... or anybody else ... *no more!*" Taking hold of the knife at his side, Curtis backed away from Seth toward the door.

Lunging forward, Seth grabbed Curtis and pulled him back. He pried the knife from the boy's hand and located a rope and a handkerchief to use as a gag. He tied Curtis's hands and tied the handkerchief in place as he said, "I wish you'd cooperate so I wouldn't have to do ya this way, Curt, but you're goin' back. Think about it, boy. How would Jessie feel if she started to come around, only to find that her brother had been killed? And that's likely what would happen if you tried to tangle with Isaac."

Beginning to cry, Curtis bowed his head and allowed Seth to lift him up onto the black horse's back. In silence they rode slowly down the long roadway to where Curt's borrowed horse was standing. Leaving Curtis in front of him on the black, Seth grabbed the mare's reins and led her as they rode back toward town, picking up the pace as they put more space between themselves and the ranch.

Feeling Curtis's downheartedness, Seth patted him, removed the gag and the rope, and said, "Don't you worry, boy. Justice will soon find Isaac Cutler. I can feel it in my bones."

Hawk could not sleep. So much had happened that day, and his mind was racing. Even though the strange man had tried to take him away, he was determined not to dwell on it because his father had promised the man was gone for good. Inside his head, he could still hear the many sounds of the birds and the drums, and he closed his eyes and visualized all of the Indian men dancing around the fire. He pictured the faces of his new younger Indian friends. Suddenly he realized he had not been able to say 'goodnight' to any of them because Raven had immediately taken him into the cabin upon his Father's return from the woods.

Throwing back the covers, Hawk jumped out of bed and quietly made his way down the stairs. A fire was crackling in the fireplace, and Hawk could see Hattie sitting there talking with his father. He tiptoed up behind them, his bare feet making no noise on the thick bear skin rug. Just as he was about to grab Hattie's shoulders, he heard Hattie ask, "Well, when are ya leavin', Dark Wolf?"

Before Dark Wolf could answer, Hawk dropped his hands to his sides and asked, "Leaving, Father? You are leaving again?"

Hattie and Dark Wolf quickly turned to Hawk, and Dark Wolf pulled his son down to sit on his thigh. He answered. "Yes, son. But only for one day. I'll leave soon, take care of my business as quickly as I can tomorrow and be back to have the evening meal with you. Hattie will stay here with you boys. You can manage with Hattie and Raven for that long, can't you, Hawk?"

Sighing deeply, Hawk leaned against his father's chest and looked into the fire. "I guess so." Remembering how hard they had worked the last time they stayed with Hattie, Hawk looked at Hattie, then up at his father, and asked, "Will we have to work all day?"

Dark Wolf and Hattie both began to laugh.

Hawk smiled and watched them.

Finally, Hattie answered, "How about this. We do whatever you fellers want to do, as long as we stay 'round here. Would that suit ya?" Rumpling his hair, she added, "Maybe *you* can even find some chores for *me* to do." Then she laughed again.

"Sounds good." Hawk jumped up from his father's lap, remembering why he had actually come downstairs. He began walking toward the front door. "I'll be right back in, Father."

Dark Wolf stood up as he asked his son, "Where are you going, Hawk?"

Now reaching for the door handle, Hawk answered back over his shoulder, "I didn't tell the Indians 'goodnight'."

"No, Hawk. Do not go out there." Dark Wolf spoke firmly.

Hattie got to her feet, curious at Dark Wolf's tone.

Opening the door, Hawk said, "It'll only take a minute, Father."

Dark Wolf rushed toward the door, but he was too late. Hawk had slipped out into the night and was running across the porch.

Hattie followed as Dark Wolf went out to bring his son back. Her breath caught in her throat, and she stopped and sat down quickly on the top step. In the bright moonlight, Hattie could see Hawk slowing his pace as he walked toward the area where the Indians had been only a short time before. Then she saw him stop and frantically whirl around, looking in all directions. Where the fire circle, the teepees, the horses, and the log seats had been, there was nothing but the grass. Had she not been there and seen it all herself, she would not have believed that the Indians had even come. There was no evidence of their visit anywhere. Only one teepee stood in the edge of the clearing; the one in which Dark Wolf had sat with his sons early that morning.

Dark Wolf stopped a few yards from Hawk and waited for him to speak.

Still looking around, Hawk asked, "Father, am I dreaming? When I wake up, will the Indians be here again?"

Dark Wolf approached his son and stooped down before him. "Hawk, I know this is not easy for you to understand, but they are gone. I told you not to come out here because I knew what you would find."

On the porch steps, Hattie listened, hoping Dark Wolf would give Hawk some kind of explanation. She, too, was confused.

"Let's go back inside, Hawk. I will tell you what you need to know."

Hawk, now becoming the little boy instead of the brave hunter, put his arms around his father's neck and said, "Okay, Father."

Dark Wolf picked him up and carried him back into the cabin.

Hattie followed and shut the door.

After they had all seated themselves on the floor before the fire, Hawk on his father's lap, Dark Wolf began. "All of the Indian people you saw here today were from your grandmother's village, which was raided by white men sometime not long after she married your grandfather and left with him to come here." Looking into his son's eyes, Dark Wolf asked, "Do you understand what I am telling you, Hawk?"

After a few moments of staring into his father's eyes, Hawk answered, "I'm not sure, Father."

Raven had awakened, and, noticing Hawk was not in their room, had come downstairs to find him. From across the room, Raven spoke. "Hawk, the people of the village were all killed many years ago. Murdered by the white men."

Hawk gave his father a puzzled look. "Is that true, Father?"

"Yes, Hawk."

Raven walked over to the fire and joined them on the rug. He looked at his brother and continued, "We have been visited by the spirits of Grandmother's family, Hawk. But it is a very good thing, so you don't have to be afraid of the truth."

Leaning back against his father and staring into the fire, Hawk began to understand what Raven was telling him. Though it made his heart ache to hear that all of those wonderful people had been killed, he was so happy they had come to spend the day and teach them of their ways. Finally, he turned to Raven and said, "They came to honor Grandmother. And they taught us so many good things. And they danced and sang in *our* honor, Raven!"

Laying his hand on his little brother's shoulder, Raven said, "Yes, they did, Hawk."

Looking through tear-filled eyes into his brother's dark eyes, Hawk said, "I feel sad and happy at the same time. Do you feel that way, Raven?"

"Yes, I do, Hawk."

Hawk wiped his tears away and sighed. "I didn't get to say 'goodbye'."

Raven stood. "You don't have to. Their spirits will always be with us. They will help us when we hunt and fish and make our journeys. And we will never forget them."

Hawk remembered their hunting and fishing games. The disappointment showing in his eyes, Hawk said, "Aw,

163

Raven, they took our hunting stuff ... the bow and arrow, the spear, and what's that other thing? The 'hummytock'?"

Amused, Raven grinned at his brother and said, "It's called 'tomahawk' But don't worry, we can make new ones. They taught us how, remember?" Reaching for his brother's hand, Raven said, "Come now. Let's go and get some sleep. Tomorrow we will practice some of the things they taught us. And we'll make a new 'hummytock'."

They all laughed as Hawk took Raven's hand. Raven said, "Goodnight, Father. Goodnight, Hattie."

As the boys ascended the stairs, Dark Wolf and Hattie heard Hawk ask, "Raven, can I sleep with you tonight? Oh, I'm not *afraid* or anything. I just want to be close to you. Can I?" They heard Raven answer with a chuckle, "Yes, Hawk, you can sleep in my bed." After a few seconds, Hawk said, "Tommyhawk, tommyhawk, tommyhawk. Hey! That's easy to remember. It's got my name in it. Tommy — Hawk. Tommyhawk."

Dark Wolf looked at Hattie and shook his head.

Hattie winked at him and said, "That Raven is quite a wise little man. He knows exactly how his brother needs to hear the truth. 'Specially when it's a tough truth."

Nodding, Dark Wolf stared at the fire and said, "Yes. They are both pretty amazing." Turning to Hattie again, he added, "You know, I am learning so much from them, Hattie. And I realize more and more how much I've missed by not being with them."

Hattie nodded, "I'm sure that's true, but ya need to put all that behind ya and move on with 'em."

Dark Wolf stood and said, "I had better go now so that I can see Elizabeth before Isaac sees me."

After they had returned the mare to the livery and tied the black to a fence rail, Seth walked Curtis to the back door of Sarah's house. He whispered, "I'm keeping the knife, Curtis. Just until you get over the notion of using it for harm." Opening the door quietly, he stepped inside with the boy and gently pushed Curtis toward the center of the room. He whispered softly, "Go on, now, boy. Get some sleep. Jessie will probably be lookin' for ya in a few hours."

Curtis decided to obey Seth, and he waved his hand and tiptoed to the room where he had denied himself sleep earlier. The exhaustion of the whole trying episode now flooded him, and sleep came quickly.

CHAPTER SEVENTEEN

Near dawn, Elizabeth awoke with a start. Her eyes wide open, she lay still, waiting for any sounds that might explain her sudden awakening. After a few seconds, one single tap sounded on a window pane. She slipped quietly from the bed, picked up her robe, and, holding it in front of her, tiptoed toward the window, staring at it as she went. Her body jumped slightly as she saw a small object hit one of the panes and heard the tap again. Finally she reached the window and carefully peered downward into the yard. In the misty morning light, she thought she saw someone standing, staring up toward her window. As she strained her eyes to see more clearly, she saw a hand go up and wave slowly. Though she could not make out who it was, she believed the person meant no harm. She quickly put on her robe and fastened it. Then she raised the window and leaned out for a better look. The stranger spoke.

"Elizabeth, it is Dark Wolf."

Her heart leaping for joy, Elizabeth smiled and motioned for him to go to the back of the house. She whispered, "Meet me at the kitchen door." As she watched him walk in the direction indicated, she whispered to herself, "Oh, no! I didn't want him to see me like this!" She hurried to her dressing table, lit an oil lamp, and grabbed her brush. Loosing the knot at the top of her head, she let her thick hair fall around her shoulders and brushed it into decent order. She wiped the corners of her eyes and mouth, pinched some color into her cheeks and went to the door. She opened it slowly, looking and listening for any signs that Isaac might be moving about in the house. Hearing nothing, she rushed toward the stairs and, keeping her back to the wall, began descending them quietly. When she reached the bottom step, she leaned forward and looked toward the study. The doors were shut, so she was not certain whether or not Isaac was still passed out in there.

She rushed down the hallway and through the kitchen toward the back door of the house. Just as she laid her hand to the latch, she heard Isaac's voice.

"Slipping out to see the stable boy, Mother?"

Whirling around and pressing her back to the door, Elizabeth gasped and said loudly, hoping Dark Wolf was nearby and could hear, *"Isaac! You scared me nearly to death!"*

Hearing Isaac's voice and Elizabeth's startled response, Dark Wolf ducked down below the window and pressed his back against the house, listening. He decided that he would only make his presence known to Isaac if he began to be rough with Elizabeth. Words could only cut the heart, but he would not let Isaac hurt her physically. He waited.

Grinning, Isaac said, "You aren't usually up this early, Mother." Looking her up and down and motioning with his hand, he added, "And you don't usually go running around outside in your night clothes."

"Well, Isaac, I had a restless night and I thought I would take a walk before breakfast." Moving toward the stove, Elizabeth reached for the coffee pot, which she found to be already hot. In her rush to speak to Dark Wolf, she had not noticed the aroma of coffee which filled the kitchen. She turned to see Isaac squinting as he sipped the steamy brew from a large mug. Finding a small cup for herself, she filled it halfway and took a sip. *"You* aren't usually up this early, Isaac, so how do you know so much about *my* morning habits?"

Pushing his chair back noisily as he stood, Isaac sat his mug on the table and said angrily, "You know, Mother, I'm growing weary of your sassy mouth! I think I liked you better when you were crying and cowering and staying in your room all of the time." He began walking toward her, slowly, his hands balled into fists at his sides.

Elizabeth set her cup down and turned to face him. "Isaac, what are you going to do?"

As he continued toward her, Isaac's piercing eyes stared into her frightened ones. Suddenly he stopped and clamped both hands against the top of his own head. His body swayed slightly as though he might topple over. He yelled, *"Dammit, Mother! Now you've got my head pounding again! Get out of here!"* Feeling for the nearest chair, Isaac pulled it out and fell into it with a thud. He crossed his arms on the table and laid his throbbing forehead down on them.

Elizabeth was thankful for the opportunity to escape Isaac's dreadful company, and she intended to take advantage of it, but she could not seem to restrain her tongue before she did. As she reached the door and took hold of the latch again, she turned and said, *"I'm* not the cause of your pounding head, Isaac. It's *you.* You can't even stand yourself. What demon lives inside of you, Isaac Cutler?"

With his head still down on one arm, Isaac slipped his free hand down to his side, drew his gun, and pointed it in the direction of his mother's irritating words. Without looking, he pulled the trigger.

The window glass shattered above Dark Wolf's head just as he jumped up to enter the house, and Elizabeth darted out the door into his arms. It was apparent that she had not been hit by the bullet. As he pulled her down with him under the window, several small fragments of glass sprinkled down upon them both. The door slammed shut and more slivers of glass fell as they heard Isaac's insane laughter coming from inside the house. It had all happened so fast, Elizabeth's head seemed to be spinning, and after a few seconds, she fainted.

Hearing the shot and the breaking glass, and now Isaac's laughter, Seth came running from the barn, his gun drawn. He saw Dark Wolf come around the side of the ranch house, holding Elizabeth's limp body his arms. He put his gun away as he ran over to them, angry tears filling his eyes. *No, Lord, God! Please don't let her be dead! I love her! Please, God!*

Dark Wolf motioned for Seth to keep silent, and he lifted Elizabeth and placed her in the big man's arms. He whispered softly, "She has fainted. Take her to your quarters. I will meet you there in a few minutes."

Seth carried Elizabeth to his room in the barn and laid her on his bed. He laid his gun on the night stand and pulled a chair over next to the bed. Sitting down beside her, he took her delicate hand in his. He stared at her lovely face and kissed her hand, inhaling her soft scent through his nostrils. Seth told himself, *When this is all over, I'm going to ask Elizabeth to be my wife. I know that I love her. I can only hope she will let me spend the rest of my life showing her how much.* He gently removed a few fragments of glass from Elizabeth's hair and brushed away a tiny one that glistened on her cheek below her left eye.

Dark Wolf crept back to the kitchen door and peered through the glass. He could see Isaac, his head still down on the table and one hand resting on his gun, which laid on the table beside his head. He assumed Isaac had passed out again. He kept his body low as he ran to the barn to find Seth and Elizabeth.

The morning sun streamed in through the windows of the cabin. Hattie stretched and yawned. She sat up and looked around. There was no sign of the two boys left in her charge, so she guessed they were still in bed upstairs. She stood and stretched again. After making her way to the wash basin below the mirror on the opposite wall, she poured it half full of water from a bucket nearby on the same table. She leaned over and, cupping her hands together, scooped the cold water up onto her face. It ran down the front of her crumpled shirt, but she didn't care. She grabbed a towel and dried her face and hands, then found a comb and went out to sit on the front porch and work on her tangled hair until the boys awoke. She remembered the events of the evening before, and was again amazed at the thought of how it all turned out. Again, her eyes swept the area where the festivities had taken place. *No sign of anything. Amazing.* Just then she saw something lying on the ground at about the same spot where Hawk had stood in bewilderment in the moonlight. Squinting, she stared at the object until she thought she figured out what it was. She could now see that there were actually several objects lying there. She smiled broadly, and said aloud, "Well, if that don't beat all." Hattie quickly pulled her hair up and twisted it into a loose knot and secured it.

She jumped up and went into the cabin and directly upstairs to the boys' room. As she suspected, they were still asleep. She walked to the window and looked down to see if the objects were still there in the yard. They were. "Hawk! Raven! Wake up!"

The boys slowly sat up. Raven scratched his head and yawned. Hawk rubbed his eyes and tried to open them. He mumbled, "What's wrong, Hattie?"

"Why, nothin's *wrong*, boys. Come over here and look. Yer Indian folks left ya somethin'."

Both boys were wide awake now as they ran to the window and opened it. There, on the ground below, they could plainly see the bow, the arrows, the spear, and the tomahawk. Even from that distance, they could see they were the same ones they had used the day before. The boys looked at each other and grinned.

Hawk hugged his brother tightly. "You were right, Raven. They *are* with us." He ran over to the bed and sat down to put on his jeans and his boots. "Come on, Raven! Let's go get 'em!"

Hawk's excitement became contagious, and Raven soon began dressing and thinking about how they would spend this day until their father returned.

Just as they were ready to go out of the room, Hattie said, "You boys go get yer things, then come in for breakfast. After that, we'll all go outside for the day and you can hunt and fish to yer heart's content."

Hawk nodded. "It's a deal, Hattie." Then off they both went.

Hattie chuckled as she heard them racing noisily down the stairs and out of the cabin. She straightened their beds, then went downstairs to start breakfast.

————

At the doctor's house, Jessie continued to sleep. She had only come around that one time late the evening before. Abigail Smith was worried. Would her husband be able to save Jessie and her baby? She wondered what would become of them even if he did. She folded her hands under her chin and bowed her head in silent prayer.

Curtis tiptoed to the door of Jessie's room and waited for Mrs. Smith to finish her prayer. When she raised her head, he entered and sat on the edge of the bed where his sister lay. "Is she any better, ma'am?"

Wearily, Abigail looked again at Jessie and said, "I'm afraid there is no way of knowing just now, Curtis. She tried to wake up once in the night." Turning to look at the boy, she continued. "She called out your name, and I made sure she knew you had been here with her, but that I sent you home to rest. Then she said her mouth was dry, and we gave her some water. Just a little bit. She asked about the baby. Then she went back to sleep. She hasn't moved since then."

"She asked about Rachel? Didn't she ask about Eli, too?"

Suddenly realizing that Curtis obviously was not aware of his sister's condition, Abigail sat forward and asked him, "Curtis, do you know why Isaac Cutler was angry with your sister?"

Embarrassed at his own ignorance, Curtis blushed and answered, "No, ma'am. I didn't hear what my sister said to him before he started hitting her."

Taking Curtis's hand, Abigail gently explained to him what had happened to his sister at the Cutler ranch, and how Isaac was angry at the thought of being a father, so he had taken it out on Jessie.

At first, Curtis just sat there staring at his sister, his hatred for Isaac Cutler intensifying with each passing moment. The sound of his heart pounded loudly in his ears, and he heard the sizzle as his blood seemed to boil inside him. After a few long moments, Curtis thought he heard a voice in the distance calling his name. Finally, the voice became louder and the sound of his heart began to fade.

Abigail pried her hand loose from his and began rubbing it. "Curtis! You were gripping my hand so tightly. Are you okay, son?"

Curtis understood many things now. He knew why his sister cried so much lately since their mother had died. She needed their mother to help her through this, and she was humiliated, having a baby with no husband. He silently wished Seth had left him alone and let him kill Isaac. But it was too late now. He looked at Mrs. Smith and said, "I'm sorry I hurt your hand, ma'am. I was angry at Mr. Cutler."

"I know, Curtis. What you have to think about now is getting your sister back. And if all goes well with the baby, you will be an uncle."

Curtis looked at her and his hateful thoughts of Isaac vanished at the thought of being an uncle. His eyes softened as he looked at his sister again. "You can go out now if you want to, Mrs. Smith. I'm going to sit with my sister for awhile."

Abigail stood and motioned toward the chair. "It's more comfortable over there."

Curtis moved to the chair. "Thank you, ma'am."

Just before leaving the room, Abigail turned and said, "Please let us know if Jessie moves or speaks."

"I will, ma'am."

The sun had fully risen when Elizabeth awoke to find herself in Seth's quarters, the two handsome men sitting nearby talking about her. She blushed and sat up. "What happened?"

Seth hurried over to her and sat beside her on the bed. He rubbed her back as he asked, "Elizabeth, are you all right?"

The embarrassment showing in her eyes, Elizabeth looked at Seth and said, "Of course, I'm all right." Remembering that her son had shot at her, she quickly asked, "Where's Isaac?"

Dark Wolf answered, "When I looked inside the house, he was still passed out at the table."

Elizabeth covered her face with her hands and said, "Dark Wolf, this is not how I wanted to present myself when I saw you again. You must forgive me."

"Forgive *you? I'm* the one who awakened you at an unusually early hour. Remember?"

Peeking out through her fingers, Elizabeth said, "Yes, you did, didn't you?"

They all laughed.

Seth pulled Elizabeth over to lean on him. "It's all right, Elizabeth. You are still beautiful, even in the early mornin'."

Blushing again, Elizabeth said, "Enough about me. What about Isaac? I'm afraid to go back into my own house."

Dark Wolf spoke first, "Elizabeth, I know now that Isaac killed my father and my wife. I also know that somehow he killed his own father, your husband. Many others have died because of their dealings with your son."

173

Seth interrupted, "Somethin' I need to tell you both. Yesterday, Isaac tried to kill Jessie, the girl that used to work here."

Elizabeth flashed him a fearful look. "What did you say, Seth?"

"Yes, ma'am. Curtis was here last night real late."

"Curtis? He came here by himself? Why, he's only thirteen!"

"Yes, ma'am, I know. I just had a feelin' somethin' was wrong. I couldn't sleep, so I was sittin' out under that big tree, and here come Curtis, sneakin' up the road. He had a knife. He was gonna kill Isaac for hurting his sister. He said she was bleedin' inside."

Elizabeth stood and began wringing her hands, "Oh, no! Oh, God, no!"

The men stood. Seth asked, "What is it, Elizabeth?"

Through her tears, Elizabeth looked from one to the other, then answered, "Jessie is carrying Isaac's baby. He raped her when she was staying here. More than once." She sat down on the bed again and continued, her voice quivering. "When Jessie's mother died, Sarah was there comforting her, and Jessie told her about it. Sarah wasn't going to tell me, but the day she came over, I was moving slowly due to some abuse I had taken from Isaac the night before, and she told me then." Shaking her head and staring at the floor, Elizabeth went on, "He must have gone to Jessie's house and she must have told him about the baby." Beginning to sob loudly, she finished with, "And he must have tried to kill it, too. The poor, dear, little thing."

The two men looked at each other as Seth took Elizabeth in his arms and rocked her gently. Both were feeling the same emotions of hatred for the evil son of this wonderful woman. Both wanted to rid the world of this menace.

Elizabeth calmed herself some and said, "I sent Seth with a note last night, inviting Jessie to come here and bring the baby and the other children to live. I would enjoy the company. But they can never come here and have peace with Isaac around." With a look of hopelessness, Elizabeth asked, "How did such an evil person come out of my womb? What did I do wrong?"

Dark Wolf knelt before her, taking her hands in his, and spoke softly, "Elizabeth, you have done nothing wrong. Please don't worry. I found the treasure Isaac has been wanting — the treasure he has been killing to get his hands on. I'm going to take him there and give it to him. And when he gets what he has always wanted, no one will ever have to worry about him again. I promise."

Isaac grinned and slinked silently from the barn where he had been listening to the last few minutes of conversation between Seth, Dark Wolf, and his mother. He hurried to the ranch house and went to his room to wash up and put on clean clothes. He laughed aloud softly as he thought of his mother's words. In a high-pitched voice, he mocked aloud, "How did such an evil person come out of my womb? What did I do wrong?" He gave a disgusted snort. Then, as he buttoned his white, silk shirt, he looked in the mirror and told himself, "Well, Isaac, they all *hate* you now. But your half-breed friend is right. When he gives you the treasure, nobody will have to worry about you anymore. And do you know why, Isaac?" He rested his hands on the dressing table and leaned in closer to the mirror. Staring into his own eyes, he answered the question. "Because once I learn where the treasure is, *they* will all be *dead*." One more confident grin at himself as he picked up his jacket and hat, then he went down to the study to wait for Jon Dark Wolf Morgan.

Breakfast long over and a few clean-up chores done, Hattie sat under a shade tree above the lake and watched the boys attempting to catch some fish. They wanted to surprise their father with the delicious smell of fish frying when he returned. Hattie grinned and chuckled to herself as she watched Hawk getting tangled in the string he had tied to his arrow, hoping to shoot it and pull it back with a fish on it. Finally, she stood and called to the boys, "Hey! Don't ya think that would work better in a small shallow stream than in the pond?"

Hawk and Raven looked at each other, then at Hattie. Raven spoke, "I know where there is a stream, Hattie, but Father wants us to stay here."

"Is it very far from here?" Hattie asked.

"No, just down in that little valley over there. Can we go there?"

Hattie stood and looked in the direction Raven pointed. After studying the distance for awhile, she said, "I guess we can. But let's take the horses so we can get there and back quicker. You boys get the horses and the things you need to do your fishin', and I'll grab some canteens and leftover biscuits and bacon in case we get hungry."

The boys ran to the corral and began preparing the horses for the short journey. Hawk said, "Raven, I like Hattie. She's nice."

Raven led his horse through the gate and to the front porch. After tying the reins around a post, he went back for Hattie's horse. "Yes, Hawk, I like her, too." In his mind, Raven added, *but I look forward to Father's return.*

Soon the three were mounted and ready to ride. Raven led the way, and Hattie kept to the rear to keep an eye open for any predators or any sign of trouble. She didn't expect any, but with the stranger trying to steal Hawk away last night, she was a bit uneasy.

Isaac waited, pacing the floor and watching out the window toward the barn. *Where is he? What is he waiting for?* At last, he saw Dark Wolf ascending the porch steps. He put on his jacket and picked up his hat. Opening the door, he gave the Indian a surprised look, then began to grin. "Jon Dark Wolf Morgan! What a surprise this is!" He reached out to shake Dark Wolf's hand.

Dark Wolf did not take his hand.

Isaac laid his hand on Dark Wolf's shoulder, smiled and said, "How many years has it been, old friend?"

Dark Wolf said, "Isaac, I will get right to the point. We have some business to discuss. I need to show you something that I'm sure will be of interest to you."

Isaac put on his hat, then pulled out a cigar, bit the end off, and spit it on the porch floor. After lighting the cigar, Isaac said, "Well, Jon, I am just on my way out to have breakfast at the hotel in town. Why don't you join me, and we can discuss our business over some steak and eggs?" In his mind, he finished the thought, *and people will see me with you, so if anything happens to me, they'll know who is responsible.*

"No, Isaac, I think we should take care of our business *now*. If you are hungry, I will wait for you to have breakfast here. I would like to visit with your mother for a little while, anyway. May I come in?"

Continuing to stand in the doorway for a few moments, Isaac stared into Dark Wolf's piercing eyes and studied what he saw there. *He's up to something. He knows Mother is not in the house. Come on, Isaac ... think ... think!* Stepping back from the doorway, Isaac grinned and said, "Where are my manners? Of course, Jon, come in."

Dark Wolf entered the house and waited.

"Why don't you just have a seat in the front room there, and I will go and find Mother. I believe she went for her morning walk." As he left the room, he called back over his shoulder, "We can all have breakfast together. That would be nice."

Knowing Seth was there to protect Elizabeth, Dark Wolf did not follow Isaac out to the barn. He hoped Seth and Elizabeth would both cooperate with Isaac and come into the house as they had discussed earlier. He stood back from the window, but still at a spot where he could observe. Finally, after several minutes, he saw all three of the others emerging from the barn and walking toward the house. He noted that Elizabeth looked more composed. Dark Wolf had ultimate respect for this woman, and he wanted to be sure her suffering would soon end.

Awaking suddenly, Jessie looked from side to side and tried to remember where she was and why she was there.

Curtis scooted up to the edge of the chair and gently squeezed his sister's hand. "Jessie, how do you feel?"

At first, Jessie stared at her brother as though she did not know him, but as her eyes focused, she smiled and softly said, "Oh, Curtis! I'm so glad to see you." She took a deep breath and spoke again, "Are Eli and Rachel doin' all right?"

Curtis moved to the side of the bed so that Jessie would not have to turn her head so far to see him. "They are just fine, Jessie."

Tears welled up in Jessie's eyes and began to drip down along her temples. "Curtis, there's something I have to tell you. And I hope you will understand and not think bad of me. It wasn't my fault. You see, ..."

Interrupting his sister, Curtis offered, "If you are talking about your baby, Jessie, I already know."

Jessie turned her head away and sobbed.

Trying to comfort her, Curtis patted her hand and said softly, "Jessie, I could never think bad of you. Look at me."

Jessie turned to look at him through tear-filled eyes.

In an angry tone, Curtis said, "It's Isaac I hate!"

Weakly, Jessie reached out her arms, and Curtis laid gently down upon her breast to receive the welcome embrace.

Jessie stroked Curtis's hair and said, "Oh, Curtis, we will be fine. When you came to get me at the ranch that day, Mrs. Cutler gave me a great deal of money she had saved up. She didn't know about the baby, but she didn't want us to have need or to worry about anything. She is a wonderful person, Curtis."

"I believe she is, Jessie." Curtis quickly sat upright. "Jessie, Mrs. Cutler sent Seth around last night with a letter! I'll go get it, and let Sarah know you are awake." He stood and bent over and kissed Jessie on the cheek. "I have to let Doc and his wife know you are awake, too. They will prob'ly want to tend to ya while I'm gone. But I'll be back soon!"

Jessie smiled and nodded. "Tell Abigail I'm hungry, too!"

Curtis grinned broadly and rushed from the room.

CHAPTER EIGHTEEN

Sarah and the two younger children were just finishing breakfast when Curtis returned. They looked at him as he entered the house.

When she saw Curtis, Rachel's face lit up with joy. Still seated at the table, she reached out her little arms and said, "Curty!"

"Hi, little sister!" Taking Rachel up in his arms, Curtis looked at Eli and Sarah and smiled. "I have great news! Jessie is awake now, and she asked about you all."

Fiddling with Curtis's curly hair, Rachel laid her cheek against his and whispered, "Jessie come home now?"

"Not yet, Rachel. It will prob'ly be a few days yet." He let her down on the floor. Her dark curls bounced as Rachel ran around squealing and clapping her hands. "Jessie! Jessie!"

The others laughed, and Sarah rushed over to give Curtis a big hug, her eyes filling with happy tears. As she released him, she asked softly, "How did she look Curtis?"

Curtis sat in the nearest chair and said, "Well, she's awful weak. At first she looked confused, like she didn't know me. But then she said my name and told me she was glad to see me." He paused.

Sarah had stepped over to the shelf to get a plate for Curtis. She turned around and looked at him. She could tell there was something more on his mind. Setting the plate and a fork in front of him, she asked, "Was there something else, Curtis?"

Curtis looked over at Eli and Rachel, now in the opposite end of the room, trying to spin a wooden top on the floor. He looked back at Sarah and spoke quietly as he said, "She told me somethin' else, too, Sarah."

Sarah sat down near him and waited for him to tell her the rest.

Looking directly into Sarah's eyes, Curtis said, "My sister is going to have Isaac Cutler's baby."

"Yes, I know. She told me the night your mama died." Reaching out to take Curtis's hand, Sarah asked, "She told you that herself, Curtis?"

"Well, she started to. She was crying and saying she had something to tell me and she hoped I wouldn't think bad of her, but I already knew, so I saved her the trouble."

"What do you mean, honey?"

"Mrs. Smith told me when I got there this mornin'. She wanted me to know how serious Jessie's sickness is." Staring at his empty plate for a moment, he said, "I still hate Isaac Cutler for what he did to my sister, but ..." Looking at Sarah again, he began to smile and said, "I'm gonna be an uncle, Sarah!"

Sarah released his hand and tousled his hair. She stood and began placing the plates and bowls of food closer to his plate. "And a fine uncle you'll be, too, Curtis. Now ya better keep your strength up. Eat hearty!"

It didn't take long for Curtis to eat his breakfast. When he put his plate and fork in the soapy water, he looked up at Sarah and said, "I promised Jessie I'd come right back. And I told her I would bring the letter Mrs. Cutler sent. Do you have it?"

Quickly drying her hands, Sarah said, "Oh, yes! I'll get it."

While Sarah was in the other room, Curtis strolled over to where Eli and Rachel were playing. He stooped down and helped them get the top spinning.

Rachel jumped up, dancing and clapping her tiny hands, squealing with glee at the sight of the spinning toy.

"Maybe later today I can take you two to see Jessie." Curtis stood as Sarah came back into the room.

"Here it is, Curtis. Take it to her. Give her my best wishes." Sarah patted him on the back. "Perhaps, later on, you might come and watch the little ones while I go and see her."

"I'd be glad to, Sarah."

They walked to the door together, and as Curtis stepped out, he leaned back and whispered, "Now you look after Uncle Eli and Aunt Rachel, ya hear?"

Laughing, Sarah motioned for him to be off and closed the door.

Breakfast at the Cutler Ranch had been very strained. While Elizabeth had freshened herself and dressed, Seth had prepared the meal. Dark Wolf and Isaac had waited in the study, Isaac making ridiculous small talk and offering Dark Wolf strong drink. No one but Isaac truly felt like eating, and they had nibbled in almost total silence until Isaac had angrily pushed back from the table and declared breakfast to be over. He had stomped out of the house, yelling that he could have enjoyed better company at a leper colony.

Dark Wolf watched from the back kitchen door where Isaac had fired his gun at Elizabeth that very morning. The breeze blew through the hole where a glass pane had once filled the frame. He saw Isaac go into the bunk house. "Does he usually go to the bunk house in the mornings?"

"No, he doesn't." Elizabeth went over to stand beside Dark Wolf at the door. "Lately, Seth has been giving the hands their orders. Then he keeps me abreast of what is going on. Isaac probably doesn't even know the names of most of the men out there."

Dark Wolf took Elizabeth's hand and led her away from the door. "It's best we are not standing there when Isaac comes out." Turning to Seth, who had started clearing the dishes away and preparing to wash them, Dark Wolf asked, "Can these men be trusted, Seth?"

"Far as I know. They've been doin' all right so far. But I suppose anyone can turn rotten for the right price." He turned back to his work and said, "Better keep an eye or two in the back of yer head today while you're with Isaac."

"Yes, that is what I am thinking, my friend." Turning to Elizabeth, Dark Wolf smiled and said, "I did not have the opportunity to tell you how lovely you are, Elizabeth. And I have a message for you from Adam Miller. The local cattle owners, friends of both Thomas and my father, are ready to help you any way possible. Keep that in mind. Thomas would be proud of how you are handling things here."

Blushing, Elizabeth said, "Well, ... Thomas would be proud of you, too, Jon Dark Wolf Morgan! And he would be so happy to know the boys are with you now." She embraced him tightly and said, "Be careful, Dark Wolf. Please, be careful."

The embrace ended quickly when Isaac entered the room and began his usual embarrassing routine. "What a beautiful sight! My mother hugging my best friend! I've heard stories of such things."

Holding a sudsy iron skillet in his hand, Seth began slowly walking toward Isaac.

Dark Wolf held up one hand in Seth's direction.

Seth stopped. "Isaac, ya better *shut yer mouth*, or *I'm* gonna shut it *for* ya. This is yer mother yer talkin' about. And ya *know* it ain't nothin' like that."

Crossing his arms and leaning on the door facing, Isaac sneered. Ignoring Seth, he pointed back and forth at Dark Wolf and Elizabeth and continued, "Hey! You lay with this half-breed, Mother, then we can have a bunch of quarter-breeds running around. Pretty soon, somewhere down the line, they will all be white again. Won't that be nice?"

Seth raised the skillet and rushed forward, enraged. *"That's it, Isaac! You've insulted yer mother for the last time!"*

Isaac quickly stood away from the wall. He drew his gun, pulled the hammer back, and aimed it directly at Seth's forehead. Calmly, he spoke, "Go and finish washing your dishes. I know you want my mother for yourself. Or maybe it's just her money you want. I don't even care what you two have going on. But I'll be *damned* if a stable boy is going to tell *me* how to talk to my mother."

At those degrading words, Seth's shoulders drooped and he hung his head as he walked back to the sink. He lowered the iron skillet into the soapy water and just stood there, unable to move. Seth remembered his thoughts of the night before when he wondered if he could ever be worthy of someone so wonderful as Elizabeth.

Elizabeth rushed over to Seth and laid her hand on his shoulder. Turning to Isaac, she said, "Isaac Cutler, this man is a *thousand* times the man you only *dream* of being. You leave this house and never come back. You are not welcome here."

With renewed courage, Seth turned and put his arm around Elizabeth's shoulders, pulling her closer to him. "I may be just a stable boy, Isaac, but I know how to respect a lady."

Isaac sneered again and put his gun in its holster. He thought to himself, *This is my ranch, and when I get back, I'm going to clean house.* "Very well, Mother. Have it your way. I don't need you or this ranch. I believe this is going to be a *very good day* for *me*." He took a cigar from his pocket, bit one end off and spit it onto the kitchen floor. After lighting it, he turned and left the room, calling back over his shoulder, "Come on, Jon! We've got business to take care of."

Dark Wolf gave an encouraging nod to Seth and Elizabeth, then followed Isaac out of the house.

Hawk and Raven had caught enough fish for a feast to celebrate their father's return later that day. Hattie had shown them how to keep the fish fresh by putting them in a gunny sack, tying it securely with a long rope, and lowering it into the water. The other end of the rope was tied to a nearby tree to keep the sack from floating away.

The boys were now resting on a large flat rock near the water's edge. Hattie watched them from her place under a large shade tree.

Lying on his back, looking up at the clouds, Hawk said, "Raven, do you think that cloud up there looks like a bear?"

Raven lay down beside his brother and shaded his eyes from the sun. "Which one?"

Pointing, Hawk said, "That big fluffy one. I think it looks like a bear."

"You are right, Hawk. And it looks like he is chasing a rabbit. See the small cloud in front of him?"

Hawk laughed. "Hey! The wind is blowing and the shapes keep changing. Now it looks like a fish."

Raven laughed and turned to look at his brother. "You have been looking at all of those fish we caught, and you must have gotten that shape stuck on your eyes."

Hawk chuckled. "Yeah, maybe." He closed his eyes. "You're right, Raven. When I close my eyes, that's what I see ... fish." He opened his eyes and looked at the sky again. "What do *you* see, Raven?"

After studying the clouds for a moment, Raven said, "I see a man on a horse. And I see ... a dark cloud following him. And when I look at his face, I see fear."

Hawk sat up and looked down at Raven. "You saw all that? You could really see his face? Who was he?"

Raven sat up and said, "How can I know who he is? He is up there in the clouds, and I am down here on the earth. If he comes down here where I am, I will tell you who he is."

Hawk stared at his brother with a look of awe.

Amused, Raven tousled his brother's hair and said, "We should go back now." He pulled the sack of fish out of the water and let some of the water drain off. They had cut the heads off of the fish so they could be sure they were dead, but Hattie had promised to show the boys how to finish cleaning them when they returned to the cabin.

When the boys started walking toward Hattie, Raven noticed she was asleep. He stopped and motioned for Hawk to be quiet. He pointed to Hattie. The boys grinned at each other. They could hear Hattie snoring loudly now. Raven bent down and whispered something in Hawk's ear. Hawk covered his mouth and giggled. He nodded his head.

As they drew nearer to Hattie, they timed their steps to coincide with her snores so there would be silence between. Finally, they stood one on each side of the sleeping woman. The backs of Raven's legs were soaked from holding the bag of fish behind him. He looked at Hawk and raised his eyebrows in a questioning look. Hawk nodded that he was ready.

Quickly Raven pulled the sack from behind him and began shaking it above Hattie's head. At the same time, Hawk shouted, *"Wake up, Hattie! It's raining! It's raining!"*

Hattie scrambled to get up as the water continued to splatter on her face and clothes. She yelled, *"Get the horses before the thunder scares 'em!"*

Both boys laughed, and Hawk fell to the ground and began rolling, holding his sides.

Grabbing her hat off the ground, Hattie stood. She pulled at her wet clothing and looked around. She saw that the sun was still shining, but somehow she had gotten wet. She noticed Raven standing near her with the dripping sack. Putting her hands on her hips, Hattie gave him a piercing look.

Hawk stopped laughing and jumped to his feet. He came quickly to his brother's side and said, "We didn't mean any harm, Hattie. Are you angry?"

After continuing her angry look another moment or two, Hattie could not help herself. She reared back and laughed loudly.

The boys watched her, and Hawk began to laugh with her. Raven stood there smiling his quiet knowing smile. His heart was lifted with happiness.

Finally, Hattie's laughter subsided. She knelt down and hugged both boys to her for a moment. When she released them, she said, "Well, now, fellers, I guess that makes us even, don't it?"

"What do you mean, Hattie?" asked Raven.

Before Hattie could answer, Hawk excitedly said, "Yes! That's right! Don't you remember, Raven? The day Father took us to meet Hattie, she got her shotgun and made like she was gonna shoot us! Remember?"

Raven cocked his head and gave Hattie a sideways glance. "I remember. Yes, I think we are even now."

All was quiet at Dr. Smith's house when Curtis returned. Abigail had met him at the door and told him that Jessie was getting stronger, but her condition was still serious, so he needed to be very quiet while she rested.

Curtis tiptoed into the room and settled quietly in the chair. He looked at his sister and determined that she was sleeping soundly. He pulled the letter from it's envelope and began reading it. The more he read, the more uplifted his heart became. His joy came more for his sister's sake than for his own. True, he believed it would be a wonderful thing to live on the Cutler ranch and learn from Seth how to do all of the chores and take care of things; however, he refused to become too excited at the idea until he discovered what his sister wanted to do. He trusted her to know what would be best for them all. There was the mention of an avenging angel to come and take care of Isaac once and for all. This one thing Curtis would pray for.

After Dark Wolf and Isaac had gone, Seth had finished washing the dishes, and was now preparing to dry them.

187

Elizabeth donned an apron and grabbed the dish towel from the man's big hands.

"Elizabeth, no. You'll ruin your pretty dress," Seth insisted.

Beginning to dry and stack the dishes, Elizabeth replied, "Nonsense! I should have been doing this instead of you. I am so sorry, Seth. You made quite a delicious breakfast. I apologize that I could not eat much of it. It has just been such a wearisome morning." In silence she finished drying the dishes, and allowed Seth to place them in the shelves and cupboards. As she began wiping the table, Elizabeth said, "Thank you for being here for me, Seth."

Seth's heart began to pound. His mouth became dry and his palms began to sweat. The opportunity was right. He knew he had to speak to her right now. *Lord, help me find the words ... please!* Fighting the weakness in his knees, Seth found the strength to take a step toward Elizabeth. He gently removed the towel from her hands and softly said, "Elizabeth, please sit down for a moment. I have some things I want to say."

Without questioning, Elizabeth sat in the chair he offered.

Sitting down in the next chair and facing her, Seth took her hands in his. Looking deep into her eyes, he began, "Elizabeth, you don't have to thank me for being here for you. There is no place on earth I would rather be than where you are. *I* should thank *you* for letting me be near you." After a moment of studying the sweet look on Elizabeth's face, Seth continued, "Isaac said some things this morning. Some he was right about, but some he was very wrong about. Elizabeth, I do want you for myself. That is true. But I don't want you for your money. That is wrong. Give it all to charity. I don't want a penny of it." Looking even deeper into her eyes, he felt himself blushing nervously as he began again. "Elizabeth, I love you. I think you already know that. But another thing Isaac was right about ... I'm only a 'stable boy', as he called it. Can you love such a man in return?" He lowered his eyes and bowed his head.

Elizabeth, tears filling her eyes, gently pulled her hands from his. She laid them on his cheeks and lifted his face gently. Looking into his hopeful eyes, she answered, "Seth, you are a giant. I have always known it. Before your Mary died, she told me what a wonderful man you are. But she didn't have to tell me, Seth. I could see it in the way you were with her. I know how much you loved her and how hard it has been since she died. Thomas and I shared the same kind of love and adoration for each other." Holding his hands again, she went on. "Our mates are gone now. We can't have them back. But I see no reason why two people, who have so much love to share, cannot share that love honestly as long as they live ... no matter who they are, or what other people say or think. I do love you, Seth. I love you dearly. Always remember that."

Relief washing over him, Seth released Elizabeth's hands and pulled her over onto his knee so he could embrace her fully. Burying his face in her neck and inhaling the soft scent of her skin, he said, "Oh, Elizabeth! How I love you!"

Elizabeth allowed her tears to flow freely as happiness filled her. She looked upward and prayed silently, *Lord, let this be real. Please, don't let Isaac destroy what I feel at this moment!*

Seth raised his head, wiped Elizabeth's tears away and kissed her deeply. After the kiss ended, Seth helped Elizabeth stand, and he knelt before her. Taking her hand, he smiled and said, "Elizabeth Cutler, will you marry me?"

Smiling down at him, her eyes sparkling, she pushed back the new tears which were making their way to the surface. "Yes, Seth Logan, I will marry you." Tugging at his hands, Elizabeth said, "We can begin making plans very soon, darling, but right now, I would very much like for you to take me into town to see about Jessie."

Seth stood and said, "I'd be glad to."

Together they walked to the front of the house. Elizabeth said, "I won't be long getting ready. Wait here for me, and I will help you get the carriage."

Heading for the door, Seth said, "*I'll* get the carriage ready, Elizabeth. It's my job, remember?"

Teasingly, Elizabeth said, "Well, if we can do dishes together, then we can surely ready the carriage together."

Seth smiled and nodded. "Okay, I'll wait." He watched as Elizabeth ascended the stairs.

From the top of the stairs, Elizabeth smiled down and said, "If Jessie is up to it, we will tell her our good news!"

As Elizabeth disappeared into the hallway, Seth decided to return to the kitchen to finish drying and putting things away. Satisfied, he walked over to examine the broken window and thought, *I might as well take this frame into town to have the glass replaced.* He began prying the window frame loose. Suddenly, a movement outside caught his eye. He stepped back away from the window and watched as two of the ranch hands came from the bunk house. They were both rough-looking, and he recognized them as the two new hands Isaac had hired only the day before. He stepped closer to the window as they turned and headed for the barn to get their horses. Seth finally worked the window frame loose and set it down on the floor. Soon he saw the two men ride out of the barn as though they were in a hurry. He thought, *It they are on a mission for Isaac, I trust it will fail.*

Elizabeth's voice interrupted his thoughts. "Are we ready, Seth?"

Deciding to spare Elizabeth additional worry, he did not mention what he had just seen. He picked up the wooden frame and said, "Yes, I thought we could have this glass replaced sooner if we take the frame into town to the merchant. He may even have some glass in stock."

"Good thinking, darling."

190

"It looks like sunshine for the moment, but would you like for me to cover the window before we leave, in case it storms?"

Looking around, Elizabeth answered, "No. There's nothing near enough to that area that a little rain would damage it."

Offering his arm to Elizabeth, Seth said, "Shall we, then?"

Smiling and taking his arm, Elizabeth said, "We shall!"

The sun shone brightly as Dark Wolf led Isaac up the mountainside. Isaac stopped his horse and complained of the heat. He removed his jacket and tie and stuffed them into his saddle bag. He removed his hat, placed it on the pommel, and wiped his forehead with a handkerchief. Then he took another swallow of water from his canteen and poured some on his head and face, letting it run down his neck and inside his white silk shirt. "You said you had something to show me, Jon. What is it? *Where* is it? Is it much further? This damned heat is making me crazy."

Dark Wolf stopped and turned his horse around. "It is not much further. You will see soon enough." He noticed that Isaac kept turning around as though he were looking for something ... or someone. He had also noticed two riders following at a good distance. He assumed it was the result of Isaac's visit to the bunk house earlier that morning. *Poor dumb fools!* he thought. He turned his horse again and continued up toward their destination.

Isaac began to try to make conversation. "Say, don't you live up here in your father's old cabin?"

"Yes."

"I guess your boys are with you up there."

"Yes."

"I didn't think your mother wanted to live up there again."

"She died."

"Oh, too bad. And now you are forced to take the brats with you, hunh?" Without waiting for an answer, Isaac went on, "Yeah, I know. I came real close to having a bastard of my own. But I took care of that little problem real quick and in a hurry."

His hatred for Isaac growing stronger with each passing moment, Dark Wolf managed to answer. "I am happy to have my sons with me. I am sorry for the time I was not with them."

Lighting a cigar, Isaac nervously looked back to see if the men were still following. Satisfied they were, Isaac decided to change the subject. "Well, Jon, 'each to his own,' I always say. Are you going to tell me what you want to show me?"

"We are almost there. Then you will know."

Finally, after several hours, Jessie awoke to find Curtis seated beside her. Reaching for his hand again, she said, "Did you bring the letter, Curtis?"

Moving to sit on the edge of the bed, Curtis pulled the letter from his pocket and held it out for his sister to take.

Jessie struggled to keep her eyes open. She said, "Would you read it to me, please? I'm going to close my eyes, Curt, but I'll be listening."

"Sure." Curtis began reading, and he glanced at his sister from time to time to see if she was hearing what it said. As he neared the end of the letter, tears began to pour from the corners of Jessie's eyes, down her temples, and into her hair. He folded the letter and laid it with the envelope on the bedside table. "Don't cry, Jessie. It will be all right. We can do whatever makes you happy."

Jessie took a ragged breath and said, "Thank you, Curtis." She wiped her eyes. "Would you go and get Sarah for me? I want to see Eli and Rachel, too. Please bring them."

Curtis could not help worrying at Jessie's tone. She sounded defeated, and so sad. He said, "Jessie, you are my sister, and I love you ... and I need you, too. You think about that while I'm gone." On his way out, Curtis told the doctor that Jessie was awake and asking for the others.

Dr. Smith nodded, laid down his pipe, and asked Abigail to assist him with Jessie again.

Before Curtis closed the door, he asked, "Is Jessie gonna be okay, Doc?"

"We will certainly keep hoping so, Curt," the doctor replied. "You run along now and get Sarah like Jessie asked you to."

Not long after they had finished changing her bindings and checking the strength of her heartbeat, Sarah came into Jessie's room carrying Rachel. Curtis followed, holding Eli's hand.

Abigail gently tucked another pillow under Jessie's shoulders to lift her slightly. "Your visitors have arrived, Jessie. They may not stay too long, though. We don't want you getting over-tired."

Dr. Smith agreed, "Yes, all of you need to realize that Jessie must regain her strength fully before she may come home. Keep your visit brief."

Sarah nodded and said, "We will only stay for a few minutes, Doc. She wanted to see the wee ones."

The doctor and his wife left the room.

Rachel reached out her arms for Jessie. "Jessie! Jessie!"

Holding her back, Sarah said, "Easy, Rachel. You must be very easy with Jessie, just like you do when you carry the eggs. She might break, just like the eggs."

Obviously puzzled, but understanding that she must be gentle, Rachel agreed to sit next to Jessie on the bed. She looked at her sister for a moment, then very softly laid her head on Jessie's chest. She whispered, "Jessie."

Jessie tried not to laugh as she ran her fingers through the little girl's dark curls. "I love you, Rachel."

Without raising her head, Rachel softly answered, "Love you, Jessie." Sarah stood nearby, ready to scoop Rachel up if she became the least bit rowdy.

Jessie reached out her hand for Eli to come closer.

The young boy walked over to the edge of the bed and took Jessie's hand. "Hi, Jessie. I miss you."

"Aw, I miss you too, Eli." Jessie lifted his hand to her lips and kissed it. "I'll try real hard to get better so I can come home. But you children need to keep mindin' Sarah and bein' real good while she's lookin' after you. Promise me you'll do that, Eli."

The boy gave his sister's hand a gentle squeeze and answered, "I promise, Jessie."

"Okay," Sarah interrupted, "that's enough for now. Jessie needs her rest. We must go."

Rachel sat up and reached for Sarah. "Go now."

Quickly Jessie said, "Sarah, I need to talk to you alone." Looking at Curtis, she asked, "Would you please take Eli and Rachel back to Sarah's?"

Now more worried than ever, Curtis nodded and picked up Rachel. "Okay, Jessie. But can I come back later?"

"Sure, Curt. But I'll be asleep again soon, so you might want to wait for awhile."

When the three children were gone, Sarah pulled the chair around so she could sit facing Jessie. "Now, tell me how you are feeling, Jessie."

With a deep sigh, Jessie began, "Sarah, Doc Smith and his wife both tell me I will be fine if I just rest and get my strength back. They say the baby is fine, as far as they can tell." She stopped talking and stared at the ceiling.

"Go on, Jessie, girl. What is it?" Sarah coaxed.

Jessie finally gathered the words she wanted to say and looked at Sarah. "Sarah, I don't know *how* I know, but I just know I'm not going to make it."

"Nonsense! Where did you get such an idea? If the doctor says you can get through this, then you will. You are not someone who gives up easily, Jessie."

Jessie sighed again. "I know that, Sarah, but there are some things you just know, even if you can't explain them. I may have this baby just fine, but I think something is wrong inside of me, and I am not going to be here to take care of my child." Tears welled up in her eyes as she said. "It will be an orphan unless someone is willing to take it in. And what about Curtis and Eli and Rachel? What will become of them?"

Sarah's heart went out to Jessie, but knowing no other way to respond to the girl's comments, except to be firm, she said, "Jessie, you had better get those silly notions out of your head and just concentrate on getting well so you can enjoy your motherhood. But you know that your baby would not be orphaned. Not as long as I'm around. And not as long as it's grandmother, Elizabeth Cutler, is around."

"Did I hear my name?" Elizabeth strolled in with a smile that could not help but brighten the spirits of those in the room.

Jessie reached out her hand. "Mrs. Cutler! I'm so glad to see you. Thank you for your wonderful letter."

Taking Jessie's hand, Elizabeth kissed it and said, "You are welcome, my dear. And I meant every word of it. In fact, on the way here, I've been making some plans."

Sarah stood and offered Elizabeth her chair. "I'll just wait outside while you two talk."

Refusing the seat, Elizabeth waved her hand and said, "No, no! This conversation includes you too, Sarah. Please sit down."

"Me?" Sarah gave a puzzled look and returned to the chair.

Elizabeth sat on the edge of Jessie's bed and looked from one woman to the other. "But first, before I tell you of those plans, I must tell you my good news."

Jessie could see the excitement sparkling in Elizabeth's eyes. "What is it, Mrs. Cutler?"

"Please, Jessie, call me 'Elizabeth'. We are friends. And besides, very soon, 'Mrs. Cutler' will no longer be my name. You see, Seth Logan has asked me to marry him, and I have accepted his proposal." She smiled brightly and looked at the other two women.

Sarah grabbed Elizabeth's hand and patted it softly. "Oh, I knew it! When I was at the ranch I could see that you were quite taken with him. He's a fine man, Elizabeth. I'm very happy for you."

Jessie reached out her arms to embrace Elizabeth. "I'm happy for you, too, ... Elizabeth. You deserve to have another good man in your life. You are a wonderful person." Looking toward the door, Jessie asked, "Where is Seth now?"

"Oh, he had some business to attend to. But he sends his best regards." Repositioning herself on the bedside, Elizabeth said, "All right, enough talk about me. Let me tell you two about my other plans!"

CHAPTER NINETEEN

The boys were hungry by the time they returned to the cabin, and Hattie began preparing a light meal while they turned the horses into the corral. She had promised that, after lunch was finished, she would show them how to clean the fish and get them ready to fry for supper.

At the corral, Hawk asked his older brother, "Why do you think that man tried to steal me, Raven?"

After closing the gate, Raven sat down and leaned against the post. "I don't know why, Hawk. But I believe it was the work of Isaac Cutler. He must have found out we are here with Father, and he wanted to cause him more pain."

Sitting down Indian style and facing his brother, Hawk said, "Do you think it has anything to do with the treasure he wants? ... the gold?"

"I suppose he thought he could use you to make a deal with Father. He would force Father to give him the gold in order to get you back."

Hawk stared at the ground for a few moments, then looked up at his brother. "Raven, do you think Father has gone to kill Isaac?"

Not wanting to answer too hastily, Raven searched for the words to describe what he felt in his heart. "Hawk, I believe that Father would like to see Isaac just vanish from this life and cause no more harm to anyone. He has hurt our family more than words can describe. But I know Father is not a murderer. I believe he has gone to confront Isaac about the bad things he has done, but I also believe that the Great Spirit is with him and will bring an end to all of this trouble."

They heard Hattie calling for them to come and eat, and Raven stood and brushed the dust from the seat of his pants. Hawk imitated his brother's actions.

As they walked back toward the cabin, Hawk asked, "Raven, do you think Father would have given Isaac the gold to get me back? Gold is worth a lot of money, isn't it?"

Raven stopped. He stepped in front of his brother and gave him a serious look. "Hawk, gold is just the same as money. But *you* are worth more than *any* amount of gold. Father would have given this entire earth, *and* the sun, *and* the moon, *and* the stars, to get you back." Looking softly into his little brother's now tear-filled eyes, he added, "And so would I."

Hawk took a deep breath, wiped away the tears, and hugged his brother. "Oh, thank you, Raven!"

They heard Hattie call out again, and Raven began trotting toward the cabin. "Last one to the table is a cow pile!"

Hawk began laughing and dashed past Raven. He shouted, "Hattie, hold the door!"

Dark Wolf was relieved when he finally spotted the huge dead tree a few hundred yards ahead. The rock face loomed above it. The cave was not yet visible, but he could hear the wind whistling at the entrance. To end Isaac's complaining, he pointed up toward the tree and said, "We are going there."

Studying the area around where Dark Wolf had pointed, Isaac said, "It doesn't look like much to me, Jon." He pulled up next to Dark Wolf and then quickly looked back over his shoulder.

Dark Wolf noticed Isaac's nervous actions, but did not verbally acknowledge them. He knew that whoever was following would not be able to interfere with what was about to happen to Isaac on the mountain.

As they neared the rock face, the mouth of the cave gaped ominously before them. Isaac urged the big, black horse ahead. Dark Wolf did not want Isaac to enter the cave without him, so he caught up with Isaac, and they both reached the tree at the same time.

Dark Wolf was surpised when Isaac dismounted, tied his horse, and waited for him. As they stepped just inside the entrance, he saw Isaac look back again. While locating the lantern he had placed there the night before, Dark Wolf asked, "Why do you keep looking back, Isaac?"

Isaac sarcastically replied, "Well, Jon ... Dark Wolf, your Indian senses must not be workin' too well today. I think two men have been following us this whole time."

As he lit the lamp, Dark Wolf said, "Don't worry about them."

Just then a glittering rock caught Isaac's eye. He ran toward the rock, which jutted out of the wall. In the lamplight it was now easy to see that the vein was very wide. Isaac's mouth began to water as he gazed all around and mentally calculated what it could be worth to him. His hands swiped over the sparkling golden wall of rock and he looked at the residue sparkling on his hands. He laughed wildly as he ran to the opposite wall and repeated the action. He closed his eyes and laid his cheek against the cold surface. His hands carressed the wall near his face. *You are mine! All mine!* he thought. Suddenly, a noise behind him reminded him that he was not alone. He spun around and looked at Dark Wolf. "Jon, when did you find this?"

Noting that Isaac had pulled the side of his jacket back and was resting his hand on his revolver, Dark Wolf answered, "Not long ago."

With as sneaky grin, Isaac said, "We can be partners, right Jon? We can mine this gold together." Still grinning, he added, "Do you know something, Jon? You'll be the richest red man in the world!"

Watching Isaac's every move, Dark Wolf crossed his arms on his chest and said, "Well, Isaac, I don't think I want any of it. I just thought I'd give it all to you." Then, recalling Isaac's words of long ago, he added, "You know, for 'proprieties sake.' I mean, what would it look like for a red man to have all that money?"

With a evil grin, Isaac answered, "That's real good thinking, Jon."

Hearing a noise near the entrance of the cave, they both turned to see two men coming toward them. As the men slowly proceeded, peeking into the dimly-lit cave, one asked, "You all right, Mr. Cutler?"

Isaac smiled widely and said, "Yeah. I'm great! Come on in, boys." As the two stepped further in, he added, "Look what my friend, Jon, just gave me! A gold mine!" Before the men could say a word, Isaac swiftly drew his gun and shot them. He walked over, looked down at them, and snorted, "Stupid fools! Too bad they won't be able to tell anyone about it." Laughing as he turned back around toward Dark Wolf, he put his gun away. Shrugging his shoulders, he said, "Well, you did give it to me, right, Jon? So it's mine. Mine!"

Though it angered him beyond words how Isaac could have so little respect for human life, Dark Wolf was unflinching as he said, "Come, Isaac. I still have more to show you." He picked up the lantern and began leading the way. A few yards further, the cave twisted off to the right. Just before they rounded the curve, Dark Wolf stopped Isaac and turned to face him. "Isaac, do you remember that barbaric fighter you were trying to buy a few months ago?"

Without giving himself time to wonder how Dark Wolf might know about that, Isaac nodded and said, "Oh, yeah. I could have made a *fortune* with that guy. But he didn't even acknowledge my offer when I sent off a letter to his agents. Son-of-a-bitch just disappeared. Nobody knows where he went."

Dark Wolf smiled and leaned closer, and bringing his face right up to Isaac's, he whispered, "That was me."

Laughing nervously, Isaac began backing away, his hand quietly fumbling at his jacket, trying to locate his gun.

Dark Wolf grabbed Isaac's collar and pulled him closer. "No, now you can't go yet. I need to show you my surprise. You will want to see this." Without letting go or taking his eyes off of Isaac's, he set the lamp down. As he came up, his hand slipped under Isaac's jacket and removed the pistol from it's holster. He tossed it away as he added, "Oh, you won't be needing this." Then he picked up the lantern again and began slowly dragging Isaac along.

They continued around the curve, Isaac becoming more fearful with each step. When they entered the large room and the light filled it, Isaac gasped and turned his face away at the sight before him.

Still holding Isaac's collar, Dark Wolf slung him toward the center of the room and released him. Isaac lost his balance and stumbled onto the ground. Frantically, he tried to scramble to his feet. Every way he turned there were corpses, their bodies leaning against the cold sparkling cave wall. Some stared at him with black, empty eye sockets. Their fleshless jaws gaped, seeming to laugh at him. Others looked at him with expressionless faces and emptiness in their eyes.

Dark Wolf set the lantern on the floor, folded his arms on his chest, and mocked, "Isaac, you don't seem pleased to see your friends. Well, I say 'friends', but you have no friends, do you, Isaac?"

Isaac finally scrambled to his feet, trembling. "Jon, ... I ..."

Interrupting him, Dark Wolf held out one arm, indicating that Isaac should look around. "Some are only skeletal now, Isaac, but these are the remains of men who died in your service. Men whose names you probably don't even remember. No, wait! You did know Zeke, didn't you? Well, he's here, too, I see."

Isaac frantically looked all around until he spotted the freshly exhumed body of his old foreman. He stared in amazement at Zeke's haunting eyes. "How did he get here? I had him buried on the ranch!"

"I'm sure I don't know, Isaac. But there he is. Obviously, he didn't want to miss your party." Crossing his arms on his chest, Dark Wolf added, "Oh, by the way, Ben Thomas was not successful in stealing my son for you. He tried, but I stopped him."

Isaac looked around again. "I notice he's not here. Did you slit his throat, or maybe scalp him?"

Dark Wolf answered, "No, Isaac. I gave him a chance to wise up and get away while he's still young enough to make something of himself. It's *you* I'm dealing with now."

As Isaac turned back to face Dark Wolf, he spotted his gun lying off to the left.

Dark Wolf noticed. He warned, "Don't even think about it, Isaac. You'd never make it that far." Taking a thick leather cord from his back pocket, he grabbed Isaac and pushed him down. He swiftly tied his hands and feet in front of him, then tied them together, so that he was forced to sit.

Isaac pleaded, "Jon, take me out of here, please. Don't do this. *Please!"*

Squatting down near Isaac, Dark Wolf said, angrily, "Did you even give any of your victims a chance to plead for mercy? Those two men? My father? *My wife?"* He stood and walked around behind Isaac as he continued, "You see, Isaac, you made it personal a long time ago. I didn't know it then. But I have come to know. And *your own* father; did *he* beg for mercy?"

Dark Wolf walked out of the room, Isaac screaming and begging him not to leave him there. He quickly returned, dragging the bodies of the two men Isaac had murdered only a few minutes earlier.

Isaac whimpered quietly, "Jon, ... please ..."

Dark Wolf placed the bodies against the wall facing Isaac and lifted their eyelids so they could stare out at him.

Isaac looked away. Trying again to save himself, he attempted to appeal to Dark Wolf's conscience in his knowledge of the law. "Jon, listen, you know you will never get away with this. The law will come afer you. They will track you down."

Dark Wolf motioned and looked toward the two fresh bodies and said, "Isaac, these are the only two people who knew where you were." Sarcastically, he added, "And I don't think they are going to say anything to anyone." Slowly walking around Isaac, he continued, "According to the law, someone would have to accuse me of something and show evidence. But first, someone would have to complain because you were missing." He squatted, facing Isaac, and whispered, "I've been hearing people talk about you, Isaac. I don't think they are going to miss you at all."

Thinking quickly, Isaac tried to appeal to Dark Wolf's spiritual nature. "Jon, vengeance belongs to the Lord ... the Great Spirit ... or whatever you call it. Isn't that what the Good Book says?"

Slowly standing again, Dark Wolf answered, "True, Isaac." He moved around behind Isaac and grabbed his hair. Pulling his head back, Dark Wolf added, "And he uses people to get his work done sometimes." Raising his free hand above Isaac's head, Dark Wolf said, "It looks as though I am an instrument of vengeance this time." His hand came down hard against Isaac's chest, breaking his sternum. He released Isaac's hair.

Isaac gasped for breath several times and fell over onto his side. He began coughing and gagging.

Just then, a deep, rumbling sound began outside, and the low tones filled the cave. A rush of cool wind came into the room and caused some of the older skeletons to shift positions against the wall. Isaac's eyes grew wider as he saw the movement of the bones. He whimpered and shut his eyes tightly.

Not wanting him dead just yet, but rather having time to think about all of the wrong he had done, Dark Wolf pulled Isaac back up into a sitting position. "That was for our fathers, Isaac, ... mine *and* yours." As he walked around behind Isaac again, Dark Wolf reflected back to how his beautiful wife, Ravena, must have felt at being tied, beaten, humiliated ... raped. His foot moved swifly, and his boot heel met with Isaac's spine and snapped it.

Isaac screamed and toppled over into a heap.

The rumbling grew louder, and an even stronger, colder rush of wind filled the room.

Dark Wolf said, "And *that* was for my wife, Ravena, the mother of my sons ... and for Jessie, the mother of *your* child, Isaac." He walked to the edge of the passageway leading to the mouth of the cave. "Oh, the Good Book also talks about honoring your father and mother. Think about that. I'm leaving now, Isaac. You wanted the gold. It is yours."

His tears falling onto the damp dirt floor of the cave, Isaac gave one long agonizing groan. Even in this room full of people with staring eyes and gaping jaws, Isaac realized he was alone. The wind blowing into the cave caused the lamp's flame to flicker, making the shadows of the bodies dance on the glistening walls. Isaac was terrified. The physical pain was unbearable. He could not move, and his tears would not stop flowing. The low rumble continued and grew louder.

Without looking back, Dark Wolf walked steadily to the cave entrance. Stepping outside, he looked at the sky. Thick, black, roiling clouds covered the sun, and the wind blew first one way, then another, causing the trees and other vegetation to dance in all directions. He mounted his horse and untied Isaac's black horse to lead it home with him. As he began to slowly ride away, a tremendous clap of thunder filled the air and lightning split the sky. He walked the horses further to a safe distance from the rock face, and he could faintly hear the sound of drums.

Stopping, he turned his head to look downward toward the cave. He blinked his eyes and looked again. There was no mistaking it. The spirit of Two Falls, his mother's brother, who had talked with him only the day before, now stood in the mouth of the cave looking at Dark Wolf. The roar of thunder continued and the wind swept toward the cave. After a few moments, Dark Wolf saw Two Falls raise his hands toward the sky, and he heard him chanting something into the wind. Another boom of thunder came, bringing with it a brighter bolt of lightning. Downward it bolted, barely missing Dark Wolf's head, and entered the cave as quickly and swiftly as an arrow is shot from a bow.

Inside the cave, the lightning swept the entire wall. It entered the large room and violently knocked each body away from the wall and toward the center where Isaac lay helpless, hearing the sound of drums and chanting, along with his own screams inside his head. Before the last body fell upon him, his terror-filled heart failed him. His eyes remained wide open and fixed as his last breath escaped his body.

Another deep rumble came and the mountain began to tremble. The sparkling goledn dust sprinkled down from the ceiling onto the heap of bodies. The lantern light went out, leaving the cave in total darkness.

Feeling the vibrations in the earth, Dark Wolf's horse danced nervously from side to side. Dark Wolf rode off to the right, to a safer distance, but where he could still observe. He dismounted and stood between the horses, gripping their bridles tightly. He knew this would be over very soon, and that the Great Spirit was finishing the necessary task in his own way. Suddenly, the rock face began to break away and tumble straight downward onto the flat ground just below. Dark Wolf watched as the entrance to the cave was totally sealed off, removing all temptation from any future passersby. The huge dead tree toppled over, landing with its roots reaching upward into the air. For several minutes he felt the ground shake, and watched as giant boulders continued to roll down and cover any evidence that a potential gold mine had ever existed there. Finally all grew quiet again, except for the sound of rain pelting the ground. A long, gentle rumble of thunder filled the air. The rain came now in its fullness to freshen the earth. Dark Wolf mounted his horse and headed toward home.

Having laid out her ideas and plans to Jessie and Sarah, and not wanting to exhaust the young girl, Elizabeth had taken her leave. On the way back to the ranch she chattered about her conversation with the two ladies.

Amused at her girlish excitement, Seth chuckled. He said, "It's so good to see you smiling and happy about something, Elizabeth. It's been a long time, and you deserve to be happy."

Elizabeth tucked her arm in his and snuggled closer to him. "Well, I am happy, Seth. Happier than I have ever been. Oh! There is so much to do! You will help me won't you, darling?"

The big man blushed and shrugged his shoulders. "Of course, I will. Why what kind of man would I be if ..."

"Stop!" Elizabeth shouted. "What is that noise?"

Seth quickly pulled back on the reins and stopped the carriage. They both turned to look at the mountain. The sky had turned black and they could hear the loud cracks of thunder and see the lightning bolts spearing the earth in one area. "It's just a storm over the mountain, Elizabeth. That's all. Now don't you worry ..."

Continuing to stare toward the mountain, Elizabeth whispered, "No, Seth. It's more than a storm." After a few moments of silence between them, only the deep hum of thunder filling the air, Elizabeth gasped and laid her hand on her chest. Her heart raced as she said, "Isaac."

Seth saw the painful look in Elizabeth's eyes. He waited for more words, but when she did not offer them, he asked, "Do you want me to go and see about him, Elizabeth?"

A louder roar filled the air and they could visibly see the mountain shaking violently. They watched in awe, neither one saying a word. When it was over, they could see the clouds releasing their sheets of rain above the area where the noise had generated. Elizabeth took a ragged breath, and tears flowed down her cheeks as she said, "It is over, Seth. I feel it. I know it." She bowed her head and leaned against his chest. "Isaac is dead."

Seth's heart went out to her. He wrapped his arms around her and held her close. "I'm sorry, Elizabeth. I'm so sorry it had to be this way." After holding her there for awhile, Seth reached over and took up the reins. He smacked the horse's hips gently with the leather, and the carriage began to move again. In silence they finished their journey. Seth knew this was very difficult for Elizabeth. He was just glad he was there for her.

On the front porch of the cabin, Hawk could not stop pacing. Just a few minutes before, they had all seen the activity in the sky and had heard the commotion on the side of the mountain down below. The boys knew it was happening in the area of the cave, and Hawk feared that something dreadful had happened to his father.

"He will be here soon, Hawk," Raven promised. "We just have to believe that and wait for him to return. He will."

Hattie tried to help comfort Hawk, although she, herself, was somewhat concerned. "Listen to Raven now, boy. And get back over here and help us clean these fish. Yer pa is gonna be good and hungry when he does get here. We're almost done and we can start cookin'." Taking another fish out of the sack, Hattie added, "Yep, yer pa will shore be proud of you boys, catchin' all these fish."

With that statement, Hawk decided to rejoin them at their task, but he could not help being afraid. "I wish he was here right now."

Raven smiled and said, "He'll come back, Hawk. I promise."

———————

Having explained Mrs. Cutler's plans to Curtis, and giving assurance that Isaac would not be able to ruin things for them, Sarah found paper and pen and began making a list of everything that would need to be done. Curtis watched Sarah's hand and saw the pen glide effortlessly across the paper. Nearby on the porch floor, Rachel and Eli played with a ball, rolling it back and forth to each other.

Curtis tipped his chair back and leaned it against the wall. "Sarah, when do you think Jessie will feel good enough to go to the ranch?"

"Oh, I imagine it will be a few weeks ... maybe a month, Curtis." She looked at the boy and saw the disappointment in his eyes. He had told her how much he hoped they could go soon. "But Doc Smith says, if she continues to get stronger each day, she can come here and *we* can take care of her until she is able to travel. We just have to take one step at a time, Curtis."

"I understand, Sarah. We don't want Jessie to lose the baby."

Sarah put down her pen and looked out at the sky. "Apparently, the storm that was brewing on the mountain has decided to pass on by. The thunder has let up now, and the sky is clearing."

Curtis looked at the rays of sun peeking through the clouds. "That was some of the loudest thunder I ever heard, Sarah! I'm glad it didn't rain down here as hard as the thunder roared up there. Rachel never would have come out from under the bed!"

Sarah chuckled. Still staring at the sky, she said, "You know, Curtis, Mrs. Cutler came along at just the right moment today."

"What do you mean?"

Sarah sighed deeply, looked at Curtis, and answered, "Well, Jessie was just telling me that, even if she made it through to having her baby, she wouldn't live to raise it. I tried to argue with her, but she just insisted, and I think she was going to ask me if I would look after it for her." She looked over at Curtis. "I truly think she was about to give up. I think she didn't want to live."

Dropping the front of his chair back to the floor, Curtis said, "Sarah, I'm afraid she won't live. Not if she feels like that."

"Well, that's when Elizabeth Cutler came in, all excited and happy, and told us of this plan she had. You should have seen Jessie's face light up. She has always enjoyed working for Mrs. Cutler, but this time it will be different. We will all be a family together. And I must tell you, Curtis, I am *thrilled* at the prospect. I never had children or family, other than my husband, since I was a young girl."

Taking on some of Sarah's happiness, Curtis said, "And I'm sure Mr. Seth can teach me a lot of things about horses and ranchin' and such."

Excitedly, Sarah said, "Oh! Did I tell you that Seth and Mrs. Cutler are getting married soon?"

Smiling, Curt answered, "No, Sarah. You didn't. That's great. They are both very nice people."

"Yes, they are, Curtis. Yes, they are." Picking up her pen again, Sarah studied her list and said, "Now, let's see. Where was I?"

After realizing the tragic demise of Isaac Cutler, Dark Wolf continued his journey up the mountainside. Rather than go directly to the cabin, he traveled off to the left, through the forest beyond the lake and around above the small graveyard. He tied the horses at the edge of the forest and stepped out into the sloping meadow. As he made his way down to the graves of his father and his wife, he watched the thin string of smoke rising from the cabin chimney below. He was not ready to see Hattie and his sons just yet.

Sitting down between the graves, he laid a hand on each of them. Aloud, he softly spoke, "Your deaths have been avenged, but my heart remains heavy. Isaac's death cannot bring you back." After a few moments of silence, Dark Wolf spoke again. "I ask the Great Spirit and both of you to be with me as I raise my sons. And I thank you for waking me out of my painful sleep to walk as the father my sons deserve." Looking off to the left at his mother's place of rest, Dark Wolf sighed. He closed his eyes and was shown a brief vision. He knew now that the spirit of his father had shared his mother's journey through life and had seen her come to know peace, even in her death. A smile curled the corners of his mouth as he opened his eyes. Trusting that the spirits knew the thoughts and feelings he could not verbalize, he stood and returned to the horses.

As he led the horses down through the meadow toward the rear of the cabin, Dark Wolf saw Hawk come down the side steps from the porch and walk toward the lake. He heard Raven's voice asking, "Where are you going, Hawk?"

Hawk turned around just as Raven reached the porch steps. He answered, "I'm just going up on this bank to watch for Father. Hattie says he should be back soon."

Raven recalled what Hattie had told him the night they had stayed with her at her cabin; about how it seems like the person you are watching for will never come as long as you are watching. He descended the steps and followed his brother up the bank. They sat down, and Hawk threw a small stone into the water. They watched the circles on the surface enlarging and moving outward to the water's edge. As Raven was about to share Hattie's little story with his brother, a movement off to the right caught his eye. He turned his head and saw their father approaching, leading the two horses. He smiled and stood. Just as he was about to turn back and tell Hawk the good news, Hawk saw his father and jumped to his feet. In their excitement, the two boys slammed into each other, lost their balance, and tumbled down the bank and into the water.

Releasing the reins, Dark Wolf ran to the edge of the pond and looked down at his sons. He laughed as the two boys scrambled out of the water and up the bank toward him. He opened his arms to receive both of his soaking wet sons in a huge embrace.

When the hug ended, Dark Wolf walked back to where the horses stood.

Raven rushed forward and grabbed the reins. He said, "I'll take care of them, Father."

Dark Wolf nodded. He and Hawk walked toward the cabin, Hawk chattering incessantly, "Oh, Father! I'm so glad you are back! We felt the mountain shake and heard the thunder, and I was afraid you were hurt! ... but Raven and Hattie told me you would be back. Hey! We went fishing in the stream and caught a bunch of fish for supper. Hattie's cooking them now. Oh! And Hattie fell asleep under a big tree, and we made her think it was raining, but it was only the sack of fish dripping on her, but she wasn't angry because now we're even ..."

Dark Wolf's laughter interrupted his son.

Hearing Dark Wolf, Hattie stepped out of the cabin just as the two came up the steps. She smiled.

Hawk began again, "Hattie! Look! Father is here! I already told him about the fish. I couldn't help it."

Hattie put her hands on her hips. "Well, it's hard to keep somethin' a secret when it smells so good a-cookin'." Noticing Hawk's wet hair and clothes, she asked, "What on earth happened to you, boy?"

Hawk pulled at his clothes. "Me and Raven fell in the pond."

Raven joined them just as they started inside. "Come on, Hawk, let's get some dry clothes on."

When the boys had gone upstairs to their room, Hattie looked at Dark Wolf. Grinning, she said, "Welcome back to life on the mountain. Supper's 'most ready."

After freshening up, Dark Wolf joined Hattie and the boys at the table. Hattie said, "We're thankful for what we have, now let's eat it!"

As the food was being passed, Raven asked, "Where did you get the horse, Father?"

"It's from the Cutler ranch. Tomorrow we must return it. And while we are in the valley, we will purchase some supplies in town."

Oblivious to the conversation, Hawk and Hattie filled their plates and began eating heartily.

Giving his father a knowing look, Raven asked, "Did you finish your business, Father?"

Looking with pride at his son's wise, discreet way of asking about his dealings with Isaac, he answered, "Yes, son." Pointing one finger upward, he said, "I had help from above, but it is finished."

Raven nodded and took a bite of fish.

Dark Wolf took a big bite. "This is delicious. Putting food on the table is a great thing. I'm proud of you boys."

Hattie said, "I told 'em you would be."

Hawk said, "Hattie even taught us how to clean the fish and cook them, Father!"

"She did? It sounds as though you learned some very useful things today." Dark Wolf jokingly added, "From now on *I* can do the fishing, and *you* can do the cleaning and cooking!"

At first Hawk gave his father a disappointed look, then realized he was teasing. He said, "And we can *all* do the eating!"

They all laughed.

CHAPTER TWENTY

FOUR MONTHS LATER:

Outside, beneath the kitchen window, Seth and Curtis were digging a hole to transplant a rose bush for the ladies to enjoy the fragrance next spring and summer. The early morning air was filled with aromas of biscuits baking and bacon frying. Seth's mouth watered, and he said, "Curtis, boy, we are a couple of the luckiest men in the Rocky Mountains."

Tamping down the last shovel of dirt around the rose bush, Curtis asked, "How so, Seth?"

"Well, we've got three excellent cooks in our kitchen." Standing and beginning to collect the tools to put them away, Seth added, "And *that's* why we have to work so hard around here." Pointing to the rose bush, he said, "We gotta keep 'em happy so they'll keep fixin' our grub."

Curtis laughed and patted his belly, "And we don't want to get fat do we, Seth?"

"No, sir!" As he turned to go to the barn, Seth said, "Now, boy, if you would kindly tie that bush to the trellis ... not too tight, just easy like ... we'll be done with this project."

"Yes, sir." Having long since received his father's knife back from Seth, Curtis cut a piece of twine from a spool and began tying the thickest branches to the white fan-shaped trellis, being careful not to prick himself on the thorns. Just then, inside the house Sarah began singing loudly. Her shrill voice, combined with the volume, caused Curtis to flinch, and he ran the side of his hand fully into a large thorn. "Ow!"

Seth had returned and was standing over the boy, chuckling. "That's the screechin'est woman I ever heard."

Curtis finished tying the string, then put his finger to his mouth, spit on the small bead of blood that had formed, then wiped it on his pants. "Yeah. That's one of the reasons I stay outside with you all the time."

Seth laughed, and patted the boy on the back. "And here, all this time, I thought you enjoyed my company."

"Oh, I do!" Curtis pinched at his finger and wiped it again. "But you just oughta hear what it sounds like when you're in there right next to that noise! Whew!"

When they began walking back toward the barn, Curtis noticed some riders coming slowly up the road toward the ranch. His first reaction was fear, thinking it might be Isaac, even though he believed Isaac was dead. He stopped and pointed. "Seth, it looks like we have company comin'."

Seth shifted his hat to block the sun and squinted as he continued walking. A smile formed on his face, and he said, "Well, I'll be jiggered! Curtis, run and tell the ladies to set four more places at the breakfast table!"

"Who is it, Seth?"

Looking back at the boy with a big smile, Seth said, "It's Dark Wolf and his boys ... and, it looks like Hattie Gray is with 'em. It's okay, now, go on!"

While Curtis ran inside to give the message, Seth began walking down the road to meet the visitors.

Becoming impatient, Hawk urged his horse on, and it began trotting ahead of the others. He yelled, *"Hello, Mr. Seth! How is everybody?"*

"Just fine, Hawk!" Seth answered. "And how are all of you?"

Now drawing near to Seth, Hawk stopped his horse and jumped down. "I'm tired of riding. I think I'll walk back up the road with you. Is that all right?"

"Yes, sir, that's just fine!"

They waited for the others to catch up with them, and they turned and began walking back toward the ranch. Seth said, "It sure is good to see all of you. Elizabeth will be so pleased. And so will the others."

Suddenly remembering that Sarah, and Jessie and her family, had moved there, Hawk said, "Oh! That's right! I'll get to see Eli and Rachel ... and Curtis!" Looking up at Seth, he explained, "I only met them one time, but we had *so much fun!*"

Seth offered, "Well, you can go on ahead if you want to. It won't hurt my feelings none."

Turning back to look at Dark Wolf, Hawk asked, "May I, Father?"

"Yes, Hawk. You may go ahead."

Raven asked, "May I, too, Father?"

"Yes, and both of you mind your manners."

Seth helped Hawk back up onto his horse, and the two boys galloped away.

Curtis stood in the yard, watching them. He could not help smiling, as his heart leapt with joy.

Eli helped Rachel down the porch steps, and they joined Curtis. Rachel clapped her hands and jumped up and down, squealing happily at the sight of the boys approaching.

Down the road, Dark Wolf and Hattie dismounted and led their horses as they walked with Seth.

Seth said, "You've come just in time for a breakfast feast. These women always cook a'plenty."

Hattie said, "Good! I'm starved! And beef jerky just don't hold a candle to good home cookin'."

"Now, that's a fact, Hattie." Seth turned to Dark Wolf. "How is everything on the mountain?"

"Good. And how is Elizabeth?"

Shrugging his shoulders and looking downward, Seth answered, "Aw, you know, she has her good days and her bad days, thinkin' about Isaac and all." Raising his head again and looking ahead, he said, "But we sure are happy together, Dark Wolf. She is a fine, fine woman."

"And you are a fine man, Seth. You will keep the grief from overtaking her."

Seth breathed a deep sigh, "I hope so. She deserves to be happy."

After a few moments, Dark Wolf asked, "How are Sarah and Jessie?"

Excitedly, Seth answered, "Oh! They are just fine. Jessie had her baby a few days ago. It's a boy! He came a bit early, but the little feller's doin' real good." Nudging Dark Wolf, Seth grinned and said, "You'll never guess what they named him."

"Not 'Isaac', I hope."

"Of course, not." Seth snorted. "No, Jessie told Elizabeth she could name him, and she came up with the names of two of the most respected men in her life." Feeling the need to explain further, he added, "Now, she respects *me*, too, but we didn't want to name Jessie's baby after *me*." Waving his hand in the air, he said, "Well, anyway, can you guess?"

Jokingly, Dark Wolf said, "Seth, it's too early in the morning to have to think so hard. Why don't you just tell me."

Hattie chuckled and nodded.

"Jonathan Thomas Cutler. That's it."

Dark Wolf smiled. After a few moments, he softly said, "It's a good, strong name."

"Yes, it is. Elizabeth said she had equal respect for you and Thomas, but the name sounded better in that order. The other was a little awkward. Jessie is real pleased, too."

They had finally reached the ranch house. Curtis had helped Hawk and Raven tend to their horses. Seth took Dark Wolf's and Hattie's horses and headed for the barn.

The next few minutes were spent in tearful greetings and much hugging, the baby sleeping through all of the attention and comments.

When they all started inside, Sarah ordered, "Now everyone get your hands washed and get to the table so we can eat!"

217

Jessie glanced over and watched as Dark Wolf brushed a bit of dust from the sleeves and front of his deerskin shirt. She watched one of his sun-darkened hands lift a beaded necklace and drop it back inside the shirt against his smooth chest. She quickly turned away and joined the others inside the house.

Elizabeth slipped her arm around Dark Wolf's waist, and he put his arm around her shoulders. As they lagged behind, slowly walking together, Elizabeth said, "I've been thinking about studying to become a school teacher so that I can help these children get an education. But I don't want to go away to do it. I want to be here with my new family. There must be a way that I can correspond with a University somewhere and complete the necessary courses here in my home. What do you think?"

Giving her shoulders a squeeze, Dark Wolf answered, "I think you would be a wonderful educator, Elizabeth. Your library here is already quite extensive as it is. And I'm certain that, *if* there is not already a program in place for home study, with your influence, you can convince them of the need for one."

Elizabeth blushed. "Really, Jon! You sound like Seth!"

"Well, it sounds like he believes in you as much as I do. And that's a good thing."

Finally, everyone gathered around the table.

At seeing the bountiful feast set before them, Hawk exclaimed, "I have never seen so much food in all my life! My eyes hurt just lookin' at it!"

Everyone laughed, then Seth said, "Well, now, let's bow our heads and thank God for giving us this food, and for the good company at our table today."

When the prayer was finished, the room was filled with the pleasant din of chatter and laughter, as well as the clanking of silver utensils against the many dishes and platters.

Dark Wolf's heart felt truly joyful for the first time in a long time as he listened to the voices and glanced at the others around the table. He sat in silence, deciding to feast on the happy memory that was creating itself in his mind. Slowly, his gaze shifted to the one across the table from him. There was Jessie, looking radiant as she, too, ignored the food and held her baby boy lovingly in her arms, smiling down at him as she gently rocked from side to side, and softly stroked his cheek. Dark Wolf studied her; her long hair pulled back on the sides and hanging from a red ribbon which matched the tiny flowers on her dress, her dainty ear above the long, smooth line of her jaw and chin, the sweet smile on her lips as she looked tenderly at her baby. He could feel and hear his own heart beating more rapidly. The noise in the room faded as long-forgotten feelings began to stir inside his heart and body.

Still enjoying her first trip to the table to be with the family since Jonathan Thomas was born, Jessie was simply thrilling at the many sounds of happiness that filled the room. She could not remember such a grand time ever before in her life. She raised her head to take in the vision of it all. She smiled broadly as she looked around, still holding her baby close and rocking gently from side to side. Her heart fluttered when her eyes met Dark Wolf's stare. Her breath caught, and she felt herself blush. She quickly averted her eyes, but they were soon drawn again to the dark eyes of the handsome man seated across from her.

Dark Wolf smiled softly and turned away, to save the girl any further embarrassment. Once again, he could hear the laughter and voices conversing around the table.

Hattie nudged Dark Wolf and said, loudly, "Ain't you gonna try any of this grub? You won't get this kind of cookin' on the mountain, 'lessen ya kidnap one of these here gals. And I don't know if they's a one that'd put up with yer quiet ways."

The others laughed.

Dark Wolf answered, "Okay, Hattie. Pass me some grub." While filling his plate, he glanced at Jessie from time to time, and also placed small portions of each dish on her plate. Softly he said to her, "You need some grub, too, Jessie, ... to keep your strength up."

At hearing his voice speak her name, Jessie blushed again. She saw Dark Wolf smile and saw him turn away to make conversation with Hattie and the others. She picked up her fork and began eating the delicious food, savoring each bite.

When the meal was over, the women worked swiftly to clean up the kitchen, while the men and children went outside. Seth, Curtis, and Dark Wolf walked around the ranch. They all shared ideas about preparation for the coming winter, as well as the purchase of more beef cattle through Seth's and Dark Wolf's association with the other local cattle owners, promising that Curtis could soon begin attending their meetings. Dark Wolf also mentioned the need to have a lawyer make a new Deed, changing ownership from Dark Wolf to Seth and Elizabeth.

Raven, Hawk, and Eli found a dusty area near the road where they began to play a game of marbles. With a brightly-colored rag doll clutched tightly in her arms, Rachel sat nearby watching the boys and squealing happily as the marbles rolled about on the ground.

When the women finally came outside to sit on the porch, Hattie took a seat on the top step and put on her crumpled hat. "Yes, ma'am, 'Liz'beth, ya got a right nice bunch of fam'ly goin' here."

"Why, thank you, Hattie. You are welcome to come here any time. Hawk and Raven have told me how special you are to them."

Surprised, Hattie blushed, looked at Elizabeth, and said, "Them boys said I'm special?"

Elizabeth smiled and said, "They sure did, Hattie. You have been with them through some very difficult times, and they love you for it."

Hattie quickly stood, nervously shook out her wrinkled skirt tail, and said, "Well, I gotta be goin' now. Got some stuff to fetch in town." As she walked toward the corral to get her horse, she called back over her shoulder, "Thanks for the grub, 'Liz'beth!"

Several hours later, Dark Wolf and the boys were ready to make their way back up the mountainside to the cabin. Sarah had prepared a large package of food for their journey. The children had said their good-byes to each other, and had extracted a promise from the grown-ups for another visit before winter set in.

As they were preparing to mount up, Dark Wolf looked around. He did not see Jessie. He said, "Wait here, boys. I'll only be a minute." He walked over to Elizabeth and asked, "Where is Jessie?"

Pointing toward the top floor of the house, Elizabeth smiled and said, "She is probably up in the nursery with the baby. It's the last room on the left at the top of the stairs."

Not sure what he wanted to say when he did find Jessie, Dark Wolf slowly ascended the stairs. When he finally came to the nursery, he found Jessie sitting in a rocking chair, sleeping. The baby was sleeping soundly in the cradle beside her. Dark Wolf looked around and found a quilt, folded and lying on a bed in the corner. He quietly unfolded the quilt and placed it over Jessie, being careful not to wake her. As he tucked the cover around her shoulders, he studied her face again and created another memory in his mind. Dark Wolf pulled the beaded necklace from under his shirt and removed it from his neck. He hung it on the cradle where he knew she would find it later, then he left the room and quickly went back outside. "Jessie and her son are asleep."

Elizabeth said, "Oh, poor dear. Today was the first day she has been out of bed since Jonathan Thomas was born. She is probably exhausted. We'll look in on her later." After walking him to his horse, she said, "Dark Wolf, you and the boys must come back soon."

Seth spoke up, "Maybe plan to stay a night or two. We have room."

Dark Wolf thought for a moment, then said, "We will come back in a few weeks. By that time, Jessie and the baby should be able to travel. I would like for you all to come and see our home on the mountain before winter comes."

Giving Dark Wolf a knowing smile, Seth winked and answered, "Sure thing, Dark Wolf."

Dark Wolf mounted his horse and they waved good-bye as they turned to go.

Hawk, just then noticing that Hattie was not with them, asked, "Where's Hattie?"

Raven answered, "She left a long time ago, Hawk. She had to go to town for supplies."

Hawk kicked his horse to make it trot, and said, "Well, I hope she's not hiding behind a big tree somewhere, waiting to jump out and scare us. It would be just like her to do that."

Dark Wolf and Raven laughed.

Several hours had passed when Jessie awoke. The sun was going down and the lengthening shadows began to fill the room. She folded the top of the cover down onto her lap and stretched her limbs. She laid a hand on her son to make sure he was still breathing, and still warm. Jessie was relieved when she felt him squirm a little under her hand. Just as she was about to stand, she noticed the object hanging on the side of the baby's crib. She carefully lifted it up and looked at it. She felt a rush of excitement, and her heartbeats quickened as she recognized the object to be Dark Wolf's necklace. Slowly, she slipped it over her head.

She lifted her hair and let it fall over the necklace. In the dimming light, she studied the thunderbird design woven into the beads. Her heart calmed, and she felt peaceful as she leaned back and again rested her head. Staring out the window, she smiled, trusting that this was a sign she would see Dark Wolf again.

————————

At their campsite on the mountain side, exhausted from their day of fun at the Logan-Cutler ranch, and having had their hunger again fully satisfied with another hearty meal of leftovers, Hawk and Raven were sleeping soundly.

Dark Wolf sat near the fire, staring into the flames. He could not help reflecting on the past. So much had happened to darken his life, and the lives of his sons. But now, he recalled Two Falls' promise that the shadows would someday leave the mountain, and the sun would shine again. He thought of Jessie, and he smiled.

Printed in the United States
989800002B